RED KNIGHT

RED KNIGHT

A Novel

J. Madison Davis

Walker and Company
New York

First published in the United States of America in 1992 by
Walker Publishing Company, Inc.

Published simultaneously in Canada by Thomas Allen & Son
Canada, Limited, Markham, Ontario.

Library of Congress Cataloging-in-Publication Data
Davis, J. Madison.
Red knight : a novel / J. Madison Davis.
p.   cm.
ISBN 0-8027-1199-5
I. Title.
PS3554.A934636R4   1992
813'.54—dc20   91-45383
CIP

Printed in the United States of America

2   4   6   8   10   9   7   5   3   1

Special thanks to Kenneth Schiff and the Mercyhurst Summer Writer's Institute for providing the space in which to be inspired.

RED KNIGHT

Prologue

No one would ever know how incredibly happy "Bantam Billy" Alberts was when he died. His cousin Dave and Skeeter McIlwray had been with him, but they were just as dead. Odds were that the mortician had shrugged, separated what little was left of them into three equal piles as anonymous as heaps of stew meat on a butcher's counter, and scooped them into plastic bags that he sealed in the cheap coffins. Parts of each ended up mixed with the others, so what the boys had felt in that last moment before they were scattered into eternity hadn't lasted very long and didn't seem the point.

Like most people at funerals, those who had known Bantam Billy thought about him only as he related to their own lives. Father Benotti calmly looked over the service, swung his censor, and began the recessional, forcefully reminding himself of the theme of his commentary: God's infinite capacity for mercy. Billy would need it. In the front pew, Billy's aunt Perlie sobbed loudly, remembering him from better times—a long time ago, from before the fall that permanently twisted his hip—chasing his daddy's bird dog up and down the central hallway of their shotgun house, his diaper hanging halfway down his rashy butt. Next to her, Daddy Alberts concentrated on holding himself steady as he silently thanked Jesus that, if it had to happen, at least his boy hadn't been gunned down by the highway patrol in front of some 7-Eleven or Shell station he had robbed. Living with Billy was the same as waiting for that. There were blessings in sorrow. Jesus had called Billy's momma home before the first time her boy was arrested. Her stroke had been mercy, he confusedly thought. Jesus had protected her from the both of them.

Farther back in the pews, two of Billy's girlfriends (Amy and Francie) were imagining that he thought of being inside them in the instant of his death and each swore secretly to God that she would never, ever, have sex again. Amy thought of becoming a nun in Billy's memory—if her period would just show up. Francie, on the other hand, wished that her own wouldn't show, so she could leave the eighth grade and raise Billy's child. A third girlfriend, Clare, couldn't help thinking that dying was Billy's punishment for calling her a slut last Memorial Day. Behind the girls, Boss Mayhew (Billy's occasional employer) was wondering when they were going to eat, and Mrs. Jones, Daddy Albert's blowsy girlfriend, hoped they could sit down soon, her shoes were pinching.

The only mourner without the weary sense that one way or another they had all been destined to be at Billy's funeral, the only one who felt startled, angry, and severed, was Bobby Alberts, Billy's brother. He should have been in the car with Billy, Skecter, and Dave. Since the shock of the state trooper's blunt words, Bobby hadn't slept. Bobby hadn't cried. Squeezing his laced fingers white, all he thought about was revenge, violent and bloody revenge. He had a job to do as soon as the funeral was over. All these people standing around, accepting Billy's death, they made Bobby sick. Billy hadn't died for nothing: he'd make sure of that.

On the afternoon Bantam Billy died, he had wanted to work on the transmission of the 1968 Mustang he'd been rebuilding, but Boss Mayhew said no. "What happened the last time I let you lock up, boy? Huh? There was Cokes missing. My tire gauge was gone. You lost three of my goddamned wrenches."

Billy limped toward the fat man aggressively, hip swinging awkwardly. "What the fuck you talking about? I didn't take nothing."

"Yeah, well, I ain't finding out by being stupid again. I tol' ya you can work on it when I'm here and it's Friday and I'm going." Boss jabbed his thick, greasy finger at Billy.

"Don't do that," said Billy.

"Don't do what?" Boss sneered, and poked him in the collarbone. Billy lurched back and wiped at the stain made by the finger. "That car ain't running 'til the Second Coming, boy," Boss said, laughing. The smell of his bad teeth momentarily fogged the smell of his sweat.

"I ought to knock your fat head off, asshole."

Mayhew waved a crescent wrench. "Who you calling asshole, you little shit? Maybe I'll get that junk hauled outta here. Maybe that's what I'm gonna do."

Billy clenched his fists. He imagined crushing Boss's face with a tire iron. A horn blew outside. Dave and Skeeter had pulled up by the island in a Chrysler convertible with enormous fins. They climbed out and jumped over the rusty pipes where the pumps had once been.

"Aw, come on, Boss," said Billy. "Just tonight. It's a Mustang. It'll be worth plenty when it's done. I'll pay you. Dollar an hour."

Boss pointed at the balancer. "You plug that tire?"

"Yeah."

"So why you leave it there?"

"Like it makes a difference in this shithole?"

"Hey, don't you lip me, boy."

"Blow me," said Billy. He was already halfway to Skeeter and Dave.

"Fuck you!" shouted Boss. "Goddamn gimpy-leg shrimp!"

Billy spun, fists tight, but Boss laughed and slammed down the bay door.

"What's up?" asked Skeeter. Skeeter wasn't big for seventeen but he was still a head higher than Billy.

"Nothin'," said Billy, his hip rocking like a bent pendulum as he hurried toward the Chrysler.

"Ain't we gonna work on the car?" Dave had legs like bamboo fly rods and an Adam's apple as big as the wattle on a Brahma bull. His voice was so low it rumbled.

"Boss won't let us."

[3]

"What?" shrieked Skeeter.

"Boss won't let us."

"You piss him off again?" asked Skeeter.

"He *is* piss. Let's get some beer."

"Maybe if I talk to him . . ." said Skeeter.

Billy nimbly vaulted himself over the side into the back seat. "Get in the fucking car."

Dave cracked his fist against his palm. "It's your Mustang. We ought to—"

"We'd never get the smell out of our hands. Let's blow."

Dave started the engine, roared it, and peeled out. Skeeter laughed and shouted, "Maybe we ought to hose Boss down, then beat him up."

"Give me a light," said Billy, flipping a finger back at the garage.

"That'd kill him, being clean!"

"All that'd be left is a grease spot!" chirped Skeeter.

"*I'm melting!*" squealed Billy. "*I'm mel-tinnnng! Ahhhhhhh!*"

"That's what Clare says when Billy gives her the hose," Dave intoned.

Billy clipped him on the shoulder. "Give me a light, shithead." The car squealed onto the ramp for I-10. The traffic was heavy, but moving. Dave blew his horn and cut in front of a Festiva. The driver shouted out his window. Billy and Skeeter flipped him the finger. Dave swerved into the outer lane, cutting off a truck. He closed fast on a station wagon. He blinked his lights, but the wagon stayed in the lane.

The Chrysler's nose dipped as it slowed. Dave pounded his steering wheel. "Asshole!" He blinked his lights like he was going to rip the button out of the dashboard.

Skeeter handed Billy the lighter. "What're we gonna do tonight, Billy? Huh?"

Billy dragged on his cigarette. "I want to kick some ass."

"Yeah!" said Skeeter. He flopped back on his seat as Dave swerved.

Dave turned up the radio so loud they couldn't hear the traffic. Skeeter changed the station four times a mile for the next five miles, then Dave swatted his hand away from the radio. "That's Madonna, man!"

"Madonna, shit!"

"It's my car, we're listening to Madonna."

Skeeter made a motion to Billy as if whacking off, then pointed at Dave. "Madonna's all he's had lately."

"Hey, shut up!" said Dave. He exited onto the Chef Menteur Highway.

"We'll get some," said Billy. "We're gonna do it all. Right? It's Friday, ain't it?" He screamed wildly, the veins like steel cables in his neck.

Skeeter howled like a wolf until he turned red.

In an A & P parking lot, Dave clicked off the ignition. "Who's got the money?"

"Shit!" said Billy. "I forgot to get my pay!"

"You shittin' me?" said Dave. "Hey, I bought last time. *And* the time before. I get mighty tired of delivering Dominos so you two can drink it up."

"Don't look at me," said Skeeter.

"How come it's *never* look at you?"

"You just got paid. I lost *my* job. We'll go back and get Billy's."

"He won't be there," said Billy.

"Okay, okay," said Dave, "but goddammit you gotta pay me back. I gotta pay for my new tire. I mean it. You pay me Monday night, Billy."

"What about Skeeter?"

"I'll get some money," Skeeter said.

"Oh, yeah, right," said Dave, leaving. "I'll believe it when I see it."

"Bullshit!" Skeeter fidgeted. "Dave should've left the key. No radio."

"He wouldn't trust Madonna with his car."

"I don't like his attitude, Billy. I wouldn't steal his car. And I can get money, too."

"Yeah, yeah. Give me another butt."

"No shit. We'll roll a queer. If we get the right one we can party for a week."

[5]

Billy slapped the door. "This battleship's too easy to make."

"Okay, we'll go to my house and I'll borrow my dad's car."

"Hey," said Billy, "we ain't rolling no queers. I've had enough of being the bait."

"But they like guys your size."

Billy's eyes flared, then the anger subsided into an evil grin. "They'd like it if they saw it."

"You know what I mean."

"Last time the sweetboy licked my ear. I could've got AIDS, man. *You* be the bait."

"No way!"

"You're too ugly anyway, pizza-face."

"Fuck you."

"Pizza-face!" Billy turned. Dave was carrying a case of Busch. "Toss me one!"

"What'd you buy?" asked Skeeter. He looked at his can. "The cheap stuff, what else?"

"It's cold and as good as anybody's. Head for the mountains, Prince Charles. And don't spill it on the upholstery."

The three cans cracked open in staccato. Dave tucked two extra under his seat and put the rest of the case in his trunk. Dave swallowed deep and sighed. "Whoo! That's cold!"

"If we rolled a queer we could be drinking Heineken."

Billy laughed. "Sucking Heiney's about your speed."

"Shut up," said Skeeter. Billy feigned terror.

"Bitch again and you'll be walking," said Dave. "I mean it."

Billy had already chugged his entire can. He crushed it with his hand. "All right, one last time. This is beer. This is your brain on beer." He erupted with a long and resonant belch. He tossed the beer can. It clattered across the path of a platinum blond pushing a grocery cart. "Sorry, baby!" he said. She looked away.

"I think I'm in love," said Skeeter.

"Grow up," said Dave. "She's a skag."

"So let's get some cack."

"It's too early," said Dave.

[6]

"What am I? I'm your social director, gentlemen!" shouted Billy. "Give me another beer."

"It's gotta last, man."

"Just give me the beer and drive. Let's see what's up on Canal."

"What're we gonna do, Billy?" asked Skeeter.

"Do I ever let you down? Drive, I said."

A typical Friday. They cruised Canal. They saw a black man with a white woman and drove by the couple three times staring and trying to talk themselves into beating him up. On the third pass the couple lingered near a police car parked in front of an electronics store and the boys gave up. They argued about rolling queers again. They argued about going down to Bourbon Street to a live sex show. Dave said they'd never let Skeeter in. Billy said Skeeter could watch the car. They decided it'd cost too much. They parked in an alley and planned the robbery of a Vietnamese grocery store about two miles from where Dave lived. Skeeter was all for it. Dave had heard the owner had a sawed-off somewhere behind the counter. They planned it anyway. Maybe a midweek when there weren't so many people out. Maybe in a rainstorm. Dave was in favor of calling Clare—stuck at home with her second kid—and giving her twenty bucks for a triple play, like two weeks ago. But Billy was in a scrapping mood. He had to live up to his name. He hadn't hit anything since he'd slapped Clare for making eyes at his brother Bobby. If Billy didn't get his fist into somebody's face soon, he'd start on Skeeter or Dave. He'd crack a knuckle on one of their cheekbones or they'd crack one on his teeth, but they'd all feel better afterward.

By now it was late. They had parked in a dark spot along the Mississippi and were urinating off a trash-strewn levee. Billy looked up at the bridge to Gretna. A light bulb went off in his fuzzy mind. "Hey," he said, "we gotta get Bobby."

"Bobby? What do we need your brother for?" asked Dave.

"Yeah, Bobby, and a big aluminum bat. A big one. A fungo."

"All right!" said Skeeter. "Nigger knocking!"

"Hey, not in my car! No way, José! That's kid's stuff."

"Fuck your car," said Billy. "I'm talking that fucker Raleigh Lee Menzies."

"Right!" said Skeeter. "Bobby's got to be in on this."

"Aw, leave your brother out of it. He shouldn't've been along."

"The man come to the house," said Billy, "acted like he had some right. If I'd've been there I'd've kicked his ass."

"He'll see my car."

"He's an old fart. He'll be in bed."

"Come on, man," Skeeter pleaded.

Dave looked at Billy, whose eyes almost glowed in the dimness. He glanced at Skeeter, then back at Billy. He grinned. "This guy's a nigger lover? Right?"

"If he comes out of the house I'll jam his mailbox up his ass," bragged Skeeter.

Dave laughed. "I hate niggers, but not as much as I hate nigger lovers. I'm in."

Billy high-fived him. "Let's call Bobby."

Bobby wasn't home. They called his steady, Jennifer. "Gimme Bobby," Billy said as soon as she answered, and she recognized him. She glanced toward the sofa where Bobby was playing Nintendo and said Bobby wasn't there. She didn't care if Billy knew she was lying but she added she thought Bobby was with Skeeter, just to cover. She told Bobby it was someone selling magazines.

About twelve-thirty, Dave, Skeeter, and Billy got back to their own neighborhood and started the game. Dave always drove. Between Skeeter and Billy, whoever took down the most mailboxes would get seconds on Carla. The loser would get thirds and pay half. The loser would also pay back Dave for the beer, which was now nearly gone, and for Carla. They pulled up to the entrance of Thibodeaux Road, about half a mile from the cluster of run-down houses where the three of them lived. Easing up to the quiet crossroad, they looked for cops. They heard the clink of the stoplight changing, then Billy raised himself on the rear seat, waved the bat, and strained out a long whoop that reverberated into the trees.

Dave's tires squealed. Billy nearly toppled backward over the closed convertible top, but he staggered upright, one hand on the front seat to keep his balance. The humid air fluttered in his face. The first long driveway was lit by a long row of low-voltage lanterns. He leaned, and just as the name Thompson flashed by, he swung. The bat missed.

"Strike!" shouted Skeeter.

"Closer!" shouted Billy. "Closer!"

Dave edged to the right. A barn-shaped mailbox appeared. Billy clipped it, taking off its door.

"A single!" shouted Skeeter.

"Door's a double!" said Billy.

"Single!"

The road wound right. The tires squealed. There would be a group of boxes close together.

A swing and a miss. Whack! "A single!" *Piiing!* The bat struck the support post and spun backward. Billy reeled, Dave braked, and Billy toppled to the rear seat floor.

Billy clambered out. "Keep it steady, damn it! And faster! Faster!"

Dave peeled out, tires smoking. Billy again nearly fell over the back. He recovered in time to make a weak stab at a metal box, but missed. He was determined now, the hot night air hissing through his white teeth. He decapitated the next box with both hands and it tumbled behind them into the street.

"A homer! A fucking grand slam, baby!" he shouted.

The road wound left. "Fucking Menzies," he pointed. "Menzies! Menzzzzies!"

The box was closer, closer. He swung with all his might. He missed and fell over the side of the car. Skeeter barely hooked the belt of his jeans, as Billy's face hung inches from the asphalt. The aluminum bat rang as it skittered over the gravel shoulder. Dave screeched to a fishtailing halt. Skeeter hauled Billy back in.

"Jesus!" said Dave. He was picturing Billy with a face of raw hamburger.

"You're out!" said Skeeter. "You dropped the bat!"

"Fuck you!" said Billy. "Back up."

"No second chances! No fair!" said Skeeter.

"Back up or I'll kick the shit out of you, Dave! This is Menzies. This is personal. *Back up!*"

"Hey!" said Dave, but Billy had already jumped out of the car, his neck silvery in the backing lights. He limped to the bat and hit the ground with it as if testing it.

"*Men-zies! Motherfucker! Come out! You want me, come get me! Hey! Yeah, You!*"

Dave stopped in front of the mailbox. "Come on! Let's book!" Skeeter pointed to a light coming on. Dogs were barking.

Billy expelled his words as if emptying himself. "*You got a new mailbox! Come on, fucker! come stop me!*" He scurried to the mailbox. He swung so hard he missed and struck only the wooden post.

Skeeter laughed. He was about to say that Billy couldn't even hit it standing still. Dave was reaching out his long arm to pull Billy back into the car. That was the instant when the bat came down hard on top of the mailbox. That was the instant in which, as if in slow motion through the blurred orgasm of his frenzy, Billy saw the curved black metal crushing under the gleaming cylinder of the bat. It was his moment of supreme happiness, of getting even with Menzies and teachers and Father Benotti and laughing girls and cops and the entire world. It was his one brief moment, in a lifetime of surly discontent, of ultimate and total ecstasy.

In the next instant, he felt nothing. There was a flash of light. Five pounds of eightpenny nails, and hundreds of fragments of mailbox ripped through them. Dave, Skeeter, and Billy were splattered like palmetto bugs hitting a windshield. When the soft plinking rain of metal and glass fragments ceased, the only sound was the grumbling of Dave's windshield-less car, still idling on its four flattened tires, bleeding green radiator fluid. It coughed, shuddered, and stopped.

After several seconds of absolute, infinite silence, a car parked in the trees just beyond Menzies's house abruptly roared and pulled away. Dogs flopped the shock wave of the explosion out of their long ears and barked. Bedroom lights blinked on up to a mile away. A retired fireman named Keefer called the gas company.

ONE

When Vonna opened the door, Honoré St. Jean Devraix was gently stroking his olive-colored cheek with the back of his delicate right hand and squinting into his tortoiseshell mirror.

She wasn't looking forward to their conversation, so she watched him for a second or two, then tapped softly on the door frame. "I'm here," she said.

"Ummm."

"It won't rub off, you know."

"Excuse me?"

"The Congo runs too deep."

"Ummm. And the Manzanares and the Loire, possibly even the Liffey. I have a, shall we say, complex family tree. In any case, they have changed its name, have they not? Zaire, is it?"

"I like the sound of Congo."

He gestured impatiently with his long fingers. "Well, come in out of the doorway, dear."

"You sure I'm not interrupting your morning love affair, *dear*?"

Devraix put down his mirror. His normally languid eyes narrowed somewhat. "Perhaps you would like some café au lait, a beignet?"

"That's a nice mirror," she offered, sitting.

He lifted it toward her. The handle was silver, the mirrored surface discolored with age. "It was my great-grandmother's. She was sort of a Grandissime." He let the last word hiss through his bright teeth. Vonna didn't ask what a Grandissime was. Devraix would expect everyone to know and would take great pleasure in explaining, something Vonna didn't want to give him this morning. When she didn't take the mirror, Devraix stuck it in his drawer. He put his elbows on his desk, spread his fingers and placed them together at the tips.

"Okay, Honoré, you called me in to chew me out, so chew."

"My dear, 'chewing out' is not my style." ,

"It was a mistake, okay? I'm sorry. It could happen to anyone. I got the red wire mixed with the peppermint."

"Peppermint?"

"The red and white."

"Ah."

"Well, what's the difference?" she said testily. "Spyder can swear to what he heard, can't he?"

"Calm yourself, my dear, and don't play at ingenuousness. You know we could never confront Mr. Clayton without a tape. Only that—or photographs—would be foolproof in proving that Mr. Clayton is the adulterer we know him to be. Mr. Clayton need merely deny what Spyder Williams—paid operative of the Devraix Detective Agency, hired by Mrs. Clayton—claims to have heard."

"All right, I know," she sighed. "So we get the bastard next week." She avoided Devraix's coal-black eyes.

"At our expense rather than Mrs. Clayton's, I'm afraid. Furthermore, I wanted Spyder on the hardware shoplifters next week. This will cost us all a penny or two."

"I know," she moaned. "I've already had this out with Spyder. I'm sorry. Can I go?"

"Actually, I did not call you in to rehash the Clayton bungle—"

Equipment had failed before, but never because of something she had done. The word "bungle" felt like a slap. She reacted without thinking. "Well, you just tell that home boy Spyder there isn't any damn reason to go running to you every time—"

Devraix raised his hand and cocked an eyebrow. "He didn't run to me. I asked for the tape. Don't blame him."

Vonna shifted in her seat.

"I have noticed what it is you have not suggested."

"What?"

"That we send Dub out with you after Clayton and let Spyder do the warehouse."

"So, send us."

"You are not the kind of person who mistakes her peppermints for her reds. I do not recall such a mistake in the years you have worked with me."

"There's a first time for everything."

Devraix rotated his chair and lifted a china cup of café au lait off the wide shelf behind him. He raised it, offering her some. She shook her head. "Do you mind if I . . . ?"

"No," she said sharply.

He lifted the cover of a dish. "Beignet?"

"Nooo!"

He glanced at the door theatrically as if warning her that her voice might carry through. He cleared his throat. He sipped, took a large bite, and dabbed at the powdered sugar under his pencil mustache. "What is the difficulty between you and Dub?"

"Who said there was 'difficulty'?"

"You, my dear, in your attitude. When you confused your peppermint with your red."

"Then it's none of your business."

"It is affecting our business."

She sighed, and rubbed her face with her hands. "Maybe I will have a half of one."

He picked up a beignet with a napkin and handed it to her.

"I said half."

"Then eat half. You are being short with me, Miss Saucier."

She sighed again. "It's just— Christ, I don't know."

"Is it a particular strain to live with a white man?"

"No. Yes. This is America, ain't it? What is this? Oprah? Of course it's a problem living with Dub. It's a strain living with anybody. Shee-yit. He's a man, ain't he?" She laughed ironically.

Devraix raised an eyebrow.

"Okay," she said sheepishly, "it's more. Here's this cracker he moves to New Orleans and all he's supposed to eat is lettuce. He can't smoke either. It's like being in hell. Like everybody in hell, he bitches."

"He looks better. He has definitely lost weight."

"But it's driving him nuts and it's driving me nuts. He's so short-tempered. I mean, he's, like, turned into Mr. Hyde." She raised her fingers like claws and growled.

"You haven't been all sugar and spice yourself, dear."

She breathed deep to prevent proving his point.

"Admit it, dear. Do you think perhaps you are exaggerating a bit? You have been rather tense."

"You know, Honoré, if people knew we was watching them, they'd throw themselves in the river." She put the beignet on his desk. "Jesus, every time I eat something I think he's watching me. I'm supposed to be losing weight, too. I promised." She squeezed her belly between her fingers. "Some size six, huh? Sometimes I can't hear myself think because of my stomach growling. Then I eat like a pig."

"I would assume," said Devraix quietly, "that there would be many innate pressures in a mixed-race liaison. These are different times from when my ancestor the Chevalier du Four bought his wife from a Dutchman."

"Who knows what it is? He threw a real fit on the phone one night because his ex-wife let his daughter go out with one of them cadets from the Citadel."

"Is this what is meant by the 'A personality'? Is the medical situation the same?"

"He's still carrying the nitro. He's never needed it. They now tell him that what happened in the White Rook probably wasn't a real heart attack. Something about enzymes in the blood. You get a real heart attack, you get these enzymes. They wanted to do more tests with some wire they run up through the heart, but it would have cost a lot and Dub said he'd had enough."

"Mrs. O'Dell insisted on paying."

"It didn't matter to him. Now he's walking around carrying those nitros like he's waiting for them to blow up. It

[14]

might've been his heart, it might've been something else. One doctor said it might've been arrhythmia. You know white boys got no rhythm."

"Very amusing," he said dryly.

"The doc at Tulane even said it could've been gas. He should've seen him drop. Do you believe gas could do that? Shee-yit!"

"He must feel as if he is walking on eggs."

"Mrs. O'Dell might as well have burned her scratch, for all she got out of it."

"Dub's work has been excellent."

Vonna squinted at him. Devraix's tone of voice seemed cold, but that was Devraix. She had never gotten used to how coolly theoretical Devraix was about everything.

"Perhaps a few days off," he added.

"He keeps busy to keep his mind off it."

Devraix studied his manicure. "I have been considering the advantages of making him my partner."

"Huh?"

"The publicity over the White Rook case brought in a lot of business. Having a visibly lily-white partner has its social advantages also. It is an unfortunate reality that we have not been able to acquire as much in the way of security business as I would have liked. I suspect certain businessmen are suspicious of those of the colored persuasion."

Vonna's eyes were wide. "You're crazy. Dub ain't got the money to buy in, Honoré. You're still paying him less than me, and every month he sends a mighty big chunk of child support to those girls of his. He'd pay that child support if he was starving."

"Oh, I would retain total control. He would be a kind of publicity partner."

"I've been with you for near ten years. You never thought of making me no partner. How long's Spyder been working for you?"

"I am merely considering it," Devraix said quietly. "In any case, neither you nor Spyder has the publicity factor. It would be beneficial to all of us."

"Well, damn you to hell." She said it with resignation

rather than anger. Devraix sipped his coffee and rotated his chair to face the window.

"Regrettably, I can see that many of our potential customers are put off by my mannerisms. They expect a detective to be more rumpled, to be more hard-nosed and tough-looking. Columbo, Sam Spade, Bulldog Drummond, by God! My refinement, my size, my speech strike them as effeminate. I accept this. I am who I am. I shall not affect the knuckle-dusting mannerisms of Humphrey Bogart or Alan Ladd. Nonetheless, having Dub in such a position might be helpful." He thought for a moment.

"And?" asked Vonna.

"And if he does indeed have a physical problem, it would get him off the streets."

"He would *hate* supervising. You just don't know the kind of man he is."

"Does anyone really know a man?"

Not me, she thought. Never figured the bastards out and never will. God, if it would keep Dub from dying of a coronary in some dark alley while some lawyer rolled with his sugar-baby in an upstairs apartment, maybe she did want him to supervise. But that wasn't Dub to her. That wasn't the Dub who'd led her out of the White Rook. She smiled at herself for thinking of him as "her hero." When you fall in love, you want the music to swell up and the lights to dim. You expect to dissolve into the sweet fog of happily ever after, but the wrestling match is just starting. She loved Dub, there was no question of that, but living with him was getting too hard to make it sensible.

"You have no comment?"

She shook her head. She gave in to the urge and finished her beignet. "So ask him. I'm not the one to tell you what he thinks. You done with me?"

Devraix was still staring out the window. His hand had strayed up to his cheek and was brushing it as he had been when she had entered. "I believe my new razor is not quite as effective as it ought to be. Do you think—?" The telephone on his desk tootled. "Excuse me." She stood and brushed the powdered sugar from her fingers. "By all means," Devraix said into the phone, "transfer her immediately."

He covered the mouthpiece. "It is Clementine O'Dell. She has been trying to reach Dub since this morning."

"Maybe she's in love with him," Vonna said coolly.

Devraix looked like he had smelled something offensive. Never mock the rich. She leaned over and squinted. "Jesus, Honoré, you look like you've never shaved in your life. You got a face like a baby's butt."

He blinked and brushed his cheek again. "Perhaps it is irritating the skin, then, does it look—?" The telephone cut him off. "Yes, Mrs. O'Dell, very, very pleased to hear from you. No, he's not in, but I certainly know how to reach him. I see. Certainly."

Vonna drifted toward the door. "Yes, indeed," she heard Devraix say as she crossed the threshold, "Raleigh Lee Menzies. I read of the incident in the *Times-Picayune*." Vonna remembered she had forgotten to say she was sorry. The red for the peppermint. How could she do that? Jesus!

TWO

Dub's hand was shaking as he extended his finger toward the doorbell. He should have gone by a drive-through for a Diet Coke, but Mrs. O'Dell had been very insistent. Something in Diet Coke seemed to trick his stomach into thinking it had eaten. Probably some chemical that wasn't good for you, he thought ruefully. They figure that out in twenty years. Nothing was good for you twenty years later. Goddamn, was living on Nutrasweet and lettuce anything you could call living? He took a deep breath, ran a thumb under the looseness of his belt, and was startled by a face behind the barred storm door.

"Come in," said a young man as if he knew who Dub was. The man was swarthy and short. His face was so clean, it shined. His lime-green Izod shirt hung loose on his back, and Dub figured he weighed about three times what Dub had lost so far. "This way, please."

Mrs. O'Dell and a second woman were under an umbrella in the courtyard. Mrs. O'Dell had been pretty rattled the last time he had seen her, composed, but frayed around the edges. She hadn't liked getting him so deep in danger. He remembered that the first time he had seen her he had sensed there was an iron will at her core. Now that she was recovered from her husband's death, it had risen to the surface. In her manner on the phone, in her bearing in her chair, in the formal quality she gave to her sleeveless calico dress, she was a "steel magnolia," all right.

"How do you do, Mr. Greenert?" she said, extending a thin hand. "Can I offer you something? A beer? Iced tea?"

He flirted with the idea of a beer. "A Diet Coke or Pepsi, if you've got it."

The little man dipped his head slightly.

"And Stavros," she added, "bring Mrs. Menzies another highball."

Dub dragged a wicker chair up to the table. "Houseboy?" he asked.

"A chef. I intend to get him situated soon," she said, a bit too calmly. Why? Maybe Stavros was a specialist with old women. He seemed the type. "Excuse me, I haven't introduced you. This is Alma Louise Menzies, my dear friend."

If Mrs. O'Dell had iron at her core, Mrs. Menzies looked as if she had custard. Her jowls drooped, her upper arms drooped, her silvery hair was teased up in a way that seemed to emphasize the thinness of her hair. Her heavy makeup couldn't hide the flush from at least two highballs.

"Pleased to meet you, Mrs. Menzies."

As he took her damp hand, she leaned her head back as if trying to find the right angle for trifocal lenses. Her eyes were clear and blue, but bobbed as if floating on a gentle tide. "Please, call me Alma Louise. Clementine has told me so much about you. What was your name again?"

"Call me Dub."

"How are you, Dub?" asked Mrs. O'Dell.

"Do you mean did you get your money's worth?" He blinked. "No, that didn't come out right. It sounded like I didn't appreciate—"

"That's not the point," she insisted gently. "How *are* you?"

Stavros arrived with a tray. Mrs. O'Dell's iced tea had a sprig of fresh mint in the top. The highball had a zest of lemon and Dub's Coke a cherry. Maybe the boy *was* a chef.

Dub didn't want to talk about his health, but she'd paid for it, he figured. "Well, they said they don't know. Could've been arrhythmia. Could've been a lot of things. They were gonna run a sight-seeing wire up through my leg into my heart, and I said forget it. You'd paid enough."

"You should take whatever tests are needed, Dub. It's

[19]

only money to me, and darned little for what you did for my Michael."

"Never mind all this, what can I do for Alma Louise here?"

Alma Louise, five notes behind the conversation, said, "My husband's cardiologist is Tony Chimino. He's the best. You should go see him. Dr. Anthony Chimino. Raleigh had the balloon thing and is like new. It cost a fortune, but it's a better deal than that other thing."

"The bypass," said Mr. O'Dell.

"The what? Oh, yes."

Dub plucked the cherry out of his drink and dropped it on his napkin. "Tell me about the bomb," he said curtly.

"It might be like the White Rook people," said Mrs. O'Dell, "or that man who was sending letter bombs to civil rights leaders."

"They caught the letter guy."

"There are more of them than one," said Mrs. O'Dell.

"My husband," said Alma Louise out of nowhere, "was a hero."

"Raleigh Lee Menzies *is* a hero," said Mrs. O'Dell, patting her friend's hand.

Alma Louise jerked it away and raised it as if making a speech. "He fought for civil rights when black men were lynched for looking at a white woman. He was helping out when it was such a strange idea that they thought he was as crazy as Governor Long. It didn't even hurt his law practice at first, the idea was so laughable."

"But then came the Little Rock thing," said Mrs. O'Dell. "He started writing articles. Alma Louise had to go into hiding. Raleigh was beaten at Ole Miss. He still has numbness in his right arm, and his knee acts up to the extent he has pain in walking. You look at nine out of ten pictures of Martin Luther King marches in Birmingham, Selma, and St. Petersburg and if there's a white man in the picture, it's Raleigh Lee Menzies."

"He survived it all." Alma Louise had amazement in her voice. She stared through the top of the table.

"And what a lawyer on these things!" said Mrs. O'Dell.

"He backed more segregationist federal judges into corners they couldn't get out of than you can imagine!"

"It was true what he said in his book," said Alma Louise. "That young boy—you know who I'm talking about—"

"Bobby Kennedy;" said Mrs. O'Dell.

"Yes, the boy really did fly him to Washington for advice on the Reconstruction laws. And J. Edgar Hoover wouldn't even talk to him. How about that?"

"All Hoover knew was his nickname."

"The 'Red Knight.' " said Dub. "I read it in the paper."

Alma Louise smiled. "When he swung that all-white jury in Bogalusa, Andrew Young joked that 'Sir Walter Raleigh' was their 'white knight.' The Grand Dragon of Texas then went on TV in his robe and everything, and said Raleigh was a well-known Communist and ought to be called the 'Red Knight.' That's the one that took." She had said this before, maybe a hundred times.

"That's the media," said Mrs. O'Dell.

Dub thought he felt one hand quivering against the other. "But, look, that was twenty years ago, or near on. How come these Klan boys or whatever would wait so long to go after your husband?"

"They are not rational people," said Mrs. O'Dell haughtily.

"Shit, I *know* that, but you got the FBI on this, right? And the local police. Three kids were killed!" He realized he was getting loud. He softened his voice. "I'm just not sure what I could find out."

"Those teenagers were placing the bomb for someone else," said Mrs. O'Dell.

"And it went off," said Alma Louise.

"You don't think those hooligans knew how to make a bomb, do you?"

"I'm sure the cops are checking all of that."

"Well, they might miss something," said Mrs. O'Dell. "You have direct experience with these fringe groups."

"Dealing with them folks wasn't exactly the best time of my life."

[21]

Mrs. O'Dell leaned forward, touching his knee. "I'm asking you as a friend."

Dub didn't like the straightforward ploy. He owed this woman plenty. She had no particular reason to have paid his medical bills. It could give you a heart attack seeing what it cost to figure out if you'd had a heart attack. And maybe it was chump change to Mrs. O'Dell, but it was more than he'd made in five years, and he didn't like owing her. He wanted to say, "Who died and made you my friend? You hired me." But he figured it would just be his stomach bitching. The woman had always done right by him. "Well, look, I can do some checking, but I don't want to mess up the other investigations, if you know what I mean. I sure as dickens can't infiltrate any of these nut groups again." He turned to Alma Louise. "But I won't take a cent for it. I mean it. This is for your friend here."

"Don't be absurd!" said Mrs. O'Dell.

"Naw, it's on me."

Her voice switched into its command mode. "You will take your usual wages. This is your profession."

"All right, then," he said irritably. "My out-of-pocket, then. But that's all."

Alma took a swallow, set down the glass, and slumped back in her chair. "There's something nobody wants to say."

"Excuse me?"

"About the bomb. Some of the coloreds might have set it."

"Coloreds?" asked Dub. It wasn't just the weirdness of hearing the term; he didn't understand.

"Oh, not this!" said Mrs. O'Dell.

"All right, the blacks, the Afro-Americans, the African-Americans, the whatever the hell they're calling themselves this week."

"Raleigh's book," said Alma Louise.

The connections between Alma Louise's thoughts were loose as an old man's slippers. "Excuse me?" asked Dub. Mrs. O'Dell crossed her legs and stared through the French doors into the house.

"The book," said Alma Louise. "The book!"

Dub sighed. "Okay. What book? I don't belong to the Literary Guild."

"You know what book. Raleigh's book!"

Mrs. O'Dell came to his rescue. "Raleigh wrote a book for the bicentennial. His memoirs of the civil rights movement."

"His birthday gift to the nation," muttered Alma Louise.

"And?"

"Raleigh was a man who never blinked at the truth of what he saw," explained Mrs. O'Dell. "There were a lot of people who didn't like what he said about others in the movement."

"In what sense?"

"He knew about some of the girlfriends. He quoted some things that had been said by some leaders about others. He mentioned a back-room deal with George Wallace. He repeated what some of the more militant types had said about race war in 1972. Things of that nature."

"It was a kind of kiss-and-tell book?" asked Dub.

"No!" said Alma Louise. "Raleigh isn't like that!" Her head bobbed as she tried to focus on him. "Read it."

"What Alma means is that the book tells facts that no one wanted public. But they are just details, Dub. Would Thomas Jefferson have been less of a president if it were true he had a black mistress? Did Stonewall Jackson's sucking lemons or Grant's drinking tarnish his victories? What have these personal habits to do with it? Raleigh was not writing John Foxe's *Book of the Martyrs*. He was trying to leave a permanent record of how it really was."

"I get you."

"He said he was their Thu—Thucydides," slurred Alma Louise.

"Who?"

"A great historian," she said. "They threw him out of the wars, too."

Dub ran his fingers through his hair. That's right—he'd had to read some of the guy back at the Citadel.

"What Alma Louise means is that after Dr. King and Malcolm X and Medgar Evers were killed, things got uglier.

The movement's leaders began to feel that blacks had to do it on their own. They were more confrontational. The young Turks pushed Raleigh aside. He was a man with a mission, and suddenly they took it away from him. He resented it."

"And he wrote this book out of resentment?"

"No!" said Alma. "He'd killed his law practice for them. He couldn't get into government because the Red Knight thing stuck. They threw him away. He didn't have anything to do, so he recorded his past."

"And he got some money for the book?"

"It didn't do well," said Mrs. O'Dell. "The northern press crucified him."

Dub leveled his hands. "All right, all right. So the upshot of it is you think maybe some black radicals done it."

"Maybe," said Alma Louise.

"Or white radicals."

"Almost certainly," said Mrs. O'Dell.

Dub sighed. "And what does Mr. Menzies think?"

"He won't do anything about it," said Mrs. O'Dell. "That's why Alma Louise is so worried. He will not go away. Whoever it was might well try again. This time it could be both of them killed, or the housekeeper, or the neighbor, or whoever gets in their way."

"Maybe all he's wanted," said Alma Louise sloppily, "all these years, is just to be a martyr. He's sitting up there in his study saying, 'I'm Raleigh Lee Menzies, kill me. I've got nothing to live for.' " She began to blubber.

Dub looked at Mrs. O'Dell. Her mouth pursed, and she offered Alma Louise a napkin. "For pity's sake, Alma, compose yourself."

"Maybe you ought to get Stavros to bring her some coffee," said Dub. "Maybe your husband's just courageous," he offered.

Mrs. O'Dell was still miffed, and the remark about coffee hadn't helped. "We went to school together. She's my oldest, dearest friend. She's had more than enough reason to drink New Orleans dry."

"I'm sorry." He finished his soda. The ice had melted and the drink was watery. He quickly popped the cherry into his mouth and wondered how many calories were in it. Mrs. Menzies sniffled for several minutes while Dub studied the twisted vines on a false Greek column.

"I'm sorry," said Alma Louise. "He's been through so much, we—"

"It's all right," said Dub.

"You will look into it, won't you?"

"Of course he will," said Mrs. O'Dell.

He glanced at her. Steel, he thought, for sure. I don't stand a chance. "I'll ask around," he said noncommittally. "But I can't mess up the police, you understand that? They take a dim view."

Alma Louise nodded.

"I'll show you out," said Mrs. O'Dell abruptly.

Mrs. O'Dell pulled him to a stop in the corridor as soon as they were out of sight of the French doors to the courtyard. "There is something else," she said.

"Yeah?"

"I don't want Alma Louise hurt."

"Go on."

"Sometimes she gets carried away."

"Drunk, you mean."

"That's not what I mean." She pursed her lips. "Well, that's part of what I mean. She hasn't been herself for some time. For the last two weeks she has been hitting the bottle very hard. She is always befuddled. She's turning into the White Queen in *Alice in Wonderland*."

"The Red Knight and the White Queen," said Dub.

"I think she wears those adult diapers sometimes."

"And?"

"She gets lonely."

"How do you mean lonely?"

"Stavros."

"The houseboy?"

"Once or twice. And he isn't a houseboy. He's free to do as he pleases. He knows if he uses Alma Louise wrong I will make certain he never cooks in this town. So far I think he just gives her some happiness."

"Who else other than Stavros?"

"She's not a tramp!"

"But she gets drunk. Maybe forgets."

She crossed to a large painting of a fox hunt and touched the dust in the gilt curls of its huge frame.

"The upshot is that you think one of these guys could have tried to get Raleigh out of the way," he said quietly.

"Don't be silly."

"Lady," said Dub, "it's the oldest motive in the book."

"Well, I won't have you hurt her," she said firmly. "I will not."

He grabbed her elbow. "If you want me to ask around, you've got to let me follow my nose."

"If she were responsible—well, not responsible—but the motive behind an attempt on Raleigh, it would kill her, Dub." She stated it as an irrefutable fact.

He ran his fingers through his hair. "If it comes to something like that, I'll tell you first. Is that good enough? Before the police, before anybody. You're my client, not her. I wouldn't touch this with a pole for nobody but you, you understand me?"

"Very well."

"I'll call you, Mrs. O'Dell." He turned, but her fingers tugged the flap of his jacket pocket.

"Thank you," she said. The way she said it surprised him. Her tone was soft. She would have been quite a belle in her day, turning on the infrared. It reminded him of his ex-wife when they were first married. It caused a twinge, but he let it charm him nonetheless.

He tried a smile. "I'll do what I can." He hesitated a moment, wanting to say he was sorry to be so grumpy, but it seemed the wrong time for it.

When he was almost through the door he thought he saw a movement by the curving staircase to the right behind Mrs. O'Dell. It might have been the lime-green flash of Stavros's Izod shirt. So the little chef was an eavesdropper, Dub thought. Maybe I should've been quizzing him.

THREE

By the time Dub had worked his car out of the Garden District it was nearly one-thirty. He already had some ideas on how to get started, though he couldn't see the point in it. Once you play footsie with the real cops (and they refuse to put out), then you annoy everyone in the neighborhood by asking the same questions the cops have. Finding out nothing new, you then try to skip the middleman by speculating on the origin and trying to work it from that angle. In this case, figure out who was most likely to have set the bomb. And then? Well, if it was a white-supremacy group, Dub couldn't go anywhere near them. His face was like raw meat to a pit bull. If it was a black perp or group, he didn't have the right pigments even to ask around. He also imagined that the old lady's highballs would wear off, she'd feel lousy and wouldn't remember sending him on this wild-goose chase. That would be par. "Pointless, pointless, POINTLESS!" he shouted, slapping his steering wheel. The man in the next car heard him and gave him a look. "Don't worry," said Dub, "I'm just your typical Crescent City loon." The man drove off as if he hadn't heard, and the horn behind Dub burped immediately.

He was hungry, he was sweating, and he was pissed off. He pulled into a McDonald's, found a seat under the air-conditioning vent, and picked at his dressing-less salad trying to avoid the cholesterol-bearing Velveeta-like shreds scattered through it. He ate slowly and nursed his Diet Coke for half an hour, never mind the sign warning a twenty-minute limit for customers. When he finished, he thought, he'd still be hungry and pissed off, but at least he'd be cooler. What in the world had made him want to move to a city like this? When you stood up on the Mississippi levees you could see that New Orleans was actually lower than the river. The accumulation of mud over the centuries had raised the river up on a natural aqueduct that was watched and cared for like a newborn. It was perverse, like the whole goddamned city. You saw it and you knew that if the levees ruptured, New Orleans would be the name of a bayou. The city was, in that sense, under water, and to Dub, it usually felt underwater.

He'd moved here to live with Vonna, he remembered. She'd invited him. Was that the only reason? Was it capital-L love? Little-L love? Or was he just afraid of being alone? Of dying alone? He stuck his hand in his sport coat and held the little bottle of nitro tablets. Maybe he could deal with it better if the doctors could tell him whether he'd really had a heart attack or not. If he knew, maybe he'd also know if he'd made a mistake with Vonna and ought to move back to Pittsburgh, where the humidity was usually below two hundred percent. He inhaled the Siren smell of the hamburgers and quickly tossed back the last of the ice from his Coke.

Back in the office, he had a note to inform Devraix about his meeting with Mrs. O'Dell, but Emma, the secretary, said he had gone for the day. A second note told Dub that Vonna wouldn't be home until after eight: she was taking over for Spyder on the loading-dock pilfering case at the mall. Spyder had picked the case right up when Mrs. O'Dell yanked Dub's leash. I should go back to Pittsburgh, he thought. Calabrese at the Keyhole Agency would give him his job back. He didn't really owe anybody here, did he? Vonna could come with him or get over it one way or another. Maybe she was already over it. This Raleigh Lee Menzies thing was already in better hands, and Dub wouldn't get nowhere with it nohow.

All right, he told himself, at least go through the motions. He found Lawrence Campbell's phone number in his black book. He was surprised the FBI agent accepted his call. He tried friendliness. "Dub Greenert here."

"So Jane told me. What do you want?"

Shithead, thought Dub. "How you doin'?"

[28]

"Pretty good until you called."

"Aw, come on, Larry."

"I don't go by Larry, and even if I did, it's Agent Campbell to you."

"Yes, sir," said Dub.

"Okay, get on with it. Sticking your nose where it doesn't belong again?"

"Aw, come on, I haven't talked to you for a year and you're still cranked off."

Campbell expelled a long breath of air. "You were playing on our court without letting us know, Greenert."

"I didn't know you guys were involved. Honest."

"Yeah, yeah."

Dub listened to the silence for a few seconds. This wasn't going nowhere. He might as well get it over with. "You on this Menzies bombing?"

"That's none of your business."

"Hey, come on, now. Nobody wants Raleigh Lee Menzies to be hurt."

"If you've got information, Mr. Greenert, we'd be glad to hear it. If not, you're wasting tax dollars by tying me up."

"Look, I can't say who, you understand, but somebody close to Menzies asked me to do what I can. Now, I know that I can't do much compared to you boys, but the client is worried."

"Who's the client?"

The question was sharp, but Dub thought there might be a toehold in it. A government guy always had to worry about influence. "I can't say that, you know, but you can imagine there's a lot of people who'd hate to see a hero of the civil rights movement get blown up."

Campbell seemed to be thinking. Maybe Dub had implied his client was the NAACP or a similar group. If he had, he was happy to let Campbell think so.

"It doesn't matter who it is," the agent said finally. "The matter's under investigation, and if you have any questions you'll have to contact our press liaison. His number is—"

"So you're on it. That's good," said Dub. "Everybody

thinks it's maybe the same guys who were sending the letter bombs, maybe the Kluxers. What do you think?"

"That was one man and we nailed him."

"So you think it's a copycat. Maybe somebody inspired by your boy?"

"I think you should contact our press liaison. Oh, gosh," he said sarcastically, "what time is that? I'm late for an appointment. I'd *love* to chat, but I've got to run. Have a nice day."

"But—" The phone clicked. "Prick!" said Dub to the dial tone. He slammed the phone into its cradle so hard, he was afraid he'd broken it. He listened again to the dial tone. The conversation would have been shorter if Campbell hadn't suspected Dub's client might have clout. Nothing struck fear into bureaucratic hearts like angry millionaires or black liberals on the warpath. Maybe if he'd gone to Campbell's office, he might have gotten something with that lever. He drummed his fingers on the desk for a minute and decided to go by Ben Hawkins's office. The case was probably outside the city cops' jurisdiction, but Dub didn't know who to contact out there, and maybe Hawkins would help. A bomber wouldn't care whose jurisdiction he was in.

Dub had to park nearly three blocks from the station and walk back. A bank sign said it was ninety-five degrees, and his shirt was soaking into his sport coat when he approached the guard just inside the metal detector. "Ben Hawkins?" he asked, wiping his face with his hand.

"Yurr bidness?"

"We're old friends."

"Sign heah. Third flow."

Dub clipped the pass to his pocket and started for the elevator. It looked crowded, so he took the stairs.

Hawkins was in his office, three open files on his desk, a gyro with feta on a piece of foil in the middle of the center one. His black face was scowling as usual, but his big hands were nimbly moving over the keyboard of his scratched Selectric as if he were playing a harpsichord.

"Hey, man, what's happening?" said Dub.

Hawkins looked up without taking his fingers off the

keyboard. "That s'posed to be Nee-gro talk, Greenert? It's out of date. You must want something."

"It's just an expression us whiteys stole from you folks. How are you?"

"Just waiting for that retirement bus. And I'm busy. How'd you get in here?"

"I won't keep you. Thought I'd say hi."

Hawkins exhaled as if tired and took a big bite out of his gyro.

"Smells good," said Dub.

"A man likes having lunch at almost three," Hawkins growled. "It's good for the ulcer."

"The feta's what makes those things," said Dub. "Cholesterol's what makes everything." Hawkins set his massive jaw and gave him a cut-the-shit scowl. "I been looking into the Raleigh Lee Menzies thing."

Hawkins silently chewed.

"Some people are kind of concerned." He was trying to sound casual.

There was a slight, very slight, softening of Hawkins's expression. "That's Jefferson Parish. Didn't happen on my watch," he said.

"No," said Dub. "But, well, I thought maybe you might've heard something."

"And then I should tell you if I had?"

"Aw, come on, didn't I tip you to that crack house last December?" It was Spyder who had noticed it, but Devraix had told Dub to call it in.

"That don't pay me back for you and the almighty Honoré Devraix shucking me on that guy you killed last year."

"I know. I know." This was going to be as useful as talking to Campbell, Dub thought, but Hawkins suddenly made a movement with his head. Dub looked at him quizzically.

"The door," Hawkins mouthed impatiently.

Dub eased it shut with his foot.

"Who's your client?" asked Hawkins.

"I can't tell you."

"Then drop dead."

[31]

"Somebody close to him."

"Riiiiight."

Hawkins lifted a file, pulled a napkin out from under it, and wiped his fingers. He was deciding whether to talk. Dub hadn't expected this at all. Hawkins didn't have a reason to talk, that Dub knew of, or he would have come into the office ready to exploit it. The most he'd thought he might get was a name to contact in the Jefferson Parish cops. He settled into a chair and waited.

"Raleigh Lee Menzies is a hero," Dub finally ventured.

"Don't tell me," said Hawkins angrily. "You know something? Like some of these shit-don't-stink white boys of yours after him?"

"I don't know."

"Well, I'm interested, you got me? And if you're onto something, you'd better fucking tell me. It's not my case, but you'd better fucking tell me."

"I know: it's a Jefferson Parish matter."

"But there are a couple of Orleans men on it, and I got a personal interest."

"Why city men?"

"Because the boy driving the car lived just inside. The bomb might have been made in Orleans Parish. And we fingered the little shit, Bantam Billy, for rolling some fudge-packers in the Quarter a couple of months back. Bad limp gave him away. The girls were from out of town, though. They wouldn't testify."

"You know anything about the bomb?"

"It was a big one."

"What do you mean?"

"It was a lot bigger than it needed to be."

"So?"

"How slow are you, Greenert? So, it ain't like it was somebody who knew about bombs."

"Or it was somebody who wanted to make sure."

Hawkins shook his head. "Stolen dynamite. They wrapped it in your regular Ace Hardware variety nails. There was a wire to the trigger attached to the door. It was supposed to work by pulling down the front door."

"So it was an amateur thing?"

"Maybe even Bantam Billy himself."

"They were setting the bomb and it blew."

"That's what the feds think. They're going to tell the press that tomorrow morning. The bomb just wasn't like the other bombs, so it don't seem like the same cruds."

"You believe it?"

Hawkins shrugged. "It ain't my case."

Dub thought for a minute. "There's something else, though. What's up?"

Hawkins sniffed, and bit into his gyro.

"If there wasn't something else, you wouldn't've told me all this. You're a good cop. You don't like P.I.'s on principle, and you particularly don't like me."

"Naw!" said Hawkins, beaming.

"So?"

"So law enforcement ain't what you see on TV, is it? Sometimes the law is just as happy to see somebody become a victim as they are to stop a crime."

"The FBI?"

"Don't act so innocent. Hoover's boys spent a lot of time back in the sixties trying to prove Raleigh Lee Menzies was a Communist, and let's just say that any asshole from my part of town knows they could've been a bit more forthright in going after the Klan. Later, they got pushed and some of them did a good job, but there are still a lot of those boys who'd like to prove that the Red Knight was really a Red."

"So you really think that if somebody killed Menzies there wouldn't be too many wet eyes over there." Hawkins set his big jaw. "And then they could get the credit for nailing his killer." Hawkins wiped his fingers. Dub was silent for several seconds. Eventually, he halfheartedly grinned. "Get serious. Where do you get this fairy tale?"

"Suit yourself, white boy. Maybe you got to have rhythm to know which way the wind blows."

"That's paranoid, Ben."

"You aren't paranoid, Dr. Sigmund Fraud, if somebody's out to get you."

"Jesus, Ben, why not say the FBI set the bomb?"

[33]

"I didn't say that, and you'd better not fucking go around saying I said it."

"Then what are you saying?"

"I'm saying Mr. Menzies has got a lot of enemies, and they aren't all low-life crackers. Some of them wear silk ties. Bantam Billy was a gimpy-leg punk. He could've kept his brains in an okra pod. Sure, he did some valve work and a ring job or two, but bombs won't his style unless somebody gave him one. Billy and his crowd go for knuckles and ax handles and sawed-offs."

Dub wiped his face with his hand. Hawkins was a hard-nosed cop. The hardest kind of hard-nosed cop. He dated the fall of civilization from the outlawing of the rubber hose. For him to be saying this was scarier than Dub wanted to admit. "Okay," he said, "but what about a black bomber? I understand Menzies wrote a book that cranked off a lot of people."

"Shit, nobody cares about that stuff."

"But he took the halos off some black leaders."

"Man, you think anybody cares how much pipe laying those men did? They were in a war, and a lot of them died."

"But it was Menzies who wrote about it."

"And so did Ralph Abernathy and so did a lot of them. Abernathy died in his bed, didn't he? Don't come around here with this 'black revenge' bullshit, or I'll show you some."

Dub raised his palms. "Hey, it's always a possibility. People usually get it from their own. A Hindu killed Gandhi. Muslims killed Malcolm X."

Hawkins stared into space. "I'd kill the brother who went after Menzies. With my hands. That ain't it, though. No way."

The intensity of the man's feelings startled Dub. Hawkins looked embarrassed, so Dub avoided his eyes. What was going on here? First he opens up in a way he never has, then he comes up with an elaborate conspiracy theory, then this bubbling, churning anger. Hawkins knew a great deal about the case. He'd made some effort to find out. This was more than just station-house gossip. How was he linked to Raleigh Lee Menzies?

"You through?" asked Hawkins quietly. He shoved his gyro to the side of his desk as if he had lost all appetite for it.

"I gotta get home," said Dub, standing. He almost bumped into a policewoman coming in.

"Oh, good," she said, ignoring Dub, "you're through. Sergeant Bailey said he thought you'd like to know they just nailed that bomber at the guy's house."

Hawkins looked like five hundred volts had shot through him. "At Menzies's house?" He sprang to his feet. "Is Mr. Menzies okay?"

The woman shrugged.

"Do you mind if I—?" Dub asked.

Hawkins was already halfway to the stairs.

FOUR

At the funeral supper, his foot patting nervously on the wooden floor, Bobby Alberts knew who had killed his brother, no question, and there wasn't any way the bastard was going to get away with it. The cops wouldn't do shit, he knew. They never go after guys with money. Daddy couldn't do shit but cuss. As the man had left the funeral limo, he'd had to cling to the open door to keep from falling. He'd finished off his pocket flask on the way over. Bobby had to choke a fit of weeping down. He couldn't bring himself to help him walk into the house, so Aunt Perlie led him. Perlie, technically his aunt but only a dozen years older, probably had the guts. The older folks liked to call her a spitfire. He thought about getting her to drive him when he went after Menzies, but she was a chick. She'd tell somebody or try to talk him out of it. This was a man's job.

As if reading his mind, their neighbor, Mrs. Jones, who about once a week woke up with a hangover in his daddy's bed, shook her head and placed a hand on Bobby's shoulder. "I guess you're the man of the family now," she said. And she was right. Bantam Billy was dead. His father was a ghost. It was time for Bobby to be the man now, the carrier and defender of the Alberts blood. No, there wasn't anybody else left in the family to make Raleigh Lee Menzies pay.

"Yes'm," he said, gritting his teeth so forcefully he thought they would shatter.

He couldn't get what happened at the graveside out of his mind. Between the raised casket and the rack, Bobby could see water glistening next to the vault down below. When it came his turn, he picked up a handful of the soil held up in a bucket by one of the undertakers. He squeezed it in his hand and took a silent oath. He turned his wrist and pressed the soil against the casket lid, then noticed the white flecks of vermiculite. Instead of sprinkling it on, he had wanted to leave his handprint on the lid, but instead of the sticky red clay in which Billy was to be buried, the funeral people had provided a bucket of potting soil. When Bobby took away his hand, the black stuff slid off like rain on a fresh-waxed Chevy.

Nobody ever done right by Bantam Billy. Nobody. They hadn't given him anything. They hadn't gotten the operation to fix his hip because it cost too much, and then it was too late. He'd watched his momma drop dead, then his daddy crawl into a pocket flask. Nobody'd even bailed Billy out when he was arrested for rolling the queer, though Bobby had begged them. Billy Alberts deserved something. Revenge, if nothing else. Bobby could give him that. This was his oath.

Bobby scanned the women unwrapping salads and casseroles. Some were chattering like it was bingo night. He turned away from them and stared out the window at the hamburger wrappers and paper cups that had blown against the rusty chain-link fence. His arms ached from his clenching his fists. Perlie sidled up to him and said something about getting something to eat. Bobby wanted to slap her. He didn't want distractions. He heard his daddy sadly say, "Well, that's over, I guess." *They* didn't deserve what Bobby was going to do for their good names, but it didn't matter because he wasn't doing it for them. He was doing it for Billy.

Bobby felt his father looking at him several times. The old man slurred out something about the weather and muddled through a story about meeting the boys' momma and how he'd had to marry her and what she had said in the last few days before the stroke finished her, but Bobby refused to listen. He'd heard the sloppy story a thousand times. He would not allow his intensity to be wasted. He walked through the mourners, past the layout of corn bread, fried chicken, potato salad, Coca-Cola cake, and other desserts, and went into Billy's room. Somebody had cleaned up while they were gone. The *Car & Driver* magazines were neatly stacked. The bed was made. The pile of T-shirts and jeans that usually lay in the corner was gone, maybe looted. Bobby snapped open the closet door and swept aside the jackets. The machete, the nunchakas, and the throwing stars Billy had kept in the dark corner were gone. What else? The wrenches. They'd stolen Billy's socket set.

Bobby almost dove for the bed. He reached under and into the hole in the cloth covering the bottom of the box springs. He was pricked by the sharp edge of a wire, then he sighed. The cold greasy feel of the metal. The twenty-two was still there. He jiggled it loose, unholstered it, and, still on his back, sighted up along the barrel. The cracked light fixture was Raleigh Lee Menzies's head. Bang, he whispered. He saw the head explode, like Billy's must have. He checked the clip. Six bullets. He stuck the pistol in his belt and buttoned his polyester suit jacket. He fished the box of bullets out of the back of the underwear drawer, scattering different-colored briefs on the linoleum.

He paused and looked around. What else? The trophies: pictures of girls nearly covered the surface of Billy's dresser mirror. In the small uncovered center, Bobby glanced at himself. You couldn't really see the gun under his jacket unless you knew it was there. A picture of Billy holding a longneck beer and standing between two chicks in bikinis caught his eye. The breasts of the heavy girl on Billy's right were level with his eyes, which were wide and smirking. "Hey, li'l brother," Bobby remembered Billy saying, "Breaking my hip was the best thing ever happened to me. You're too tall. You have to look at their *faces!*"

Bobby started to laugh, but it choked. He wasn't going to cry. It might let the feelings out, and he needed every drop. He pointed at the photo. "This is for you, man!" he shouted. "This is for you!" He snapped open the door, went into his own room, and snatched his big hunting knife out of the closet. He roughly shoved people aside making for the front door, then had a sudden thought, reached under the kitchen sink, and took out the nearly empty pint of cheap bourbon.

"Bobby, Bobby," pleaded Mrs. Jones, but Bobby drained it

and pushed her back. The mourners gathered around him, limply holding their plates piled with food.

"What are you looking at? Huh?"

"Poor boy," whispered one old woman to another, as if Bobby wasn't there. Boss Mayhew wetly cleared his throat.

Bobby sneered. "Well, don't let me stop you! Stuff your faces! Forget Billy! None of you cares a shit!"

"Now Bobby, Bobby," soothed Perlie, but the boy punched open the screen door and stalked out.

"He'll be all right," he heard Boss Mayhew say. "The boy's upset."

Bobby was almost in the car when he remembered he hadn't taken the keys. He wouldn't go back for them. His license had been revoked almost as soon as he'd gotten it, and there might be a wrestling match over the keys. The other cars blocked it in, anyway. He shortcut through Mrs. Jones's garden patch, stomping her scrawny pepper plants and kicking dirt on her okra. He reached the main road and walked resolutely. He did not want to be out of breath when he got there. On the other hand, he didn't want to move slowly in case anything might interfere. He concentrated on calming himself. His hand had to be steady. His mind had to be ready. It was like hunting deer, that's all. A two-legged, murdering, son-of-a-bitch deer. You had to be ready when you got your chance.

After about half a mile walking along the dusty shoulder buffeted by the blasts of air from passing trucks, he reached the stoplight and the brick pillars flanking the entrance to the subdivision. As long as he could remember, there had always been rumors that as soon as the sewer pipes were approved, the subdivision would spread west and wipe out the little community in which Bobby had grown up. The bastards just wanted to clean them off the land like mildew off a bathroom tile. Blowing up Billy had been their big mistake. Once Bobby showed the way, everybody'd know there wouldn't be any treating them like dirt. This was for Billy, but it was more than that, too. It'd be Billy's best memorial.

He was concentrating so intensely, he was startled by a movement in a black car parked in the trees just before

Menzies's driveway. Did they have cops watching the house? When he peered directly at the man behind the wheel, he could barely make out his features because of the mottled reflection on the shiny windshield. The man raised a newspaper in front of his face as if reading it. Try and stop me, thought Bobby. I'll kill you, too, if you get in my way. The objective is Raleigh Lee Menzies. At any cost.

He paused at the end of the driveway. The street had been cleaned. Other than the glitter of some grains of glass and the splintered mailbox pole, there was no sign that anyone had been killed there. Skeeter, Dave, and Billy had been washed away so that the neighborhood could get on with its cookouts and pool parties. Bobby patted the pistol on his left side and the knife on his right. First the knees, and he can't run. Then the elbows. Then three slow ones in the guts. The pain will be so bad he'll beg to die, and when I get good and ready, I'll slice his throat.

He climbed the driveway. The big window curtains were all closed. He should check the gun. He pulled it out. Hiding it close against his hip, he clicked the first shell into the chamber. Sweat stung his eyes. He felt like he was going to throw up. He inhaled deeply and could taste his father's cheap bourbon at the back of his throat. He shook his arms to loosen up, then pressed the doorbell. He waited. Maybe no one was home. Shit! He pressed again.

He heard some movement, and then the peephole blinked. He weakly smiled and licked his lips. The door locks clicked. An older black woman had chained the door and was peering through the slot. A strong sweet perfume was carried on the cool air pouring out.

"Yes?"

"I'd like to see Mr. Raleigh Lee Menzies."

"And what is the nature of your business?"

"That's between me and your boss."

"What is your name, son? He don't want to talk to the press today."

"I'm not the press, and I want to talk to Mr. Menzies right now!"

"Well, you won't see nobody unless I hear a name and see some identification. Mr. Menzies is an important man."

"I'm— I'm—" His mouth didn't seem to work. "Open the door, damn it! Open the door!"

The woman saw the gun. When it registered what it was, she whispered "Lawd!" and rolled out of the opening. She must have thrown her body against the door. It slammed, and Bobby heard desperate fumbling with the locks. He threw himself against the door with a thud. It opened hard against the chain, which held nonetheless. He thrust his arm through the slot and flailed against the woman, shouting, "Open it! Open it! I won't hurt you! I want Menzies! Don't make me—"

Something cracked against his forearm. He heard a shattering like glass and was blinded by pain. The door then clamped his upper arm against the doorpost and he pulled in agony, trying to get it loose. He flailed the gun wildly with his free hand. It went off with a deafening pop, and the bullet split the soffit. The door opened enough for him to pull his tortured arm loose, then slammed. He kicked against it, then bent over, pressing his injured arm with the pistol. He looked down at the street and thought to run. "You pussy!" he heard Billy say. He twisted his head from side to side, then scurried past the bushes to circle the house. He reached the gate of a high fence.

He heard the woman screaming into the backyard. "Mr. Menzies! Mr. Menzies!"

Bobby snapped back the gate. About twenty-five yards away he saw a tall, silver-haired man by the edge of his swimming pool, spraying his roses with a hose and a plastic fertilizer mixer. The man seemed confused by both Bobby's appearance and the woman's shouting from a door that Bobby couldn't see. Bobby lumbered forward, his right arm dangling limp, the gun extended out in front of him.

"Go inside, Martha," said the man calmly.

Bobby reached the corner and glanced to his right. The woman was standing under a large patio canopy.

"Go inside, Martha," the man insisted.

The woman looked at Bobby. Bobby kept his eye on Menzies. She backed through the glass sliding door.

"You know what?" said Bobby. "You're thinking she'll call the police. But I let her go."

"Thank you," said Menzies. "She's got two boys."

"You care more about a nigger's kids than Billy."

"Billy?"

"Billy Alberts. My brother. Don't make like you forget."

"No. I had to come to your house. You can't go around smashing mailboxes."

"And then you killed Billy."

"I?"

"Over a goddamned mailbox! And you're going to die for it. You're gonna suffer. I'm going to wait until the cops are in the driveway before I put you out of your misery, you . . . you—" His mouth was tangling up again. In desperation he pointed the pistol at Menzies's knee.

Menzies turned. The gun went off as the spray from the hose burned into Bobby's eyes. Bobby fired, then stumbled back, then fired again. He tried to raise his broken arm to rub his eyes, was punched by the pain, and lost his bearings. He wiped at his face with the sleeve of his gun arm and saw the blurred red, yellow and green of the rosebushes. Something sharp clipped him in the calves and he lost his balance, spinning out of control to a grating noise.

He tumbled through space. There was a rush of sound, then utter silence. He was in roiling water, sinking, flailing with his gun arm. He wanted to swim, but his broken arm wouldn't move and the thrashing spun him chaotically. He knew he was drowning. He gasped for air and tasted chlorine. He felt wonder as the pain began to deaden and float soft as a feather. The sunlight splintering the murky water turned velvety gray, then faded to warm violet and silent black.

FIVE

Dub tried to get Hawkins to talk about Menzies as they ripped
through traffic, siren hooting. Hawkins had no authority out
on Thibodeaux Road. He wasn't even one of the men working
on the bombing in the city, but he had bolted out of the
station house without telling anyone where he was going and
he radioed the dispatcher four times to find out what the
situation was. The first report said three people, unidentified,
had been shot. The second report said that only Menzies had
been shot. The third said the boy was dead. The fourth time
the radio barked back, "We'll let you know, Hawkins! We got
work to do here! We'll let you know. OUT!"

Dub tried to probe casually when the traffic slowed, but
slowing only made Hawkins's jaw set hard as a Mayan god's.

"You two must go back some ways."

"You wanta walk? How'd you get in this car? You don't
belong—" he swerved around a bus and through a red light
"—in a police vehicle, Section Two-thirty-whatever-the-fuck."

"I'm invisible," Dub said. "Hear no, see no nothing."

Hawkins screeched to a stop behind a TV news truck. He
flashed his badge, and Dub followed him through the cluster
of curious neighbors and reporters. They both stepped under
the yellow tape and started up the driveway. "Those are city
cops," Dub heard a woman say. "Sir! Sir! Will you talk to us?
What's the city's interest?" Dub glanced back and saw an
immaculate blond who reminded him of his first wife, Beth,
at the prom. The blond was waving a microphone and fid-

geting like she couldn't find a bathroom. At the ambulance the paramedic was getting ready to close the door.

Hawkins showed his badge. "Menzies?"

"Around back," said a Jefferson Parish deputy. He sported a large, very waxed, handlebar mustache that probably pissed off every traffic violator he stopped. It was as stiff as the newswoman's hair, from the look of it.

"Who's the boy?" asked Dub.

"Robert Ray Alberts, 'Bobby.' Broken arm, damn near singing at the pearlies."

Dub got just a glimpse before the door closed. The boy's arm was in a sling, but he was not resisting the heavy nylon straps binding him to the gurney. He stared up at the ambulance ceiling, his lower lip quivering.

"What happened?" Dub asked the deputy.

"Damn near drowned. Why're you boys out here?"

"Oh, liaison stuff," said Dub. "Politics. We'd rather you done it all, but hey—" He shrugged helplessly. He turned to check for Hawkins. "Great mustache!" he said, walking away quickly. He hadn't *said* he was a cop, exactly.

He started for the front door, then noticed another uniform guarding the gate to the back. He walked toward him as if he knew what he was doing. The deputy seemed to assume he was Hawkins's partner and even held it open for him. "How're you?" asked Dub.

"Good," said the deputy coldly.

As he approached the pool, he saw that a tall, dignified man was straddling a pool lounger, shaking Hawkins's hand and clutching his elbow. His shoulders were covered by a long, striped towel. Water dripped from spikes of hair at the back of his neck. A squatty man in a suit leaned toward them.

Hawkins's voice was warmer than Dub had ever heard it. "Are you all right, Mr. Menzies?"

"Oh, now, Ben," said Menzies, "you know I want you to call me Raleigh."

"Are you all right, Mr. Menzies?"

"Damp!"

Hawkins turned to the squatty man. "Why don't you let the man go inside and dry up, Bill?"

"Never mind that," said Menzies. "The sun is warm. I needed the dip." He noticed Dub. "How do you do, sir?"

"Fine," said Dub. Hawkins gave him a look but didn't say anything.

"How is the boy?" asked Menzies.

"He'll be all right," said Bill.

"His eyes?" asked Menzies, settling to the lounge.

"His dip," snorted Bill, "rinsed him purty good."

"Good," said Menzies. "In a way, I wasn't even thinking. There he was with the gun, looking more afraid than I was. I turned, and the stream hit him in the face. It was a mixture of that fertilizer with the blue label in the shed back there—forget the name—and Thuricide. You make sure the hospital knows."

"We tol' 'em," said Bill.

"Nobody was shot?" asked Hawkins.

Bill shook his head. His double chin flapped.

"Mumbo Jumbo," said Menzies.

"Huh?" said Hawkins.

"Mumbo Jumbo shall never be the same." He pointed across the pool at a large black wood carving, an African totem with angular grooves for features. About half the face had split off, exposing a light wood interior. "We'd just won the settlement in St. Petersburg and lots of the papers were—you know, Ben—calling me 'godless' and so on, and I was on the Klan's hit list. Some of the ministers and Rathman—he was a Jew—decided I needed a god to protect me, so they bought this big thing and got Dr. King himself to present it. They called it Mumbo Jumbo, god of the just cause." He wiped his face with the end of his towel. "It's supposed to be a witch doctor's totem, actually. A medical god, like Apollo or Aesculapius. The story's in my book."

"I know," said Hawkins, with a wistful grin.

Menzies's mood changed. "I don't guess ol' Mumbo has much power."

"You're alive, ain'tcha?" said Hawkins.

Menzies looked up and weakly smiled.

"Looks like Mumbo took a bullet meant for you," said Dub.

"Yes," said Menzies thoughtfully. "They told me he was ebony, but the inside looks like ash or oak. I guess he's a fake."

"You're *alive*," repeated Hawkins. "Hey, I know a wood guy over to Chalmette who'll make it like new. I'll take it myself."

"It's all right," said Menzies. "It's just an old trophy." He closed his eyes tightly like a man trying to suppress a migraine. "Is that all?"

"Well, Mr. Menzies, I reckon so," said Bill. He flipped his notepad closed. "We'll bring the complaint around to sign this afternoon."

"No, no," said Menzies. "I won't sign it. The boy's distraught over his brother. I went over to their house once to warn the older boy not to smash people's mailboxes, but only Bobby and his father were there. There were words, the old man had put away a few, and he threatened me with a bat. I don't think charging the boy will solve anything."

"With all respect, Mr. Menzies," said Bill, "if you had turned Billy Alberts in, maybe he wouldn't't've eat that bomb and maybe young Bobby wouldn't't've been waving that pistol in your face."

Hawkins raised his hands as if exasperated by a stubborn child. "The boy tried to kill you. Maybe both of them tried to kill you."

"The boy wasn't in his right mind. Grief can do that."

"We gonna charge Bobby whether you want it or not, Mr. Menzies," said Bill. "Your bleeding liberal heart could be bleeding literally!" He softened his tone. "One of them bullets could've hit a neighbor kid. S'pose Mrs. Johnson hadn't—"

"Oh, Raleigh! Raleigh!" Dub was clipped hard on the shoulder as Alma Menzies rushed past him, one hand on her broad-brimmed hat. "Are you all right?" A mixed odor of florid perfume and sour mash swirled in front of Dub.

She collapsed on one knee and clutched her husband's shoulders, kissing his cheek. "I'm fine, Alma Louise, I'm fine," Menzies said. He pulled back from her, trying to peel off her embrace.

"I'd never forgive myself—"

"I'm okay, Alma Louise."

"I was shopping at the Riverwalk."

Maybe with Stavros, thought Dub.

"I'm fine," he said sharply. "Don't make a spectacle of yourself!" He looked apologetically at Hawkins. "My wife's so—"

Alma Louise had looked up at Dub. "Why weren't you protecting him? You knew somebody was after him."

Bill, who had begun leaving, had regained interest. He looked at Hawkins. "He ain't with you?"

"He came with me, but he ain't with me, no."

"What the hell does that mean?" He came after Dub. "You *knew* that this boy was coming after Mr. Menzies?"

"Whoa," said Dub. "I didn't know anything more than you boys did. I knew there'd been a bomb, that's all."

"He was supposed to protect you, Raleigh," said Alma Louise. "Clementine told me they were good detectives."

"Detectives?" Menzies shook his head. "You went out and hired some Pinkerton? Oh, really, Alma Louise, I told you—"

"She was worried about you, Mr. Menzies," said Dub.

"And didn't you think I'd be interested that there was a private eye watching me?"

"We hadn't even started," said Dub. "We were just looking into it."

"Well, you're just finished with it," said Bill. "We can protect our citizens out here."

"Your deputies did a fine job today," said Hawkins. Dub was startled to hear someone even partly take his side.

"What the hell you mean? You think you city cops'd done better?"

Hawkins's nose flared. "Three days ago there was a bomb down that hill, and you don't even have a man on the property."

"Mr. Menzies didn't want one on the property, wouldn't take one. That don't mean we weren't watching the place."

"Has everybody got to watch me?" asked Menzies. "I'm no zoo animal. I won't have it."

"That boy tried to kill you," said Alma Louise. "Twice."

"Hey, look," said Dub to Alma Louise, "it's up to you. I can keep looking into it or not. I warned you I didn't think there was much I could do that the police couldn't."

"Pay the gentleman his expenses, Alma Louise," said Menzies, peeling his wife's arms off his shoulders again. "And give him a bonus for his trouble."

"We're even," said Dub, wondering how he'd explain refusing payment to Devraix.

"I insist," said Menzies.

Hawkins leaned over and touched Menzies's shoulder. "Keep him a few days." Menzies looked at him quizzically. So did Dub. "He knows something about these white terrorists."

"But the police are on it."

"Even if *I* were on it," said Hawkins, "I would tell you to keep him."

"No," said Menzies. "I'm an old man. I've been threatened a thousand times. I'm not going to cave in now."

"Suits me," said Dub. "Who needs this shit?"

He was halfway to the gate before Alma Louise caught him. "You are not off the case. Never. Clementine promised, and I mean to have you stay on it. You and everybody at your agency."

"It ain't my agency," said Dub. "It's the Devraix Agency. What do you want? Somebody to baby-sit your husband? He don't want it. We could put somebody on the street down there, but as soon as we take him away, bang. Maybe these kids are all there is to it."

"I'll just hire someone else, then. You found out who murdered Clementine's husband, you can find out who's after Raleigh. I don't care what it costs. I have my own money, believe it or not. My papa was in wholesale shrimp and oil and gas."

"Maybe you ought to drink some strong black coffee first, Alma Louise, then think about it."

Her mouth dropped, the standard reaction of an insulted belle. He expected her to say, "Well, I never!" but her face twisted. She covered it with her hands, then scurried into the house.

Oh shit, thought Dub. Let's say the wrong thing again.

Goddammit, he was so hungry he could walk back to Hawkins's office to get the fragrant gyro the cop had abandoned there. He noticed the exchange with Alma Louise had been watched by a black woman from a casement window. The circle around Menzies was breaking up. Bill, flushed with anger, stalked by Dub without looking at him. The deputy at the gate eyed Dub nastily. Menzies shook Hawkins' hand enthusiastically and said, "Say hello to your dad for me, tell him he's in my thoughts." Dub checked the casement window again, but the woman was gone.

"Well, that worked," said Hawkins.

"Huh?" said Dub.

"There'll be a squad car parked in the driveway at night."

"Good," said Dub. "And thanks for the kind words."

"Shit," said Hawkins. "That was just to make Bill do it. He hates rentacops even more than I do."

"Thanks loads." Dub glanced back at Menzies, who had settled back in his lounge chair and was staring sadly at Mumbo Jumbo. "What is it between you two? He knows your dad?"

The jaw set again. "I guess you're expecting a ride back at taxpayer expense."

"What's the big secret?"

"Rolling," said Hawkins, opening the gate.

"Aw, come on," said Dub. The gate closed. He thought about Alma Louise and the woman who'd been watching through the casement window. He opened the gate and shouted after Hawkins. "You go on without me!"

"Damn your smart ass, Hawkins," he muttered to himself. "Tell me nothing. I don't care."

SIX

Goddamned taxi'll cost me a fortune, Dub soon thought. He reached to check his wallet, but had the sensation of being watched. Menzies, however, was still by the pool, scrunched at the low end of the lounge chair staring at the shattered African god, the broad-striped towel still draped over his shoulders. The man had just had a brush with death, and it was only now sinking in. He didn't know Dub or anyone else existed. Menzies crossed his arms on his knees and rested his head on them. He closed his eyes and squeezed them hard. All during the civil rights movement Menzies must have thought about dying often, but he had been young then, and dying seems less real the younger you are. Now, limber as he was, he was in his sixties and death had walked in with a sixteen-year-old's angry face.

Dub remembered coming face-to-face with death, the grasping, the panic terror. You didn't think so much about the good things you'd lose—the feel of a breeze on a summer's day, the taste of a woman's lips, the smell of fresh coffee. Good didn't matter, just life. Life on any terms. Burnt coffee, pouring rain, nightmares, sad memory, the aching of a muscle too old to move like it once did. You'd take anything that would slap you in the face and make you feel. You'd take what you could get, as long as you could feel.

He slipped in through the patio doors. He wasn't sure why. He knew he ought to try to apologize to Mrs. Menzies and see if he still had the job. She had been insistent, but who knows? And then he'd need to call a cab or Vonna to pick him up. He was startled as he closed the door by the chopping of an enormous knife to his left.

The woman who had been watching him through the window was mincing celery. "Yes, sir?" she said without missing a beat.

"I'm Dub Greenert. Mrs. Menzies hired me to—"

"I know who you are. Can I he'p ya?" She swept the celery off the white chopping block into a Pyrex cup.

"You must be Mrs. Johnson. That was a brave thing you done today."

The knife paused in midair. "Ha! Brave ain't the word. It was stupid. I never should've opened that door."

"You ought to sit down and relax. It's been a rough day."

"I don't like sitting down. That's why I don't like TV. Oh, I watch it while I'm doing something else, but sitting there clogs you up, don't you think?"

He thought of all the long nights he'd sat in a car watching some building while John or Joan Adultery did the dance of the seven sheets. His hand caressed the nitro tablets in his jacket pocket like a talisman. "Yes, ma'am, I suspect it does." He glanced around the kitchen. It was large, furnished with all the amenities—icemaker, microwave, countertop stove— but it wasn't luxurious. The saucepans were steel, not copper. The floor was vinyl, not tile. From what he could see of the dining room and the living room beyond, the furniture was nothing you couldn't get at Sears—nice, but probably not solid wood. "You know, I expected when I come out here that Mr. Menzies would have a fancier house."

She swept more celery into her cup. "This ain't good enough for you?"

Dub grinned. "Too much for me, but, you know, him being a lawyer and so famous and all."

"His family goes way back, you know. He could've gone on being the country squire. He had his plantation. I had my own little cottage there. It was one of the old converted slave quarters. It was nice, but I felt a little strange in it at night. Anyhow, Mr. Menzies sold the whole thing about 1972, took an apartment in the French Quarter, then when he got his book money bought this. He wanted a place in a mixed neighborhood."

"This is mixed?"

"There's a judge up the street and a mayor's assistant farther on. Last week some, I don't know, Vietnamese or Koreans or something moved in next to the judge."

"You've been with the Menzieses for a long time. You must know them as well as anybody."

She clattered the lid off a large stock pot on the stove and dumped in the celery. From what he could see, each chunk of the vegetable looked like a perfect cube. "I know the man's a saint. I know that he's paid a terrible price for everything in his life. He's a man who carried his cross. That's all the Lord asks us to do, but most people don't. And most people's cross ain't all that heavy."

"I know what you mean."

Mrs. Johnson glanced at him as if trying to judge whether he was condescending to her. "It's true," she said.

"I know it's true. He doesn't even want to charge that boy."

She opened a bin and took out a bag of onions. "Then I hope you do a better job of protecting the man. He cain't rely on an old woman like me to save him." She laughed.

"You done good, honey. You don't look that old to me. You must have been working for Mr. Menzies since you was born."

"My daddy was a mean man when he got hold of the hard stuff, which was easy since he minded the still for the parish bootleggers. I run away and Mr. Menzies took me in. He tried to talk me into going back to school, but I wouldn't. I was just twenty. I thought I knew everything! Well, I didn't. A couple years before Mr. Menzies sold the old plantation, I went out and married a man just like my daddy. Only worse. He was so worthless he didn't even know how to make liquor, just how to drink it. Mr. Menzies didn't have to fire him, he just disappeared." She sniffed and wiped her eyes on the towel. She saw Dub looking at her. "The onions," she said. "I don't care about John no more."

Dub nodded.

"I'm sorry. I'm just running on."

"It's okay," said Dub. "I like listening."

She studied him for a minute. "You look like you had a rough night. A lot of rough nights. Your woman got another man?"

"Huh? Naw."

"You got to stop worrying and put your trust in God."

"I reckon you're right."

"You're probably not eating right. Let me give you a jug of this soup when it's done."

"I've been eating too right, Mrs. Johnson. Too right." He sighed. "It's giving up smoking, you know. It rattles you."

"So I hear. Put your burden on the Lord."

He crossed the aisle, leaned against the cooking island, and lowered his voice. "So, listen, you're a smart woman, you see what's going on. Mrs. Menzies puts away a lot of liquor herself."

She didn't say anything, just hesitated in her chopping.

"I'm just an outside observer, you know, but from what I've seen there ain't a lot of affection between them."

"They been married a long time."

"Excuse me for saying so, but she's a drunk."

"I know a drunk when I see one," she said forcefully. "She don't put away that much. It just hits her hard."

"And drunks sometimes don't know what they're doing. They do stupid things. They know they're stupid, but they do them anyway."

She concentrated on her onions. "So? You think you already know what you're saying. So why ask me? I got nothin' to say."

"Because I've got to know stuff to figure who might've planted that bomb."

"You don't believe that boy done it?"

"Maybe. Or maybe he done it for somebody else. It seems mighty strange to me that this Bobby Alberts comes busting in here screaming that Mr. Menzies killed his brother if his brother set the bomb in the first place."

Mrs. Johnson thought for a minute, walked to the hallway door, and looked. She then went to the patio door and checked on Mr. Menzies. "Don't go sniffing up the wrong tree and get people hurt for nothing. There's a lot of white people would like to see Mr. Menzies hurt. You hurt Mr. Menzies and I'll come after you like a blender."

"Goddammit, Mrs. Johnson," he said with a smile, "I believe you would."

"Don't you cuss around here."

"I apologize."

She crossed her arms. She was thinking. She was going to talk to him or she wasn't. He waited. She began slowly. "Mr. Menzies was gone a lot, you understand. They was deep in love. She wanted to go with him, but he couldn't bear the thought she might get beat up or worse. Look what they done to Mrs. Liuzzo. Shot her head off without even blinking. So Mrs. Menzies sat home a lot, waiting for the phone to ring, afraid for the phone to ring. Hoping to hear from the man she loved, scared she'd hear the man had been killed. Soon she'd get sloppy a couple nights a week. She'd go to town and stay with the O'Dells just to have somebody around." She lowered her eyes as if she'd regretted saying that much and assumed the "I don't know nuthin'" expression blacks have used to keep secrets from whites since the first slave hit Virginia. "She don't drink that much."

"Later," Dub coached, "she'd just go to town, right? Sometime in there she found some companionship, right? A woman needs companionship now and then."

"Everybody does," she said.

"Who was the man?"

"I didn't say it was no man." She looked him in the eye. "It wasn't any man in particular. It was different men. Not every night, mind you, but once in a while. Then she'd feel so bad about it when Mr. Menzies come home she'd get three sheets in the wind and he couldn't stand to see her that way. He'd go back to his protests and trials as soon as he could. It was love what ruined them. If they didn't've loved each other so much it never would've come to this."

Love'll chew you up and spit you out, thought Dub. "Would any of these men try to get Mr. Menzies out of the way?"

"Gracious, you do have an imagination!" She chuckled.

"It's the oldest motive in the book."

"Well, maybe it is, among reg'lar people."

"Do you know who these men were? Any of them?"

She shook her head and moved back to the chopping board. "I might've knowed one or two names, but I forgot them."

"Aw, come on," begged Dub.

It was the wrong approach. She began peeling the last onion.

"Do you know about Stavros?" he asked.

"Who?"

He couldn't tell whether she didn't or whether she had decided to clam up. "Listen, Mrs. Johnson—" he touched her arm "—I'm not out to hurt anybody. I'm out to keep Mr. Menzies from being hurt. Do you believe me?"

She chopped as if he weren't touching her at all. "It's been quite a day and I'm getting behind on dinner and you're wasting both our times. Mr. and Mrs. Menzies's private lives ain't what's behind this. It's some of them Klan boys. I mean one of them's in the state legislature, maybe he'll be president. Don't think some of you people don't still hate Mr. Menzies with a passion. That's where your bomb came from."

"You're probably right."

"I mean, sweet Jesus, if Miss Jane was still alive you'd be pestering her."

Dub started to ask who Miss Jane was, but something clicked. Mrs. Johnson had overestimated him. She had assumed he knew who this woman was. She had said Mr. *and* Mrs. Menzies's private lives. If he didn't know, Mrs. Johnson was certainly not going to tell him. "I guess you're right. I would be pestering her. How long's she been dead now?"

"Three years a week. You can see it when the anniversary gets near." She leaned toward the window. "He sits there like he is now. Staring. Missing her."

For a second Dub thought maybe he was wrong, that Miss Jane had been a maiden aunt or someone else. He played the bluff. "But he wouldn't leave Alma Louise?"

"He's a saint. I know that. And not just in public. He tried everything for Miss Jane, flew her to Mexico and then France for those special treatments. It cost him plenty. None of it done any good. The cancer was in her brain, and they thought they'd got it. Then it was all over, in the blood and everywhere. She was fifteen years younger than him and still went first. That's a hard thing. A heavy cross. Only the Lord can lift that burden, and He will. Like I say, Mr. Menzies is a saint. I know that. Someday everybody will. White people, too. They called him a Communist, but he was the real American. They'll know that what he done was for everybody, black and white and every color. We're all God's children."

"Amen, Mrs. Johnson." He was so deep in thought he said it listlessly, but he wanted her to feel it had conviction. "Amen," he repeated. "What was her last name?"

She studied him again. "What kind of private detective are you? You buy your license at the toy counter in the U-Tote-Em?"

"Maybe I'd better say good-bye to Mrs. Menzies."

"She's probably asleep." Mrs. Johnson went through the door into the corridor. Dub padded quietly along behind her. Mrs. Johnson stopped halfway down and noticed the rumbling of the bathroom fan. She reached in the door to turn out the light, then spotted Dub and abruptly slammed it. Dub had seen one leg with a stocking around it.

"She's asleep," said Mrs. Johnson coolly.

"On the john?" said Dub.

The hall suddenly dimmed. Menzies was blocking the evening light passing through the kitchen. "Where my wife sleeps is none of your damned business," said Menzies. "Now, you have ten seconds to get your rear out of my house, or I'll have you arrested."

"I think I hear my cab," said Dub.

SEVEN

Coattail flapping, Dub crunched down the long white gravel driveway, swayed by the gusts of wind. Clouds were racing across and over each other like shoppers at a fifty-percent-off sale. "Okay, sky," he muttered to himself. "Open up. Dub Greenert's walking, so let's just bring a few million gallons in off the Gulf and fill up them streets."

Just as he crossed the fallen yellow police tape, someone touched his elbow. "Is Raleigh all right?"

He faced an older man with very little hair and a maplike scattering of red veins in his nose and cheeks. His madras shorts and loose shirt decorated with bananas were stiff and immaculate, like he had them laundered with industrial starch.

"I live across the street. Donald McHugh. I heard the chief tell the TV people he was okay, but I was wondering if it's true." He took an awkward step back as if afraid of violating the invisible barrier the tape had once represented.

"He a friend of yours?"

"I wouldn't exactly call him a friend—keeps to himself mostly, but he and Alma Louise sent a beautiful present for my daughter's wedding and they were very gracious at my wife's charity garage sale party."

Dub resisted the temptation to ask what that was. "He's fine. I don't think he wants any visitors, though."

"I don't think I would, either. Just as long as he's okay." The man shuffled back like he was going to leave.

"Say, buddy," said Dub, glancing at the ever-darkening sky. "I think I got ditched by mistake."

"You're not with the Federal Bureau of Investigation?"

The momentary confusion over what the man had asked irritated him. All he said was, "I'm from the city." He pointed as if the city line were visible, just over there. "Would you mind if I used your phone?"

"Certainly not, officer. Certainly not."

Dub followed him. There were actually creases ironed into the back of his shorts and banana shirt.

"I just assumed you were with the Bureau. There are a lot of you working on this, aren't you?"

"Mr. Menzies is important to a lot of people. I imagine it makes you a bit nervous having a bomb go off in your neighborhood, and then a shooting."

"Well, we won't be buying a new mailbox every week. I was surprised the boys got past the Bureau man."

Dub took several steps trying to grasp whether this man with starched leisurewear had said anything significant. "Excuse me? The Bureau man? You mean there was an FBI guy out here that night?"

"Well, I assume he was, unless he left for coffee or something."

"Where was he?" He nearly shouted because of the wind.

"Where he always is, parked in the trees down there, just around the curve."

"There?" Dub squinted. "In those trees?"

"Yes. Is this another example of different agencies working at cross-purposes? I've noticed that is a staple of television shows, but I never thought it made sense. Is your impression of *Kojak* that it is the most authentic of the—?"

"He isn't there now, is he?"

"He left as the squad cars and ambulance first appeared."

"But he was here *before* the bomb went off?"

McHugh pursed his thin lips. "Friday, Thursday . . . I first noticed him Wednesday night."

"You're sure?"

"He just sits there, looking up to Raleigh's, his back against the car door."

"And how do you know he's with the Bureau?"

"Smashing mailboxes is a federal offense, and lord knows we've complained enough."

"Anything else?"

"He dresses like it. The car is like it. I was walking Toodles—"

"Your wife?"

"My cat." A cluster of leaves skittered by.

"You walk your cat?"

"Cats need exercise, too."

"Well, yeah, sure they do." Dub shrugged.

"I waved to the agent. He didn't wave back, but he didn't try to hide himself, either."

"And this was two days before the bomb went off."

"Absolutely. He was there again Thursday, and Friday during the day."

Damn their butts, thought Dub. They knew there was going to be an attempt on Raleigh Menzies. They must have an informer inside one of the kook groups. But they goofed. They let the punk get blown into dog chow. Now they'll never admit they knew in advance. No wonder Campbell was so charming when Dub had called him. He noticed McHugh waiting. "The FBI's like a private club. They've got an attitude, if you know what I mean," he said lamely. "I wouldn't talk it up too much."

They climbed up the long Japanese-style walkway to McHugh's front door. How could a cat-walker who probably starches his socks and briefs know an FBI agent by sight? Dub asked himself. Dub's impression of FBI guys when he'd worked in Pittsburgh was that they were mostly midwestern types, straight arrows, with a polish of innocence over a righteous anger. Enforcing the law was a religion with them. But a few agents Dub had known were like big kids who wanted the deluxe Hopalong Cassidy set—with six-guns, hat, *and* spurs. They liked the game more than the conclusion. They liked to spend government money on dressing up as telephone repairmen, or ice-cream vendors, or housepainters. They liked listening gizmos and different guns. They'd stake out paint drying as long as they got to put on a costume and play with some toys. On the other hand, why assume the stake-out was FBI? And if the watcher wasn't FBI, who was he? With the bombers? Then why come back afterward? Why make such a worthless effort at concealing himself by parking in the trees?

If he could just eat a half-pound cheeseburger, he could probably figure it out, Dub thought miserably. People were all trying to eat healthy—oats and greens and various kinds of Italian weeds. That was the trend he'd read. That's why the IQ of the general population was so obviously in a nosedive. They'd soon have the brains of herbivores and he'd be thundering along merrily, but healthily, to the water hole with them.

The rain started. Big fat drops that burst on the pavement like water balloons. The cat-walker let him wait inside and offered him camomile tea. Dub made a few calls to hospitals and located Bobby Alberts. By the time the cab arrived, the sky was beginning to clear. He had the driver pull up at an instant cash machine that printed out a snotty little chit that told him he couldn't have twenty dollars, but let him have ten. He got out at a Popeyes fried chicken and bought two large coffees while trying to breathe some sustenance out of the air dense with fragrant multisaturated fat. He walked the two blocks to the hospital, strutting like he owned the dark neighborhood to discourage any of the tough-looking kids lounging on the shadowy stoops. He continued his strut up to the main desk and a nurse who looked meaner than the kids.

"Deputy McClelland still watching the Alberts kid?" He held up the bag.

"We have perfectly fine food here," said the nurse.

"He has a thing about Popeyes coffee. Maybe they put hot sauce in it. What room?"

She made him spell out Alberts, probably just to be officious, but she didn't ask for his badge. He was lucky again when he got upstairs. The guard in the hallway was the deputy with the enormous waxed mustache who had been at the ambulance when Hawkins and he had approached the house.

"How's it going?" said Dub.

"Could use a whiz," he said. "How're you? Still on the liaison?"

"Always. Brought you some coffee."

"Coffee'd out."

"I'll leave it anyway. What's wrong with the boy? I thought they'd have charged him by now."

"Worried about the eyes. He's fine. It's bullshit. I hate this kind of duty. The bad guys aren't standing still out there."

Dub gingerly lifted out a cup and snapped off the lid. He savored the coffee like it was five hundred dollar champagne. "I know what you mean: you join up for action and they sit you on your butt. Listen, kid's not asleep, is he? Why don't you get yourself some magazines while I talk to him? Take your time. I'll wait."

"Sounds good to me. What's your name again?"

"Greenert."

"Thanks, Lieutenant."

Right, thought Dub. Just don't tell anybody about Lieutenant Greenert.

Bobby Alberts lifted his head as he entered. He blinked at Dub and then settled back. The boy's eyes were very red. Gray nylon straps like car safety belts ran across his chest and restrained his arms, even the one in the cast. "You come to take me to jail."

"You're a juvenile."

"They don't have to call them jails to make them jails. That's what Billy said."

"Billy was right." Dub pulled up a chair. "Can I get you something? Want the TV on?"

"I'm s'posed to rest my eyes."

"They hurt?"

"Just itch."

"Must've been scary, though. You must've thought you were going blind."

Bobby turned his head. "Raleigh Lee Menzies don't scare me."

"I didn't say he did."

"But he scares you."

"Me?" asked Dub.

[61]

"The police. Everybody. They're afraid of all the niggers behind him."

"Get serious," said Dub, sipping his coffee.

"Fuck off."

"No, Bobby, explain it to me. Why do you think you've got to shoot an old man like Raleigh Lee Menzies?"

"Because he killed my brother, and you know it!" He strained against the straps, winced, and flopped back.

"Your brother was blown up, Bobby."

"By Raleigh Lee Menzies's bomb!"

"How do you know it was his bomb? What sense would that make? The FBI thinks maybe Billy was setting the bomb."

"They're shitheads, then."

"Maybe Billy really wanted to hurt Menzies. He just thought he was an old nigger lover, didn't he?"

"He didn't have no bomb."

"Why not?"

"Because I would've knowed about it."

"Maybe he didn't tell you."

"He was my brother."

"Maybe he made the bomb himself. Maybe he screwed up when he was putting it in the box."

"Billy was a fucking genius with cars and shit. If he'd've made the bomb, it'd be Raleigh Lee Menzies who's dead!"

"Yeah, Bantam Billy Alberts, a regular Einstein."

"Fuck you! Raleigh Lee Menzies wanted to kill Billy."

"But why?"

"Oh, shit!" said the boy in exasperation.

"Explain it to me. Make me believe it. What would this man care about your brother? What would make him so pissed off against Billy? Explain it and maybe I'll believe it."

"Because he threatened us. He threatened my dad."

"When?"

"A week ago. Maybe two. I don't know."

Dub sucked in a slurp of coffee and waited. "So?"

"So, Billy and Dave and Skeeter went out. They were s'posed to wait for me, they wanted me to meet a chick named Carla, but I was cleaning up at KFC. They wiped out most of the mailboxes along Thibodeaux. So, like, old Menzies come to our house. Billy was at work at Boss Mayhew's, but Menzies comes in like he can't stand the smell and he's giving me shit and threatening to turn me over to the post office."

"He was mad?"

"What am I saying?"

"He was yelling? He was waving an Uzi? What?"

"He kept sticking out his finger, like, and his eyes were like slits and he was talking through his teeth. He said that I'd better give the message to Billy that if he messed with any of the mailboxes on Thibodeaux again, he'd never do it a third time. Those were his exact words: 'You and your brother will never do it a third time.'"

Dub stared at the boy for several seconds. "Bobby, how would the man know that your brother would be whacking boxes last Friday, huh? How could he make a bomb and plant it out there just in time for Billy to come along? He'd have to know Billy was coming."

"Well, how did he know it was Billy in the first place?"

"You tell me."

"He knew."

"How?"

"I don't know, but he knew. He got loud and woke up Daddy, who was—" he hesitated "—sleeping off a drunk. Daddy come out with my aluminum bat and waved it at Menzies and then he threatened Daddy and he finally left."

"You Alberts are real big on baseball bats, ain'tcha?"

"Daddy can't hurt nothin'." There was disgust in Bobby's voice.

Dub stood up and tugged at the loose waist of his pants. "Bobby, you're going off half cocked and getting yourself in a shitload of trouble. Why would Raleigh Lee Menzies go to the trouble of blowing Billy up? All he had to do was call the postal inspectors if he knew who was doing it."

"So why did he come to our house?"

"So he wouldn't have to put you boys in real trouble. Sounds like he was just scaring you off."

"But I wasn't with Billy when he and Dave and Skeeter done it and he said I done it, but I didn't. So he didn't *see* who done it, so he couldn't get us arrested."

[63]

"You don't kill a waterbug with a wad of dynamite, Bobby. Think about it."

The boy sprang against his restraints like a mad dog on a leash. "You calling Billy a bug?! I'll get you, too! I'll make you sorry for saying that! He's my brother and—."

"Shut up!" said Dub, shoving Bobby's head back. The boy grimaced and hissed through his teeth. "You want to be an asshole like your brother? Big-shot Billy Alberts was eighteen, and all the fuck he can think to do on a Friday night is swill beer and beat up on a bunch of mailboxes! And you're talking about him like he was all-American halfback for LSU. Your brother was an accident waiting to happen, so don't give me this righteous-vengeance shit! Boy, you're just lucky you were cleaning out the toilets at KFC."

Bobby Alberts made one more growling assault on his straps, the sinews in his neck tight as piano strings. Then something snapped. He fell back against his pillow, his eyes squeezed tight. He choked, then began sobbing. "I should've been with them. He promised to take me. He promised. I was s'posed to be with him."

Dub picked up the water glass on the end table and offered Bobby the straw. The boy twisted to avoid it. "Both times, right? Both times Billy didn't take you along. Both times. How many other times? How many times did he promise to set you up with this Carla or some other chick? Did you get any? Do you even know there *is* a Carla?" The boy sobbed painfully. "Sounds to me like Billy didn't want you along. He didn't want his little brother tagging along, ain't that right? You know it. Big man couldn't stand his kid brother tagging along while he did these big man things like whacking mailboxes. Shit, that's only for *real* men with *real* balls."

"I should've been with him," wailed Bobby. "I should've been with him."

"You want to be in hell with him? You want to be with him so much you'd like to follow him into hell? Well, unless you get some sense, boy, you will."

The door opened. The deputy. "What's going on? Nurse said there was noise."

"Bobby's upset about his brother," said Dub. He backed slowly out of the room. "He's got thinking to do."

The corridor lights had been dimmed for the night. Dub had a headache. The boy had been squirted in the eyes with rose fertilizer, and now he'd been kicked in the gut. The boy had known the truth about him and Billy all along; he just couldn't allow himself to face it. Bobby had only one person he could fantasize into someone who cared. Everybody needed that until they grew up. Now, for a while maybe, staring into the ugly face of the truth about his brother would keep Bobby from doing anything else stupid. Maybe it was time for him to grow up some. It might keep more lives from being destroyed. Or maybe by morning Billy would be back as his idol and Bobby'd be hating himself and planning to shoot Menzies again. Who could tell? The justifications for cutting out Bobby's heart were good ones, but Dub still felt shitty about being the surgeon.

EIGHT

Vonna was instantly awakened by Dub's key sliding into the lock. "Damn!" she said, sighing. On the television, four teenagers were planning something in a kitchen that was much too large to be real. The audience oohed over something one of the girls said, which was supposed to be either risqué or a clever retort, then applauded as if Langston Hughes had written it. How could you sleep through this shit, the sounds of people going up and down the stairs, and that idiot Guzman's boombox on his balcony, yet instantly know the click of the pins inside your deadbolt? Like a black cat, she thought, settling back on the armrest and closing her eyes. Like the last of the Mohicans. Like Superwoman. Yeah, that's me.

The door thunked shut, startling her. "That you?" she said through a yawn.

"No, it's the president of the Zulu Social Club." He threw his keys on the dinette table and they slid with a purr across the Formica.

She batted her eyes, trying to get the sleep out. Dub was in a great mood again. The Zulu Social Club? The "Zee" was a venerable black fraternal club. In her dating days, she'd been dancing at the Zee with a light-skinned lawyer who'd been a member since he was sixteen. She had been so impressed with herself for being invited there. Had she told Dub about that? Dub always threw his keys on the dinette when he was cranky. Maybe it'd be better to go back to sleep until he ate something.

"So how'd it go?" she asked.

"Shitty," he said. He was looking through the mail. "Did you know you've won a steak-knife set or a Pontiac Grand Prix? All you've got to do is drive out to Bayou Nowhere and listen to a brief sales presentation. What an opportunity!"

"You just wade out to your property." The mention of the Zee had put the song "Down by the Riverside" into her head. She knew it'd be playing over and over half the night.

"Oh, no."

"What?"

"My Visa went over again."

She gave up and swung her legs down, nearly stepping on a plate with the scattered tails of a dozen fried shrimp. "You got to be careful with that thing."

He spun around with the blue notification. "Well, what the hell am I supposed to do? I'm out there somewhere and I'm out of cash and—"

She nodded.

"And now the bastards charge me ten bucks, plus interest, because I go twelve bucks over!"

She yawned again. "What you gonna do? They got you either way."

"I'll bet they don't soak Trump when he goes over his limit."

"Hey, be kind," she joked halfheartedly, "po' man's got to live on $450,000 a month to get his whatever-billion-dollar loan." She had an impulse to cross the room and massage Dub's neck to relax him. The inertia was too much to overcome.

He took off his sport coat and dropped it on one of the chairs. "I didn't get a letter from Carrie and Elizabeth?"

"Wasn't one in there."

"Jesus, it's been a month."

She was sure his daughters had written only a couple of weeks ago.

"Well, I'm not gonna beg them. Hell, if they don't want me to know how they're doing—"

"Now, Dub, kids get busy. Where you been? You didn't eat supper, did you?"

"Maybe they don't care how I'm doing, then."

[67]

"You gotta eat something, baby. You want me to fix something?"

"My stomach's still rolling around from that bus ride."

She looked down at her feet, then hefted herself up. "I'll fix you something."

"Just wait awhile, okay?" The sharpness of his voice startled him. He wiped his face with his hand and plunked down on a dinette chair, his elbows on his thighs, head lowered. "The damn bus took forever." He'd offered the explanation as a kind of gruff apology for his mood, she thought. She padded across to him and put a hand on his sweaty neck.

"Spyder got the guy today."

"At the warehouse?"

"Uh-huh. A delivery man at the Metairie store would pull up to get his usual load, but then Ralph, that big guy with the beard—"

"The supervisor?"

"Right. He'd put in extra VCRs or CD players or whatever and then the deliveryman would drop them off on his way back to Metairie. That's why we didn't see nothing unusual."

Dub clenched his hands together. "Well, that figures. I sit on my ass out there for three weeks and then Spyder slips in for the kill."

"That's teamwork, remember? We all get the credit. Devraix said the VP over there was really pleased. We may get a lot of work thrown our way because of this." She stepped behind him to massage his shoulder muscles. He didn't seem to want it, but he didn't resist.

"So I'm out chasing bullshit while the final scene is played. Son of a bitch!"

She worked the tight muscles in his neck for several seconds. They stubbornly remained tense. "You gonna tell me what Mrs. O'Dell's got you on now?"

He made a puff of air, almost like spitting. "She's got a friend who's a lush who fools around."

"Divorce thing?"

"Can I finish?"

She wanted to slap him on the ear, but she suppressed it by digging deeper with her thumbs.

"Somebody tried to blow up her husband. Some kids got killed by mistake."

Vonna's hands stopped moving. "Lord! This is the Raleigh Lee Menzies thing in the news?"

He nodded.

"The police will be all over that," she said, "the FBI—"

"That ain't enough. Mrs. Almighty O'Dell calls Delbert Greenert the fourth—and last!—to the goddamned rescue."

"The paper makes it sound like it's one of your white cuckoos."

"Why are they 'my' white cuckoos? Shoot, if I get mixed up with those people again, I'll just be a turd waiting for the flush. And anyway, we got a client who starts boozing at eight A.M., a man who'd rather get his ass shot off than be protected, and a sixteen-year-old who imagines his dumb brother was important enough to kill. Who gives a damn?"

"It seems to bother you."

"No, what bothers me is having to take a damned bus all the way from that hospital back to the station because I don't have the money for a cab."

"What hospital? You should've called me."

"Well, I didn't."

She crossed her arms. "I think maybe you need a good shot of momma's vodka to settle down."

"What I need is a new life."

"You want it with ice?"

"Forget it."

"Ice?"

"Forget it! Vodka. Empty calories. Delbert's got to live on seaweed and dandelions, because he maybe, but probably not, had a heart attack."

Okay, the hell with you, she thought. She retreated to the television and idly turned the channels. "The doctor said to lose weight. He didn't say 'don't eat.'" She flicked several more channels.

Dub made a noise of irritation and went into the kitchen. "Damn Raleigh Lee Menzies!" he said. She heard the refrigerator open forcefully. There was a pause and the crinkling of some foil. "Jesus!" he said. "How long has this chicken been in here?"

"I don't know. A couple days."

"Huh?"

"A couple days!"

"It's got mold on it!"

"Well, throw it away, scrape the mold off, do what you want. I didn't plant the mold."

The freezer door opened, then slammed. A cabinet opened, then slammed. Another. The freezer again.

He charged into the dinette. "Is this all we got?"

"What do you mean? We got food."

"There isn't a fucking thing *I* can eat."

"There's that oven shrimp. That's what I ate. Ain't it good enough for you?"

"Shrimp's got cholesterol."

"It's seafood, ain't it?"

"I'm supposed to eat fish. Fish! I'm supposed to eat it until I grow gills."

"Now you know damn well that shrimp hasn't got all *that much* cholesterol in it."

"But this is that breaded shit. They dip it in grease, then cover it with greasy bread crumbs. It's worse than pork rinds."

"Well, then don't eat it!" She turned off the TV like she wanted to rip off the knob. "I don't know what your problem is, but you'd better straighten up or you can just get your white ass out of here!"

His eyes widened as if he'd been slapped, but then they tightened. "Why the hell don't you buy some food? There's frozen french fries in there, the damned shrimp, some mummified fried chicken—don't let's forget the 'fried' part—and a couple of cans of some kind of lousy collard greens. With bacon." He brought the can out of the kitchen and flamboyantly pointed at the label. "With *real* bacon."

"I do buy food. I buy more than enough food. I buy more than my share, don't I?"

"Don't you start on that. You knew when I moved in here exactly how much child support I was paying. You knew that."

"Well, maybe you care more about those girls of yours than about me."

"That ain't fair, Vonna. That ain't fair. Don't set me in the middle. They're my blood."

And what was she? "I'm tired of this," she said. "I'll take you to Gator's." She bent over for her shoes.

"There's nothing there I can eat."

"Get red beans and rice. What the hell's with you? A little meat won't kill you."

"I don't want to waste your big salary. Just forget it, I'll eat the fucking greens." He spun into the kitchen.

She had been restraining herself, but now she didn't care. She wanted to slap him silly. "The fucking greens? You got something against collards? Or is it you don't want nigger food? Is that what's bothering your ass? That Zulu shit not good enough for you? Huh? You think I don't know. You think I don't see. You're just like every other honky. You're willing to put up with us only as long as you can get something out of it." Her voice rang off the kitchen ceiling.

"That isn't true!"

"You go straight to hell," she said. "*Straight* to hell." She wanted to hit him, and when she saw her arms were raised, she stared at them like they were strange animals that had suddenly attached themselves to her. Her eyes blurred with tears, and she fled into the bathroom directly across the corridor.

She locked the door and buried her face in a long wad of toilet paper. She choked down her sobbing to keep him from hearing. She heard a thud as he banged the kitchen counter, and then he repeated the word "Shit!" six or seven times, each time getting louder. It was over, she was thinking. It was better before. Get a man when you need one. You can't live with them, not white, not black, not purple. Why'd she get mixed up with him like this? She saw herself in the mirror on the door. Her thighs were heavy, her puffy cheeks glistened with tears. She had promised they would lose weight together. He had, but she hadn't, not much anyway. And how could she think he would even give her a second thought when compared to his pink daughters? It wouldn't matter that their "new daddy" made two or three times as much as Dub. He'd still pay that third of his salary. If he had three dollars left, he'd send them one of them. The bastard!

She covered her face again. No, he wasn't a bastard for doing that. Most men just run off on their kids whether they had money or not. He was a bastard because he wouldn't eat collards and because he hated to ride the bus and because just because. Because he was acting like a bastard and she'd wish his bastard heart would stop, real heart attack or not, she wished he was dead. She had let him into her life and he . . . She leaned back her head and looked up at the whirring exhaust fan. She tried to put her mind on something else. She hated to lose control. She had spent so many years trying to keep herself in control: everywhere, in every situation, at work, in bed. When was the last time they had made love? She tried again to think of anything else. All that surfaced was "Down by the Riverside": "Ain't gonna study war no more, Ain't gonna study war no more, Down by the riverside."

She heard him rattling a paper bag and moving into the bedroom. The bathroom was getting stuffier by the minute. A while later he came out of the bedroom. His steps hesitated by the door. He tapped.

She wiped her nose. "Yes."

"Could I get my razor?" he asked quietly.

She looked around for it and located it behind the water glass. He tapped gently again. "I got it," she said. She wiped her nose harshly and pulled in all her strength to control herself. She looked in the mirror and recognized her old self, before she'd gotten mixed up with this man: all surface, hard, her feelings totally hidden by the mask of her face.

She opened the door and held up his cheap, disposable razor. Maybe it was just an excuse to get her to open the door. He was holding a grocery bag with his clothes stuffed in it. A pair of yellowed boxer shorts covered the top. He took the razor. Their hands briefly touched in the exchange, but she turned away and handed him his toothbrush and shaving cream. "You'll need these, too."

"Thanks." He shoved the can into the bag and stood there

holding the toothbrush like he was trying to think of something to say. "I drank some of your vodka," he said.

She nodded. "No sweat. Just empty calories."

He clutched the bag a little closer, then started for the door. He turned the knob with the toothbrush still in his hand.

"I guess—" she said. He turned his head only halfway and peered over his shoulder. "I guess we just fooled ourselves."

He lowered his eyes. "No," he said. "Anyway, I don't think so. It's just that sometimes love ain't enough. It takes a while to learn that. We should have known it all along, though. Sometimes love ain't enough." He shrugged, and seemed to be searching for something else to say. "See you" was all that came out. The door thunked behind him.

She drifted toward the dining-room table. The vodka bottle sat open on it. She swallowed deep until it burned from her tonsils to her toes, then she crossed to the curtains over the sliding glass doors. She peeked through the end. Dub was by his car. He fumbled the toothbrush into the hand clutching the bag, then probed his sport-coat pocket for his keys. He came out with the vial of nitro tablets and paused, weighing them in his palm. He glanced up at the balcony. She stepped back so he wouldn't see her. "Ain't gonna study war no more, Ain't gonna study war no more," she mumbled, then eased forward. When she looked out, he was shaking his head and had started back up to the apartment. When he stepped upon the sidewalk, however, something made him stop. He glanced back at his car, seemed undecided, then returned to it. He ground the starter, then backed out.

"Well, that's that," said Vonna, and was suddenly aware of the roaring of Guzman's boombox machine-gunning the parking lot with salsa rhythms. "Shut that motherfucking thing off!" she shouted. It continued as before. She crossed her arms. "That's that," she sighed. "The end." The bastard was right: sometimes love just isn't enough. If she tried real hard, Superwoman wouldn't feel a thing.

NINE

Sometime during the third draft, there was a movement in the mirror behind the bar. It was only a bearded man—from the looks of him an offshore oil worker—crossing to the jukebox, but the cross motion startled Dub. He had the sensation that the room had spun. I should've ate, he thought ruefully. Getting old, can't hold my brewski, as they say in Pittsburgh. He leaned his cheek on his hand and stared at himself as if his head were one of the items on the shelf, stuck between a bottle of Bushmill's and a tip-down decanter of Seagram's 7. He looked old up there, haggard, and tired, immeasurably tired. I oughta eat something, he thought, eat something I haven't allowed myself for a long time. A bacon cheeseburger. Chili, no beans, topped with onion and cheddar—real cheddar, lumpy and hard and not like the plastic stuff, cheddar so sharp it'd cut your tongue.

Every once in a while, the Greek-looking woman hurried out of the back with french fries or some other deep-fried lumps in a little paper tray and delivered them to one of the tables. All Dub had to do was ask for a menu. It would come, hand-typed and yellowed in a cracked plastic folder with pencil corrections over about a third of the prices. He didn't move, though. He just stared in the mirror. Look at you. You know these places too well, don't you? You belong here like the cigarette burns in the bar. Like the old Pirelli calendar behind the jukebox that still says November 1963. The girl on the calendar, covered meagerly in strategic locations, would be pushing fifty by now. She'd have thunder thighs like the

Greek waitress. She'd know too many things too well, too. She'd wonder what happened to the girl who posed for the calendar. She'd wonder where her life had gone, too.

But in here, the jukebox played a whiny country song about a cheating husband, and time was suspended. You could look in the mirror through your beer and you could see yourself young and middle-aged at the same time. You'd stare in the mirror trying to see what other people saw when they looked at you. The shiny forehead. The blue discoloration under your eyes. The thinning widow's peak. The sagging in your cheeks. You'd wonder who the hell you were.

A bleached blond with the oil worker cackled. It seemed out of place, like burping in church. This is Limbo. Have some respect! Dub wordlessly signaled for another beer and wiped his face with his hand. He licked the sweat on his lips and it reminded him of the dimples behind Vonna's knees. He stared at the sad face in the mirror. Oh, man, what the hell got into you? What the hell you gonna do now? I'd crawl back on my knees, but she won't want me. I've been a son of a bitch and would deserve it if she cut off my pecker. He thought about Beth, his first wife. Then Janet. Then that client in Pittsburgh. The redheaded secretary. He was always fucking up with women. He was too hot or he was too cold. The thermostat was always wrong. Always fucking up.

The woman cackled again. Some people were happy drunks. It was a blessing to be a happy drunk. A real blessing.

"It ain't funny!" he said to the mirror, and started on another beer.

"Housekeeping!" Thunk, thunk, thunk. "Housekeeping!" There was a clinking of keys and a slash of sunlight. "Oh, sorry! I'll come back later."

"Whu—? Who?" Dub raised himself on his elbows. The room reeled. He flopped back on the bed, arms spread. No one on the next pillow. It felt very empty. His skin tingled with his tiredness. He had to pee. All right, just give me a few seconds, he told himself, a few seconds. What've I done? What've I done? No one on the next pillow. Thank God!

The motel he had chosen smelled musty but not dirty,

and the TV looked decent and there was stationery on the desk. His "luggage"—the grocery bag—was on the floor. He had the impression of having driven for a long time. He had gotten sloppy about his little girls. He might have tried to call them. Jesus, that would have been a great thing to do in the middle of the night. He didn't do that, did he? He knew he'd fumbled with his change on the bar thinking about it. Then he'd decided to visit Elizabeth and Carrie one last time before he died. He wasn't sure why he'd decided the Grim Reaper was lurking in his immediate future. Maybe he'd had a chest pain. He leaned on the desk and blinked at the stationery. He was on Interstate 10, but he was still in Louisiana. He'd hardly left the city. His guts were tied in a knot, his head hurt, and he didn't like his own smell. Coffee, he thought. The man needs coffee. But he slipped off his boxers and stood under the shower until he was almost awake, holding on to the shower nozzle like it was the only reliable thing in the world.

It was almost two in the afternoon when he left the motel diner and huddled up next to the pay phone in the lobby. It was time to do something. He'd quit. It would be best for all concerned. He'd move back to Pittsburgh and back to work for Calabrese at the Keyhole Agency. Maybe he'd dump the whole P.I. business and get into something real. Let people with too much money get divorced without him. There must be fifty ways to leave your lover, and not one of them involves a stakeout. Maybe he'd locate somewhere near his girls. Get a job with health insurance.

"Hey, Emma darlin'," he said to the secretary, "gimme Devraix. This is Dub."

"Oh, Dub," she said, "where are you? I've got six messages for you. Mr. Devraix's been calling everywhere."

"Never mind that. Let me talk to him."

"Hold on."

Devraix came on quickly, his usually languid voice almost squeaky with excitement. "Dub, thank heavens it is you. We have been looking all over. We thought something might have happened to you! I was about to put Emma on the hospitals."

The assumption that he'd had the big heart attack everyone was waiting for irritated him. "I'm a big boy and can take care of myself. Listen, I—"

"In the back of my mind there is always the thought that one of your white supremacists has mind enough to remember you."

"They're not *my* white supremacists, Honoré. I've got something to—"

"Nonetheless, we were all quite worried about you. Mrs. Menzies has been telephoning since lunchtime. She is quite distraught—"

Oh, Lord! thought Dub. "She's not my problem anymore. She's probably just having d.t.'s."

"And Mrs. O'Dell has called several times also. They are extraordinarily desperate, but will not say what is disturbing them."

"Listen, I didn't call to—"

"Actually I would have gone myself, but I have an appointment at three that I simply cannot miss."

His manicurist, thought Dub. "I didn't call to—"

"It is imperative you get over there immediately. I shall inform them you are on your way."

"Over where? I'm not—"

"Mrs. Menzies's, of course. I shall notify them."

"Honoré I'm quitting, goddammit! Honoré!" His yelling roused the desk clerk. There was a click, then the dial tone.

"Goddammit!" Mrs. Menzies was being visited by the Ghost of Bourbon Past, and he wasn't jumping to every panic the woman had. He fished in his pocket for another quarter, but only came up with lint. He slammed the receiver into its hook and started for the desk clerk. "Have you got—?" He pulled out his wallet.

Mrs. O'Dell, he thought. The woman had paid his medical bills. It might have been pocket change to her, but it was enough to put Elizabeth or Carrie through college. And the doctors had found nothing but maybes. Maybe a heart attack. Maybe arrhythmia. Maybe gas—yeah, right! Keep these nitro tablets in your pocket, just in case you feel like you're gonna croak. You bought a lot for your six figures, Mrs. O'Dell! If

Alma Louise was just seeing things, why would Mrs. O'Dell call for him?

"Yes?" said the desk clerk.

Dub had stopped in the middle of the floor with his wallet open. "Oh, uh, you got any aspirin? Say, three aspirin?" He sighed. "And which way's the on-ramp west?"

He was closer to Thibodeaux than he had thought. He came around the bend by the woods and noticed the FBI stakeout was not parked in the trees. A long, glassy Lincoln was in the driveway and Vonna's red Chevette: the "sputterbug," as she liked to call it. Mrs. Johnson opened the door. "Thank Gawd!" she said. She had been weeping. Her hands were trembling. She took him by the arm before he could get a word out and pulled him toward a large den.

Huddled tightly around a large winged chair were the three women. Vonna sat on a Queen Anne ottoman. Alma Louise was collapsed in the chair, wearing white deck shoes, oversize tennis shorts, and a flowery peach blouse. Clementine O'Dell was positioning a wet towel over Alma's forehead. "He's here," said Mrs. Johnson, wringing her hands. "Thank Gawd!"

"Raleigh Lee!" said Alma Louise.

For a moment he thought Alma Louise had killed him.

"Where is he?"

"Right off his own veranda!" said Alma Louise. "And it's all my fault."

"Oh, now, that isn't true," said Mrs. O'Dell, patting her hand.

Dub glanced at Vonna. She looked away.

"Will somebody tell me what the hell's going on?"

"You best calm down for a change," said Vonna without looking at him.

Her voice gave him the same feeling he'd had when he'd been caught chewing gum in elementary school. Mrs. Johnson brought her handkerchief to Alma Louise's face. Her shoulders heaved.

Mrs. O'Dell straightened up. Thank God for her steel backbone. "Raleigh Lee has been kidnapped."

"What?"

"Alma Louise and he were having lunch on the front patio and they drove up and grabbed him."

"Who?" asked Dub.

"It is all my fault!" wailed Alma Louise.

"It ain't your fault, Mrs. Menzies—you know that!" Mrs. Johnson rushed to her and they cried, hugging each other tight.

Dub's head swam against the tide. He shushed them and turned back to Mrs. O'Dell. "Where was the cop?"

"There never was a policeman."

"Excuse me?"

"They don't have the manpower. They parked a squad car in the driveway at night."

"They say all you really need to do is make people uncertain whether there's a guard here or not."

He wiped his face with his hand. "Holy Jesus! Maybe we can just put cardboard cutouts on the beat and end the crime problem."

"Federal revenue-sharing is over. Oil prices are down."

He waved his palms. "With all respect, Mrs. O'Dell, save it for *Meet the Press*. Just tell me what the fuck happened. No, first tell me where the police are now."

"She won't call the police," said Vonna.

Dub shifted his eyes toward Mrs. O'Dell, then realized Vonna had meant Mrs. Menzies.

"They said they'd kill him," said Mrs. Johnson.

"We can't call the police," said Alma Louise.

"Are you nuts?" said Dub. "I want somebody calling the FBI right now. This ain't something you can dick around with."

"We waited for you," said Alma Louise.

"You're all crazy! Every minute you waste is—" He didn't know what to say. "Jesus!" He turned on Vonna. "You let them wait?"

Her look was withering.

"That's what I said," said Mrs. O'Dell. "I'll do it immediately."

"No!" said Alma Louise, sitting up. "If you do that, Clementine, I'll never speak to you again!"

"Look, Alma Louise," said Dub, "how long has it been since this happened?"

"About one-thirty," said Mrs. Johnson.

"And you've waited around an hour and a half?" He wiped his face with his hand. "Gawdalmighty, call the FBI, Mrs. O'Dell. You ask for Agent Lawrence Campbell and you make a breeze getting to that goddamned phone."

"Absolutely," she said, less like she'd taken an order than that she was vindicated.

"No!" said Alma Louise. "They'll kill him."

Mrs. O'Dell paused, but did not look back.

Dub grabbed Mrs. Menzies by the shoulders. There were tears puddled at the bottom of her bifocal lenses. He had to make her understand, no matter how much it hurt. "Look, I'm gonna tell you straight and you're gonna listen. If they want to kill him, the man's already dead. He might've been dead a minute after they snatched him." The woman was stunned he was saying this. "The second thing is that the FBI handles these things, not private eyes. And whether they're called in or not, it's about fifty-fifty whether a kidnapping victim gets back alive. If the kidnappers even get their ransom, it's fifty-fifty. You understand?"

Mrs. Johnson made a strong, twisted noise into her handkerchief.

"We need all the help we can get, Alma Louise. Raleigh Lee needs them FBI boys."

Her eyes rolled as if she were going to pass out. She slumped back and nodded. "Raleigh Lee's been kidnapped, Dub. Oh God! Oh God!"

"That's right," he added. "He'll need God, too."

Mrs. O'Dell was back. "They're on their way. I told them to come in without drawing attention."

"Good," said Dub. "Real good. I should've thought of that myself. See? We need all the heads we can get on this." He slumped onto the settee. "Have you heard from the kidnappers?" Heads shook. "It's wired?"

Vonna pointed to a desk. Her recording equipment was on the blotter. "I had it in the car." It seemed unnecessary to say. She always kept her electronics there.

"Good," said Dub. God, he'd been an asshole last night. His brain took a spiral. He blinked it off. "So," he asked, "what happened?"

"It's all my fault," said Alma Louise. "Raleigh Lee said it was such a nice day, with the sun coming over the . . ." She choked up.

"So she asked me to bring their lunch out front," said Mrs. Johnson.

"You eat out there often?"

Mrs. Menzies nodded.

"Once in a while," said Mrs. Johnson. "The house shadows the close end of the pool on sunny days, so they sit on the flagstones out front."

He glanced up at Mrs. O'Dell, who was still standing, arms crossed. She nodded. "Raleigh liked to sit in front, wave to the neighbors."

"Like Colonel Cotton Dixie in his rocker."

She seemed perplexed by the image. He wasn't sure what he'd meant, either. "Public men like to be in public," he said.

"But I suggested it," wailed Alma Louise. "It's my fault. We should have listened to Mrs. Johnson."

"Huh?"

"I said with all's been going on I'd feel better wheeling the lunch out to the back of the pool in the sun. Then Mr. Menzies he say he wouldn't make me do that."

"He wasn't going to let a bunch of ignorant savages drive him off his own front patio," added Alma Louise.

"Okay, so lunch is out there."

"And I'm just telling Raleigh Lee to eat his cucumber sandwiches before they get warm, and . . ." She choked up again.

"He was reading yesterday's paper, all spread up in front of him," said Mrs. Johnson. "The stock pages."

"And I don't even think he saw the van coming up the driveway. I said, 'Oh, Raleigh Lee, there's a package coming.' "

"A package?"

"She told me it was painted like a Federal Express van," said Mrs. O'Dell.

"Why 'painted like'? Alma Louise?"

[81]

"It— I don't know. The paint was all dull. And I didn't see them until it pulled away."

"See what?" asked Dub.

"The bumper stickers."

He waited, but she mopped her brow.

"Okay?" said Dub loudly.

Vonna's eyes flashed. "The one said, 'Make the President a Duke.' The other said, 'Help the Homeless: Ship 'em Back to Africa.' "

"Is that right?" Dub asked Alma Louise. She nodded, her eyes closed. "Did you see them?" he asked Mrs. Johnson. She shook her head, then refused to meet his eyes. He thought the reaction was strange. "Was there something else?"

"I wasn't paying attention to the van," she said.

"Duke is that Klan motherfucker in the legislature," said Vonna, almost grinding her teeth.

"I know," said Dub.

"It was some of your white-supremacy boys."

"Why the hell does everybody call them *my* boys? Jesus!" He wiped his face with his hand.

"I don't think Federal Express would allow bumper stickers on their vans," said Mrs. O'Dell.

"Naw? You're kidding me," said Dub nastily. He shouldn't've said that to her, he thought. "Okay, okay, so what exactly happens? You see this van come up the driveway. It pulls up front?"

Alma Louise nodded. "And a man jumps out with a gun."

"What kind of gun?"

"A big gun, like a cowboy gun. With a big barrel."

"A revolver? Like with a round thing toward the back?"

She nodded. "And he says, 'Okay, nigger lover, you're mine!' and I thought he was going to shoot, but he grabs Raleigh Lee by the arm and shoves him in the back."

"And then?"

"He points the gun straight at me. I thought he was going to kill me, but he saw Martha and seemed confused. Then, he says, 'Call the police and he's dead. You'll hear from us.' "

"Is that exactly what he said?" She nodded. "Is that how

he said it?" She shifted. "I mean, did he have an accent or anything? Did he sound like a cracker or a Cajun or a lawyer from Harvard or—"

"I don't know, I don't know. . . . He didn't sound like anybody. I can't remember." She broke down again. Mrs. O'Dell crossed to comfort her.

Dub hefted himself up. His leg was falling asleep. He moved toward Mrs. Johnson, who was still lost in her thoughts. "Did you hear him?"

"Not really," she said.

"Where were you?"

"I came to the window when I heard the china breaking on the flagstones."

"And you saw?"

"The man pointed the gun at her and stared at me. Then he warned her and jumped in the van and off it went."

"So there were two men?"

"Must've been a driver."

"Would you recognize them again?"

"I never got a good look at the driver. They wore masks," she said. "The rubber kind that cover your whole head."

"The driver's was a John Wayne, Alma Louise thinks," said Mrs. O'Dell. "The gunman's was a Stan Laurel, like in Laurel and Hardy."

"Stanley with a six-gun," muttered Dub. "Must've been a hoot. And where were you?"

"Me? I was at home. Alma Louise tried to call you, then she called me. *I* didn't do it," she said petulantly.

"They wore gloves, like big work gloves," added Mrs. Johnson, "and a jogging suit. They were all covered up. Everywhere."

The doorbell rang insistently. Mrs. Johnson hurried off to answer it.

"You should have called the police right away," said Dub. "Right away!" He didn't know why he was saying it. So they could get it right the next time someone was kidnapped in broad daylight off the front patio?

Alma Louise suddenly grabbed his coattail and pulled

him toward her. "They set a bomb in our mailbox, did you know that? A *bomb!*"

Dub nodded impatiently and tugged loose. He slumped into a chair and avoided Vonna's eyes. God, when was that aspirin going to kick in? He felt lower than a retired Teamster's balls.

TEN

FBI Agent Campbell charged in with three men. The one wearing horn-rimmed glasses was carrying tape equipment. They were all wearing the same suits, and only their different ties and the glasses indicated they weren't identical triplets. Dub thought of those kids' games in which you're supposed to pick out what is different about several drawings of teddy bears or clowns. As if he could read Dub's mind, Campbell gave him a cold glance, pushed past him, and quickly introduced his three companions to Alma Louise. They each nodded with a snap of the chin and a "Howya doin'?" To FBI guys a kidnapping was like a five-dollar prime rib to a fat Shriner.

"You shouldn't have waited so long to call us," said Campbell. "Private gumshoes aren't really up to handling something like this."

"The kidnappers said . . ."

"You could have increased the danger to your husband by listening to inexperienced people."

Mrs. O'Dell threw up her chin like a duchess. "They both told Alma Louise to telephone the authorities immediately."

He eyed her as if she were contradicting his opinion on the death penalty. "Well, then, we've got things in hand now." He stared straight at Dub. "You can go now. And take your girl with you."

"Girl?" said Vonna, rising.

"See you," said Dub.

"No!" said Alma Louise. "I want him here. He's been helping since the beginning."

"Bureau rules forbid us working with private cops."

Alma Louise looked confused, but shook her head no.

"We'll go," said Dub.

"No," said Mrs. O'Dell, "he's a friend of the family. He stays."

Campbell seemed to be trying to stare her down, but the steel pillar of southern womanhood had spoken. There would be no further argument.

"What are you waiting for?" he said sharply to Horn-Rims. "Get on the wire."

"I've already—" said Vonna, but the agent was already pulling her equipment loose. He banged the tape recorder, setting it aside.

"Hey!" she said. "You'll pay for that if it's broke."

He ignored her and started fiddling with the wall socket. Dub eased his way to the wide den door and leaned against the lintel. Through the sheer curtains, he could see a van out front and a man headed up the telephone pole by the street. Real subtle, he thought, like the guy who parked in the woods. The high-percentage stuff—kidnapping, bank robbery—had always been meat and potatoes to the FBI. This kind of case could get Campbell promoted. The boys weren't likely to do anything subtle, even if doing it might save Menzies. Never bet a man's life against anybody's promotion, Dub thought grimly. Aw, hell, Menzies was probably already reliving old times with Martin Luther King. Somewhere in Valhalla the two dead heroes were folding in their wings together and saying, "Do you remember when . . . ?"

The thought had made him uncomfortable. He shifted, turning his back to the den. Mrs. Johnson was slumped on the sofa, looking up at him. Their eyes locked for what seemed a long time, not as if she were going to speak, but as if she were trying to send him a telepathic message. Her eyelids drooped, she lowered her chin. An agent brushed past him to go outside. She was scared for Menzies, he thought, but scared for herself, too. She loved Raleigh Lee Menzies. She had worked for him for decades, had cared for him like a mother or a sister, and cleaned up after his dipso wife. But not only that, she was probably in love with him. A lonely woman dreaming about a man she can't have, about a man she couldn't even bring herself to tell her feelings to, by Dub's guess. She probably brought Menzies sandwiches and late-night cups of tea when the mistress she had mentioned was dying. Had Mrs. Johnson mentioned the woman's name? That's right: Miss Jane. And she died three years ago of cancer.

Dub tried to visualize it as a diagram with Menzies at the center. Alma Louise and Mrs. Johnson devoted to him, the two corners of a triangle, lines converging on Raleigh Lee. But he, up on the point, sent his dotted line out toward a dead woman. If this included all the love relationships, it was complicated, but it wasn't anything like a chart of all the individuals and organizations who had their reasons to hate him. In either diagram, Raleigh Lee Menzies was at the center and Dub didn't know much about him, or not enough. It was the old question that people always asked about the famous: "What is So-and-so *really* like?" As if there was an answer. In many ways, the truly accomplished, the great, the saints and the devils, weren't like anyone else. If they were, they wouldn't have been great people. Ultimately, they were unknowable.

Alma Louise and Campbell had another exchange on whether Dub should be present while he questioned her. He might have been hinting that Dub himself could be involved with the kidnapping, but Dub ignored it. Alma Louise would let neither Dub nor Mrs. O'Dell leave the room. Dub leaned in when he noticed Vonna was gone from where she had been standing. He grimaced as he once again remembered last night. Mrs. O'Dell noticed his expression. He wiped his face with his hand. She said nothing.

He distracted himself by listening carefully to the accounts of the kidnapping again. Nothing new. Alma Louise made no substantial changes in her story, and yet, fumbled through it in such fits and starts, backing up and starting over several times as if she were reconstructing it. It sounded like a bad actor trying to find his lines. Campbell told the man at his left that they should check on where you could get Stan Laurel and John Wayne masks. Christ! thought Dub, that was pulling your pud. Didn't Campbell notice how many masks floated around a town like New Orleans? Most of its inhabitants thought that fifty-one weeks of the year were for recovering from the previous Mardi Gras. Dub thought about slipping out to question the neighbors. Maybe they'd seen something. But Alma Louise had fought so hard to keep him there, it would have seemed like desertion. He hated waiting around, though. His head pounded and he was sleepy. Nearly three hours now, and the kidnappers hadn't called. It was looking more and more like a straightforward killing.

Campbell moved his interrogation show into the living room. He acted like Dub was an annoying hank of drape covering the doorway.

"Can I get you gentlemen something?" asked Mrs. Johnson.

"No, thank you. We're here to talk to you, to get all the details we can. How's your son?"

"Excuse me?"

"Your son. Rasheed M'fulu, a.k.a. William Johnson. Have you heard from him lately?"

She was obviously confused, then angered. "Well, no. Of course not." She glanced at Dub. "He sent me a postcard all the way from the Cameroons last December. I guess it was kind of a Christmas card, but it didn't get here until the middle of January."

"But he doesn't contact you regularly?"

"No," said Mrs. Johnson.

"Now, tell me about it from the beginning. . . ."

Dub listened to her account for several minutes, then casually moved back into the den. "Clementine," he said. She reacted to his using her first name as if she understood it was important. Good girl, he thought. "You like some coffee? Let's make some coffee. How 'bout you, Alma Louise? You?"

Alma Louise mumbled about caffeine upsetting her stomach. Horn-Rims shook his head. His expression was like a ten-year-old's planning his next move in Dungeons and Dragons. Dub and Mrs. O'Dell went into the kitchen.

"What do you think?" whispered Mrs. O'Dell, opening a cabinet. "He's dead, isn't he?"

"I don't know," said Dub, but her look told him she

didn't believe him. "Well, okay. Every minute the call doesn't come is probably another nail in the lid. It isn't like he simply disappeared. They know she saw it. And if you got any sense at all, you don't wait around until they're ready for you."

"Why abduct him only to kill him?"

"I don't know. Ritual. Mock trial. Torture."

"But they said they'd call."

"A bluff? Hell, I don't know. I'm only guessing. Maybe they want to keep him for twenty years, like they do in Beirut."

"Does Raleigh have a chance?"

"God knows, Mrs. O'Dell. It really is fifty-fifty. Probably worse, because of who he is."

She opened another cabinet. "Where do they keep the coffee?"

He tried a door near the sink. "Here it is." He took out the can. "You'd think they'd buy something fancier than Luzianne. Maybe go after the boutique stuff: café almond Benedictine, decaffeinated with Perrier."

"Raleigh is no gourmet," said Mrs. O'Dell. "It's one thing Michael—my husband—never understood about him. He hated to come over here for dinner. Raleigh couldn't tell chuck from sirloin."

"And Alma Louise?"

"She used to be very particular about what she ate. When we were in prep school together, she always was the one who would pass up chocolate because it would make you break out, or tell you things like Jell-O was good for your nails. Did you like school?" she asked.

"Me? I hated it. In fact, I didn't even know half how lousy it was. I wouldn't be sixteen again for all the tea in China. Basic training was better."

Mrs. O'Dell paused in rinsing out the coffeepot and stared out the window. "Maybe it's different for boys. It was golden for us. We were going to marry princes and live in marble palaces. Everything was in front of us."

"I'd say you did okay."

"I guess we did." She shrugged. "But now she hardly cares if she eats at all. I'm a widow trying to keep her husband's restaurants afloat, and she's . . . I don't know. It's all slipping away from her. What's the point?"

Dub noticed Vonna outside at the far end of the swimming pool. She was inspecting the rose beds and the fence behind them. She stopped periodically to look back at the house. What the hell was she up to? He handed Mrs. O'Dell a spoon. "There you go," he said, easing up close to her. "Listen," he said in a whisper, "what do you know about Mrs. Johnson's son?"

She did not look up from filling the percolator bin. "Thank God," she said, "I thought you were sidling up to make a pass. Ha!"

"I got enough woman trouble." Vonna, he noticed, had disappeared. What the hell was she up to?

"What was his name?" she asked herself. "Rasheed M'fulu."

"That's it."

"Mrs. Johnson's son."

"Right. A.k.a. William Johnson."

"He took the name himself. It means something. I forget what. Raleigh put the boy in the best schools. Montessori. He was a free spirit and inevitably went too far."

"What do you mean?"

"There was a shoot-out. The gadgets for making bombs were there." She stopped dipping coffee, spoon in midair. "The bomb?"

"I don't know," said Dub. "I just know that Campbell was asking about him."

"Raleigh had to get a court order to stop them from harassing her. Most of the time Mrs. Johnson doesn't know whether the boy's dead or alive. She hasn't seen him for—" she squinted, "—a dozen years, anyway. More than that."

"Any chance he . . . ?"

"What would be the political rationale in Rasheed's killing Raleigh Lee Menzies?"

"Hell, I don't know." Dub sighed. "Kooks are kooks. But Mrs. Johnson knows more than she's saying." He rubbed a water spot on the stainless-steel sink. "What about—I don't know—I'm just groping on this . . ."

"What?"

"Rasheed Whatsizname: he couldn't be Raleigh Lee's son?"

Mrs. O'Dell straightened up like she'd been jerked. "Good Lord! Whatever gave you that idea?"

"He treated him like a son, you said. And he and Alma Louise—"

"That was a long time ago. Alma Louise and he were close in those days!"

"No kids, though."

"You could never look at Rasheed and imagine he was a mixed-race child. Lord!"

"Ssssh!" said Dub, tilting his head toward the door. "It don't always work out like mixing coffee and cream. And unless I'm mistaken, there's more than mere admiration of Raleigh Lee by Mrs. Johnson."

"She adores him, but that doesn't mean . . . Lord! Ask her, if you must," she said tersely, "but for God's sake don't repeat it. It is just like the sort of thing they used to tar him with. It's ridiculous!"

"No it ain't." Dub raised his hands. "But I'm not out to hurt the man."

"I know," she said. "What's the matter with this burner?" She moved the pot to the back burner. It lit. "But you could hurt him. Even if he is dead. If you knew him, you'd know he couldn't be hypocritical about his own child."

"You're right," he said. "I don't know him. All I know is he wasn't thrilled to have me in his house." He drifted to the door leading to the corridor and remembered Alma Louise conked out on the toilet. He then crossed to the other door and heard Campbell.

"—and you didn't see the bumper stickers?" he asked rapidly. "But you just told me they said—"

"Well, everything was going so fast. I might've seen them, but it didn't register right away. . . ." Alma Louise's voice drowned in a sob.

"God, they're grilling her like she done it. They ought to sober her up, but I guess there ain't time." He shook his head.

Mrs. O'Dell moved toward the door as if she were going

[91]

to interrupt the questioning. Dub touched her upper arm. "No," he said.

"They shouldn't treat her like a common drunk," she muttered, but then went back to lean against the counter and watch the percolator on the stove.

"What about Miss Jane?" Dub asked quietly.

She looked at him nastily. More gossip. The Red Knight. The Communist philanderer with no morals. "What about her?"

"Mrs. Johnson mentioned her."

"I knew that. She was the only one who called her Miss Jane."

"She thought I already knew. She didn't tell me intentionally."

"I knew that, too. Mrs. Johnson wouldn't do anything to hurt Raleigh. She's no blabbermouth."

"How long did that thing with this Jane go on?"

"At least a decade. Alma Louise knew about it."

"A 'civilized understanding.' "

"Yes," snapped Mrs. O'Dell. "Jane Thuxpin had a good heart. She never wanted to hurt anyone. She would never have been anyone's secret mistress."

"But she was, wasn't she? If Menzies's enemies had known about it . . ."

"What I mean is that she wouldn't have allowed it to be a secret to anyone who mattered. That meant Alma Louise."

"Nice crowd. Nobody wants to hurt nobody. And you knew about it?"

The water began boiling. She turned down the burner. "Alma Louise told me. She said Raleigh had told her. She told me it was her own fault because she had gotten pickled and had a few 'encounters.' She imagined she'd gotten AIDS, but it was just guilt."

"He knew about these flings?"

"If he did, he didn't do anything about them that I know of."

"Why didn't they just divorce? Best wishes, see you around?"

"Alma Louise still loved him. Maybe he still loved her.

Or maybe he just felt a need to care for her. The patrician impulse: he is a gentleman of the Old South. He took care of Mrs. Johnson, he took care of Rasheed, he took care of Alma Louise, and he took care of Jane Thuxpin."

"And what did he do for himself?"

"Took care of others. That *is* Raleigh Lee. Noblesse oblige." She spoke mechanically, as if about to fall into a hypnotic trance, watching the second hand sweep around the clock face. She probably hadn't made coffee in anything as simple as a percolator for a long time, but even if it was ordinary Luzianne, it was going to be perfect.

Alma Louise still loved Raleigh Lee, and Raleigh Lee, thought Dub, might still love her. He peered out the window. Where the hell had Vonna gone? Love just wasn't enough to make things right in a whole lot of situations, was it? It was too bad everyone had to grow up and find that out.

ELEVEN

Two hours passed, then three. Everyone drank too much of Mrs. O'Dell's coffee because it was so good. Alma Louise even stayed on the coffee, saying, "I have to be ready for the call." After a while, she was the only one who couldn't sit still. Everyone slumped into whatever chair or sofa was convenient and flipped through their thoughts like they were browsing old *Reader's Digest*s in a dentist's office. Occasionally Campbell inaudibly consulted his office on his cellular phone. Dub dozed off several times in a big winged chair by the fireplace, only to be awakened when his chin hit his chest. The case made him more nervous than the coffee (which he had already decided would substitute for dinner). There were too many factors coming from odd directions. If he could just *do* something, check out this Jane Thuxpin, Rasheed, all these people who were supposedly too thoughtful to hurt each other . . . Nobody was going to tell him anything here. He couldn't even make inquiries over the phone without the FBI nosing in. Here, Dub was just a pimple on Campbell's butt.

His leg was going to sleep. Dub shook it, stretched, and noticed the FBI guy with horn-rims playing chess on the settee with a pocket computer. Your tax dollars at work! He went into the kitchen and out through the sliding glass doors. It had just turned dark and the insects were swirling frantically around the lights under the eaves. The air was Vietnam heavy, denser than the water. He could almost hear the *thup-thup-thup* of the Hueys. He wasn't going to let that get into his head again. There was enough brewing in there already: Jane

Thuxpin, Rasheed, Alma Louise's drinking companions, the Alberts boys.

And what about Stavros, the nosy little bastard at Mrs. O'Dell's who had put the granny grope on Alma Louise? He hadn't thought much about him. Kidnapping was sort of a Sardinian specialty, wasn't it? Sardinia was kind of close to Greece. Kind of. Were Greeks big on kidnapping? Fake kidnapping? Stavros gets Raleigh Lee bumped so he can move in on Alma Louise as soon as the inheritance comes through? Weirder things had happened. There was the woman who hired a hit man to get her daughter on a cheerleading squad. Dub also remembered a case in Pittsburgh. A shoe-salesman Lothario had killed a car-parts king. But when the widow inherited (she wasn't in on the murder) she suddenly decided Lothario was beneath her and dated any man with class enough to wear a tie. He strangled her with an eighteen-inch pair of strings from some kind of rhinestoned tennis shoe. And then hanged himself in the closet? Ate a Smith & Wesson? Threw himself in the Monongahela? Dub couldn't remember.

He leaned over and smelled the bud of a tiny white rose in a narrow vase on the Queen Anne pie table. It was strong, sweet, like the perfumes Vonna preferred. He checked the house. No one seemed to be watching him. He made his way around the far end, past the aluminum shed, and up to the area where Vonna had slipped away. He thought he saw the impression of her foot in the mulch. He climbed up on the landscaping beams that raised the rose bed and peered over the fence.

Trees. Maybe the sound of a stream down below. It sloped down, he figured, to where the FBI had staked out Raleigh Lee's house. Nobody'd mentioned the stakeout. A screwup? The guy was snoozing when the snatch happened? Or he was out getting a po' boy? That would be par. But why had Vonna slipped out over this fence? Goddammit! All he had was questions. Questions and more questions. You eliminate the possibilities and whatever is left, no matter how improbable, is the solution, Watson. He hadn't eliminated a fucking thing except that *he* didn't do it. And then, he wasn't too sure of that after all the beer he'd sucked up last night. Goddammit!

The coffee had drained through and he needed to piss again. That's what he needed: elimination. He shook his head. "That's a bad one, brother," he muttered out loud. "A baaad one!"

When he slid back the glass door, he was startled to see Mrs. Johnson with a large cook's knife cutting the crust off sandwiches. He watched her for a few seconds.

"You best come in," she said. "We don't need them bugs."

He nodded and closed the door. "No call, I suppose."

She shook her head.

"You ought to be resting. You had a bad day."

"I feel better on the move. When I was a young girl, just a skinny thing, there was an old man on Mr. Menzies's plantation. William. He used ta talk about the old days and said he was looking forward to dying so he could catch up on his sleep. He'd say he'd picked cotton and cut cane and the Lord knows what all from sunup to sunset until he was too tired to sleep. Got in the habit and couldn't sleep much no more. I guess he's finally resting now. I reckon I got some of William's blood in me. I got to keep moving, especially when I'm weary."

"I never could get that old saying right. Is it 'No rest for the weary'? Or 'No rest for the wicked'?"

"Huh?" Her mouth curled in amusement. "You saying I'm wicked?"

He moved closer to her. The cook's knife gleamed like a four-foot broadsword. He was breaking one of his primary rules: never press someone who is holding a major weapon. "You're not exactly wicked," he said in a low voice, "but you're not telling everything you know."

She glanced through the open door at the FBI men. "What you mean?" she asked with studied calmness.

"I mean you're not telling something. Maybe something about your son."

"Shoot! I ain't seen the boy almost twenty years. He said he was off to join the PLO, then I get cards here and there. Willie might as well died when he turned into Rasheed."

"But you've seen him?"

She hesitated. "No."

"You have. You might know something that could save Raleigh Lee Menzies."

She sighed as if relieved somebody knew. For a moment Dub thought she was going to open up, but then she shook her head and placed the last sandwich on the platter.

"I'm begging you. You know something."

She gripped the rims of the platter like she was going to throw it. "They was wearing gloves and masks. But the man with the gun, when he turned to go in the van—"

"You saw something," said Dub. "He was black."

She closed her eyes and bit her lower lip.

His voice was gentle. "You think it was Willie."

"No," she said. "I don't think so. I don't think it was his voice. He looked, I don't know, heavier, moved liked he was older than Willie."

"How old?"

"Older than Willie. It wasn't him."

"Older than me?" Nobody feels older than me, thought Dub.

"No. I don't think so. I can't be sure." She crossed her arms and scratched at the ashy dry skin on her elbow. "Willie ain't got no call to snatch up Mr. Menzies. That's just foolishness. He and my Willie get along fine."

"What do you mean 'get along'? I thought you haven't seen Rasheed for twelve years."

"I gave him his name and it is William, no matter what he wants to call himself. You can't refuse Christian grace once it is given."

"You haven't answered my question."

"You never hear of postcards? My Willie's in Africa. He ain't with no kidnappers."

Dub rolled his eyes skeptically to provoke her more, but she remained stone-faced.

"Okay, then," he whispered. "How did you know he was black? Maybe you're just imagining it."

She shook her head. "His sleeve. Here." She pointed to

the slit below the button. "And then his mask rode up at the collar when he bent over to jump in the van."

Dub thought about the possibility of a dark, long-sleeved undershirt. Would white supremacists color their skin to throw everyone off? And then wear masks, too? It seemed too subtle for them.

"The man with the gun was a brother," she said firmly.

Dub tossed his head toward the living room. "You've got to tell them."

"They'll just throw it on my Willie."

"But you said you know it wasn't him."

"You know better than that. I'm the wrong color to know anything, as far as they're concerned. I'm just an Indian; they're just the cavalry."

"The FBI means well." It came out even lamer than he meant it. "So why'd you tell me?"

" 'Cause you won't tell them."

"Now, how the hell you know that?"

"Well, if you do, I'll just say you're making it up, and it looks to me that the man out there likes you even less than he likes brown sugar."

She raised her head in a formal way, and Dub knew that they were being watched. "Sandwich?" she asked Campbell.

"We've sent out," said the agent.

"I make 'em with mayonnaise, not strychnine."

"Policy," said Campbell, moving back into the living room.

"Go ahead," said Mrs. Johnson to Dub. "Tell the man."

He spat out a short laugh. "Yeah." As she lifted the platter, he snatched half a sandwich off the top. Okay, so coffee wasn't going to be dinner. Ham. The kind made in Denmark of all the scraps hammered down in a can. How much cholesterol was in it? Well, it was only *half* a sandwich.

Blacks had snatched Raleigh Lee. Only, they had tried to make it look like white kooks by putting the bumper stickers on the van. So why? To get even for the gossip in Menzies's book? After—what was it?—a dozen years? So maybe they figure to draw attention to what the papers always called "the rising tide of racism" by snatching this retired civil rights lawyer and blaming it on the Klan. Maybe they got the idea from reading about El Salvador and the like. Kill one of your own and blame it on your enemies.

On the other hand, could this be a simple money snatch? All the political stuff could be a boatload of red herring. What kind of terrorist would use some kind of cowboy revolver? It's the age of the Uzi and the assault rifle. Mrs. Johnson hadn't gotten a good look at the driver. He could have been black, white, Chinese, or Martian for all anybody knew. Simpler was better. What was that called? The razor. But that would simplify things too much. If it was a money snatch, why didn't the pricks call? They'd got the package, why not sell it? Dub's headache was ratcheting up a notch. He checked the kitchen clock sweeping relentlessly forward. It was ten-seventeen. What else was Mrs. Johnson not saying?

He wanted to talk to Devraix. Dub sure as shit wouldn't be able to make any inquiries about black terrorists, and even though Devraix thought of himself as a downtown Creole whose pedigree wouldn't permit mixing with the hoi polloi of the uptown blacks, he had lots of mysterious connections. And he could put Spyder Williams on it. Just talking it over with Devraix would be good. The man had a way of wiping away the steam on the mirror. But Dub couldn't do it over a tapped phone. He and Vonna and Devraix had juggled around the Wilkton case and come up with the woman's boyfriend like that. Vonna and he had talked a lot of cases clear. Ah, well, this one was too much of a mess for him and Vonna to sort out, even if she'd talk to him. And where *had* she gone, anyway?

He decided to wait until midnight. This waiting around was boring and getting him nowhere. They weren't going to call, he told himself. This was a killing. But who? Why? He thought of Menzies's book and decided it might be good to give it a look. At the very least he'd know about the man who was at the center of the case. Know the root, maybe you know the tree. He knew there were no books in the living room. There were some in the den, but they had looked like old law books, and anyway he didn't feel like dealing with Alma

Louise's fidgeting. She was getting pretty rattled withdrawing from her regular fortifiers.

He wandered down the corridor past the bathroom where Alma Louise had conked out on the toilet. There were two bedrooms. The woman's was sloppy, with dusting powder on the vanity. The man's was tidy, brushes and cologne neatly lined up on the dresser. Around the corner were two more doors. Another woman's room, Mrs. Johnson's, and across from it a crowded office. A word processor. Gray file cabinets. A worn leather swivel chair and about a dozen copies of *Go Down, Moses: Memoirs of the Civil Rights Movement* by Raleigh Lee Menzies in a box on the floor. When Dub lifted one, dust came off. On the back of the book was a picture of Menzies leaning against a fence, with a horse behind him in the distance. He was younger but not much different: gaunt, as now; hair a bit darker; more life in the eyes, as if he enjoyed posing. The credit in small letters said "Photo by Jane Thuxpin." Most of the light had gone out of Menzies's eyes when Dub had seen him, and it wasn't from Bobby Albert's attack. The death of your lover would do that, though: make you see how pointless everything is. Especially a cancer death.

He flipped open the book. In the center of the binding was a photograph section. Menzies sitting in the pew of a black church with several black men in suits and ties, and Hosea Williams in overalls. Sheriff Bull Connor with his flat-brimmed hat. Below, German shepherds and fire hoses savaging marchers. A boy being viciously beaten by a cop with a riot stick. Menzies jubilant at a press conference on the federal courthouse steps. Menzies huddled close with Martin Luther King and A. Philip Randolph over a legal document. Menzies exhausted, his eyes wet, holding his hand to block the camera on the morning he heard of the murder of Lemuel Penn. Menzies shaking hands with Nelson Rockefeller. A collage of headlines: GO BACK TO RUSSIA! SAYS SHELTON; RED KNIGHT TO SPEAK; MADDOX THREATENS MENZIES WITH AX HANDLE; KNIGHT SPONSORED BY KREMLIN, HINTS HOOVER; HIGH COURT UPHOLDS HOUSING PLAN; KING DEAD: NATION MOURNS. On the opposite page, there were pictures of Menzies at the funerals of John Kennedy, Martin Luther King, Robert Kennedy, and Malcolm

X. The police had warned him that someone might try to hurt him at the last ceremony, but he went anyway. On the final page of photos was one of Menzies at a playground. He was sitting on a seesaw, his linen jacket hanging on the jungle gym behind him. At the other end four black children and one white, or possibly, a very light-skinned black child. They were gripping the sides of the board intensely, leaning their bodies forward like jockeys, and Menzies was carefully, slowly, rais- ing them, his mouth open wide in a triumphant laugh, his arm raised like a rodeo rider.

Dub stared at the picture for some time. A number of feelings had washed over him as he had scanned the section. He remembered his father throwing an ashtray at the televi- sion when Eisenhower sent the National Guard into Little Rock. He had been too young to understand. No one would explain except Opal, their black housekeeper, who said that the Colonel, still in the Guard, was only worried that he might be called into a dangerous situation. He remembered cadets at the Citadel sitting in the dark and planning a new Civil War to keep the "nigra" from ruining the country. He remembered the laughing face of the boy who'd told him that "someone plugged Kennedy." He himself hadn't been that outspoken, one way or the other.

Everything that happened before Vietnam seemed to him to be in an age of blissful, innocent ignorance. He wasn't threatened by blacks; he'd felt sorry for them in their run- down houses. He didn't see what was so terrible about James Meredith going to Ole Miss. Probably his mother's sentimen- talizing about "all God's children" had taken more than he'd known. He had been too naive to recognize evil, too young to fight it, and too untouched by any sense of loss to fret about the passing of the Old South. From what he could tell, the South was a hell of a lot better now than it had been when he was a kid. Why shouldn't he live with Vonna if he could? He felt a momentary tingle as he recalled the texture of the inside of her thigh. But when you've lived a certain time, when you've nearly been killed a couple of times, when you are carrying nitro tablets in your jacket, the passing of any part of your life—even the poverty-stricken, segregated, cruel and bigoted Old South—seems sad. Now the South had malls and Burger Kings and wasn't really that different from Pennsylvania or Connecticut. The end of any part of your life is another nibble off your existence. Nibble, nibble, nibble, then there's nothing left.

The photograph of Menzies on the seesaw had been blown up to eight by ten and hung on the office wall next to some plaque he had received. When had it been taken? In the book, again the credit was to Jane Thuxpin, but there was no date. Was the cancer in her when she snapped the picture? Did the joy on Menzies's face remind him of caressing her knee under the table at Le Ruth's? She would have been alive when the book was printed. She'd had a knack for capturing him on film, stripped of his public pose. She knew him like no one else. The seesaw photograph was a reminder of the innocent time, when Menzies still had the joy of the warrior, when he attacked with a heart full of exhilaration, when changing the racial situation was just a matter of pushing the seesaw with enough gentle pressure. Dub had an innocent-time picture like that somewhere. He was sitting on the stones at the Fort Sumter national monument wearing his uniform. Beth was hugging him around the neck. He was smiling. In two days he would leave for Saigon.

He drummed his fingers and peered around the office again. He tugged on the drawer. It was full of letters from book publishers: "I'm afraid we'll have to pass on this one"; ". . . so, this doesn't present any new angle on the situation"; "thank you for considering us"; "Despite the importance of this issue, Mr. Menzies, we do not think that this would break onto the Best Seller list, and the midlist I'm sure you understand is no longer sufficient to sustain nonfiction in a climate of . . ." And so on, and so on. Dub hadn't realized there were so many publishers who could say no in so many different ways. Menzies had been trying to sell a book called *Crime of Omission: The Failure of the American Health Care System*. The letters were about two years old. A new crusade, thought Dub. The old bull elephant looking for a scrap. He didn't see any manuscript. Maybe it was in the file or on computer disk.

He felt too tired to rummage in the file, so he propped his feet
up and began reading chapter one of *Go Down, Moses*.

WHEN I WAS GROWING UP AT RIVER BEND, MY FAMILY
PLANTATION, MY FATHER AND HIS BROTHER BEN SPOKE OF
"THEIR COLOREDS." A GENTLEMAN ALWAYS TOOK CARE OF
"HIS COLOREDS." HE WOULD MAKE CERTAIN THAT THE
CHILDREN HAD ONE GOOD PAIR OF SHOES FOR SCHOOL
AND CHURCH, THAT THE OLD WIDOWS HAD ENOUGH COAL
IN THE WINTER, AND THAT THE A.M.E. CHURCH WOULD
GET A BRIGHT COAT OF WHITE PAINT EVERY FEW YEARS,
COURTESY OF RIVER BEND. IF ONE OF YOURS GOT AR-
RESTED, YOU DID WHAT YOU COULD FOR HIM, THEN TRIED
TO MAKE SURE HIS WIFE AND CHILDREN WERE PROVIDED
FOR WHILE THE HUSBAND DID HIS TIME ON THE CHAIN
GANG OR IN THE STATE PENITENTIARY. LEGALLY, THE
"COLOREDS" WERE FREE MEN, BUT LIKE SLAVES, IT WAS
SAID, THEY STILL NEEDED SOMEONE TO CARE FOR THEM.
WHAT I, GROWING UP THERE AMID THE SPANISH MOSS
AND FRAGRANT FLOWERS OF RIVER BEND, COULD NEVER
QUITE UNDERSTAND WAS THAT IF WE WERE TAKING CARE
OF "OUR COLOREDS" WHY WERE THEIR LIVES SO MISERA-
BLE? *WHY WEREN'T WE DOING A BETTER JOB?*

Dub read on. Menzies told of incidents of relatively mild
injustice he had seen that had affected him deeply: an insult
to a black minister, a white boy urinating off a bridge at some
children swimming below. He told of hiding under the gazebo
one afternoon and hearing talk of a lynching in the next
parish. His father had said with disgust, "Don't these people
know what the law is for?" But his uncle had said that there
wasn't any question that the "boy" had done it. "That's not
the point, Ben," his father had said. "The law is the point."
And Raleigh Lee was so impressed with the invocation of the
word he had decided to make it his profession.

Dub wondered if Menzies wasn't dressing up his daddy a
bit and if he'd gone into law more because his daddy was a
lawyer, the same way Dub had drifted into the army because
of his father. People were both more complicated and more

simple than they liked to make out. Dub was too tired to go past chapter one. It was nearly eleven-thirty. The book might give him a clue into who this man was, not so much for what he said, which was pretty predictable, but from the way he said it. The book would certainly tell him who Raleigh Lee Menzies wanted to be and maybe, between the lines, who he was. Then, maybe from that, Dub might get a handle on who was trying to kill him. Or who had already killed him. Or why. Well, okay, that was pretty farfetched, but after all, you did like to know something about your client. Dub closed his eyes for a few minutes to get up the energy to go home. Oh, shit, he had no home. Another lousy motel. Damn! Maybe he'd just sleep in the car.

A phone ringing nearly made him topple the chair. He checked his watch. Midnight. The witching hour. It rang again. He picked it up gently to listen in. Nothing. It rang again and he realized it wasn't the one in Menzies office, but a phone in a nearby room. He charged into the hallway, saw the phone on the bedstand in Mrs. Johnson's room, and picked it up.

"Hello," said a voice. There was loud music playing in the background. "Hey, I know you're there. You stall me and your boss man is dead."

Still no one broke in as Dub expected.

"No one's stalling!" said Dub quickly. Where the hell were the FBI guys? "I thought somebody else was picking up."

"Are you the cops? You best not be the cops."

"I'm not a cop. I'm a friend of Mrs. Menzies."

"Put her butt on the phone."

"I've got to get her."

"The bitch loaded again? Maybe I'll just kill the man right now."

"No!" said Dub. "She's in the other room. I don't know why she didn't pick up."

Alma Louise fluttered in trailed by Campbell and one of his men on the cellular phone. They were all red-faced, as if they'd run around the block.

"Here she is now," said Dub. "Here she is." He covered the mouthpiece and held it out to her. "It's them."

Campbell gritted his teeth, glared at Horn-Rims, and brought his fist down hard against his thigh.

Alma Louise hesitated, hands shaking as if she were trying to move but couldn't. Dub pulled her around the desk and slapped the receiver in her hand. She slowly raised it to her ear.

"Yes, this is Mrs. Menzies. Yes. Yes. I'll remember, yes."

Campbell jerked Dub by the arm and whispered through his teeth. "Why the fuck didn't you tell us Mrs. Johnson had her own line?"

"When did I know that? Get your goddamned hand off me."

Campbell sneered at Dub, then rotated both his hands to indicate that Alma Louise should keep them talking.

"You're in charge. You should have known," said Dub.

"Shut up." Campbell grimaced. Horn-Rims's butt would be in a sling over this.

"Yes," said Alma Louise patiently. "Yes, I understand. Yes." She looked at Dub and bit her lip. She seemed to avoid looking Campbell in the eye.

"A million dollars!" she suddenly exclaimed. "My God! I can't get a million dollars!"

She listened.

"No! Don't kill him. I'll try, but I don't think I can. We don't— Yes, I understand. Yes."

Campbell was trying to get her attention. He mouthed at her, then desperately snatched a piece of paper off the desk and wrote, "Talk to him!"

She nodded. "Excuse me? No." She stiffened up. "You can trust me. No. I haven't touched a drop! I want to speak to Raleigh." She sagged into the chair. "He's dead, isn't he? You've already killed him!" Her lower lip began to quiver. She stared as if she were paralyzed.

Dub quickly snatched the phone before she dropped it. "Hello," he said.

"Put her butt back on!" said the man.

"She can't talk."

"What does that mean?"

"She's upset. She wants to be sure her husband is alive. Are you going to put him on?"

"Maybe later. You just make sure she comes up with the bread or the old man is dead. Got it?" The music was bumping at top volume; the kidnapper had to shout.

"Yes, sir," said Dub. The dial tone seemed loud enough to break glass.

Alma Louise reached up to get the phone back. Dub shook his head.

"Well?" said Campbell.

"They're gonna call back."

"Good! Great!" said Campbell. "We'll be ready for them." He turned to the agent on the cellular phone.

"Gottem! A bar in the French Quarter: Les Amis. City cops on their way."

"Les Amis?" said Dub. "That used to be something else. Uh, I forget. Now it's strictly for the boys."

Campbell looked like he'd just smelled feet. "Go there often, do you?"

"How'd you trace the call so fast?"

"This is the twentieth century," said Campbell.

"Computer chips," said Horn-Rims.

"But you didn't know there was another line into the house," said Dub.

"Hey," said Campbell, "you can just leave, mister."

Mrs. Johnson shoved her way into the room. She glared at Horn-Rims sitting on her bed. "What did they say?"

"A million dollars," mumbled Alma Louise. "We don't have a tenth of that. Not a twentieth."

TWELVE

A new energy filled the house. Maybe it was coming off the FBI men, whose lips had curled up at the ends as if they were suppressing a whoop. *All right! Way to go! Kidnapping!* The goat was on the stake, and those who thought they were tigers smelled the blood. They conferred in a huddle on the front patio, then came back licking their chops. Campbell called on the cellular phone for sandwiches. Alma Louise wandered nervously through rooms squeezing her hands to keep them from shaking, sometimes mumbling to herself. Her eyes were pinpoints of fire, and the men stood back from her when she wandered by, as if a touch would turn her into jelly.

Dub was by the kitchen door when she passed. ". . . there for you, Raleigh. I'll be there for you," she was saying.

"Alma Louise," he said quietly. "Alma Louise."

Her right eye lifted slightly. She must have heard him, but she continued her ghostly stroll. The FBI man in horn-rims spoke in Dub's ear.

"She lost it?"

"Huh?"

"Cucamonga, Section eight, Looney Tunes?"

Dub looked back at the man as if he'd just discovered lint on his shoulder. "The woman needs a drink. You've got no bad habits, I suppose. Anal retention's on your job description."

"Hardy har har," said Horn-Rims flatly. "The woman needs a doctor. She'd better not queer the action."

"And what you gonna do? Arrest her?"

Horn-Rims wandered off.

"Geek," muttered Dub. He went back to the stove, where Mrs. O'Dell was delicately touching her lower eyelid as if, with the tip of her finger, she could wipe the sleep out of her eyes like an irritating mote of mascara. The coffeepot had not yet begun to perk. Dub sidled up beside her and leaned with both hands back against the counter. "How's the queen of café?"

She drew her head back. "Oh!" She blinked. "I thought you said the 'queen of Cathay.' "

He dipped his head. "Whatever you say, ma'am."

"It's past my bedtime," she said apologetically.

"I think it's past Alma Louise's, too."

She widened her eyes to indicate *No kidding.*

"We gotta do something with her. Give her a drink to tide her over or get her to sleep until the call comes tomorrow."

She placed her hand on his sleeve. "She just buttonholed me in the bedroom and tried to get me to lend her seven hundred and fifty thousand dollars. Then she wanted me to call bankers to get them to open up. I was never so grateful for these agents' infinite desire for coffee."

"Hey," said Dub, "what you make deserves a better name than coffee. The ghost of Antoine couldn't make Luzianne taste like you do."

She adjusted the flame. "If it's done right . . ." She checked the clock. "I'll see what I can do with her. I might have a Percodan in the bottom of my purse from when I sprained my ankle last year. If she hasn't been drinking, it shouldn't hurt her."

"If she won't take it, get a shot in her. If she unravels . . ."

"She's not well," said Mrs. O'Dell thoughtfully, then stared into the blue flame. "Listen," she said without looking at him, "I appreciate all you've done, but you don't have to stick this out if you don't want. You have no obligation to me."

"I ought to be making *you* coffee. It's just too bad you got so little for your money. A week in the hospital in Helena, and then all that stuff at Tulane, and then all they can say is 'could be stress,' 'could be arrhythmia,' 'could be gas.' " He held up his nitro tablets. "They leave out 'You could drop any damned minute, Mr. Greenert, for all we know.'"

"Well, that's not the point as I see it. I don't want you to feel you are obligated to come running—"

"Shut up and make coffee, Mrs. O'Dell. I owe you."

"But—"

"And even if I don't, I'm kind of interested. I hate things as mixed up as this. It's got more loose ends than a fur ball. There's got to be a simple explanation." Yes, he finally admitted to himself, he *was* interested—even though all this pacing made him feel like a tiger at feeding time.

She gave him a tight, wry smile and turned off the burner.

"Say," he asked, "have you got any idea where Vonna got to? Did she say anything?"

Mrs. O'Dell shook her head. He heard Mrs. Johnson trying to talk Alma Louise into lying down.

"When she buttonholed you for the loan, she didn't say anything about the call, did she?"

"Like what?"

"Like something she's keeping to herself."

"Why, no. What do you mean?"

"I don't know. I just had a feeling. Of course, I've been feeling that with a lot of people here."

Mrs. O'Dell looked away. That told him something, but not enough.

"Of course, maybe that's just the way Mrs. Menzies is, huh? She ain't wrapped too tight." He cleared his throat to keep from sounding like he was making a joke. "If you know what I mean."

"I know," she said firmly. She shook her head as if she were comparing the pretty girl she had gone to school with and her present frazzled friend.

Dub went back to Menzies's office, nodded to the FBI guy dozing by the phone, and picked up *Go Down, Moses*. He then quietly slipped into Menzies's bedroom and lay back on the man's bed. The notion of reading passed quickly, and he wiggled off his shoes with his toes. When he closed his eyes he felt watched, just as he had felt for the first few weeks in Vonna's apartment. There it was her velvet painting of Martin

Luther King hanging beyond the foot of the bed. Staring like an icon of Jesus Pantocrater in a Pittsburgh church, it had given him a weird sensation to lie there in his boxer shorts. Irreverent. Blasphemous. He raised his head and scanned the room. Maybe the feeling came from Menzies's big dresser mirror, or one of the antique oval pictures of the Menzies sugar barons. Maybe it was just lying in the great man's bed and knowing he could never fill it.

Dub dropped his head back. He ought to turn out the light, but he didn't have the energy. The kidnappers should be watching the house. They must be. But if they're watching it, why didn't they react to the FBI being there? Dub's car was in the driveway. The FBI van. Vonna's car. Shit, he should have checked if the sputterbug was gone. Piece of junk! Not now. Later. But it would be obvious to anyone who had watched the Menzies house on ordinary days that the police had been called in, contrary to the warning. The kidnappers didn't care? That wouldn't be too strange. They expected to get away with it, regardless. They had to expect somebody to call the law. Of course. That was why they called on Mrs. Johnson's line. They knew Menzies's line would be bugged.

But why wouldn't they expect Campbell and his boys to bug the housekeeper's line? And where did they get the number to her private line? From Rasheed? From Menzies? And that would mean he was alive. At least when they got the number he was alive. Shit, it did not. There were a dozen ways to get the number. Campbell should have known about her line from the phone company, shouldn't he? That was pretty stupid. Weird theory: the FBI had snatched Menzies. They had watched the house, right? Horn-Rims traced the call to the gay bar so quick, they must have known in advance.

No, everyone was in on it. Everyone in the world. Mrs. O'Dell. Mrs. Johnson. Rasheed. Horn-Rims. Devraix. President Bush. God. This was all just a test to prove what a lousy detective Delbert Greenert IV was. Thank you, Tricky Dick, for giving us faith in our government! Yell at your woman and this kind of thing happens to you, he thought, yawning. *My* woman? God's got to be a woman, or Mrs. O'Dell couldn't turn that chicory stuff into coffee. Got to be. It's a bigger miracle than water to wine.

There was some kind of excitement in the front of the house. He blinked at the gray light coming under the blinds and tried to remember how he'd gotten from the veranda into the master bedroom. He had been sitting on the veranda in a ladder-back rocking chair sipping a mint julep through a straw. He was master of River Bend, and Vonna was the mistress. His daughter Carrie was being pushed by Elizabeth in a swing decorated with garlands of cornflowers, and each time the swing reached the zenith of its flight, Carrie's petticoats flashed like a smile in the bright sunlight slashing through the canopy of live oak. Somehow he knew that the girls were now his and Vonna's children, not his and Beth's. He knew this didn't make sense, but he knew it was true all the same.

"I'm just gonna die of thirst," said Vonna in the voice of Scarlett O'Hara.

"Thas all right, ma'am," said the butler, "Ah's bring you a mighty fine drink, Ah sho' will. Ah gone save yuh, Ah is." Raleigh Lee Menzies leaned over with an enormous tumbler on his tray. He was dressed like Uncle Ben on the rice boxes.

"Thankya, Moses," said Vonna. "You're evah so kind."

There had been another flash from Carrie's petticoats, but it wasn't her petticoats. It was a woman with a 35-millimeter camera and an electronic flash. When she lowered the camera, he didn't recognize her, but he knew she was Jane Thuxpin. Her eyes were ringed with dark violet circles and her skin was gray, and he knew she was dead and still taking pictures.

She shrugged. "Raleigh Lee can't save everybody. He's an old man. Everybody ends up like me." When the flash went off again, Dub had covered his face and she disappeared. Raleigh Lee had shuffled up with another mint julep, and Carrie had gone on swinging as the Mississippi eerily slid by River Bend for a hundred years.

Dub pushed himself off the bed and went toward the

living room in his stocking feet. "What's up?" he said to Horn-Rims.

"A package."

Two FBI men had cornered a gangly boy in a messenger's uniform by the front door. He was making strange faces and tripping over his words as he tried to explain. "I dunno," he heard the boy say. "I dunno."

In the den, the padded envelope was lying on the desk blotter. Campbell was carefully moving the tip of his rosewood pen along the seam. He sat back. "I don't see anything. What do you think?"

Horn-Rims pushed his way into the room. "Gotta X-ray it."

Campbell looked at his watch.

Alma Louise rushed forward until Horn-Rims blocked her way. She looked as ragged as Dub felt, all of her flesh sagging toward the floor, but judging from the wrinkles in her blouse and the wingspread of her hair, she had slept some. "It says we have until nine-thirty to respond," said Campbell. "No time."

Dub checked his watch. Jesus, it was eight-seventeen. He *had* slept.

"Open it!" said Alma Louise.

"This might not be from them, Mrs. Menzies," said Campbell. "Suppose the bombing and the kidnapping are not connected? How far is the nearest hospital?" he asked no one in particular. "I'll get on the horn with the radiology people on the way over."

"Larry," said Horn-Rims, "if it goes off in the hospital . . ."

Campbell tapped his finger on the table. "Yeah," he said slowly. "How about a bomb dog from the airport? Can we get Holman from—?"

Alma Louise shoved Horn-Rims aside and snatched the package off the desk. She clutched it to her bosom like a Raggedy Ann. "It isn't a bomb!" she said.

"Don't do this!" said Dub.

"Now calm down, Mrs. Menzies," said Campbell. "Calm

down. Just gently put the package back on the desk here. Gently."

Her head moved from side to side as if afraid they were going to rip it out of her arms. "It's from the kidnappers. It's the message they promised."

"But they telephoned last time," said Campbell. Dub had to give it to the guy, he was the only one who didn't seem to be tasting sand. Mrs. O'Dell suddenly came into the corridor. Dub grabbed her by the shoulders and shoved her toward the kitchen.

"Give me the package!" said Campbell firmly.

"No!" she said. Like an animal, she took the envelope in her teeth.

"DON'T DO IT!" screamed Horn-Rims.

Dub rolled along the wall and dived for the floor. His face skidded into the carpet. He smelled the pine in the carpet cleaner and heard a ringing from his whopping his hands over his ears. He opened his eyes and saw the jungle of carpet pile as if he were a centimeter tall. He was soaked with sweat, and he felt like the air had turned to water. He slowly lifted his right hand away, then his left. He went up on one arm and settled on his rear, gasping and cupping his free hand over his heart. "Shit!" he said, swallowing, waiting for the heart attack. He reached for his nitro tablets, then realized he had left his jacket in Menzies's bedroom. He glanced back toward the door, but didn't get up. Up the hall, Horn-Rims was crumpled just inside the bathroom door. His glasses were askew and his tie had flipped up over his shoulder. His true being, thought Dub.

Dub crept up to the den door. Alma Louise still had a strip from the top of the envelope in her mouth. Campbell's head peeked up over the arm of a wing chair. "Fer Christ's sake, lady," he said. "Give me the envelope."

Alma Louise stepped forward and dumped the contents on the blotter. Then she remembered to take the strip out of her mouth. "If it's a question of Raleigh Lee Menzies's life or all of ours," she said, "we're nothing."

"Speak for yourself," said Campbell. "I put *some* value on

my own." He dropped into the desk chair and used his pen to move what lay before him.

There was a letter printed in dot matrix on sprocketed paper, and a triple-A map of the city. Highlighted in fluorescent yellow was a route down the interstate to Business 90 and across the river. It curled along the shore past the wharfs in Algiers, ending in a neat circle around the U.S. quarantine station.

"Gotcha!" said Campbell. "They don't know we're here."

Dub cocked an eyebrow.

Campbell hooked one of the sprocket holes of the letter with his pen and lifted it. "Well, looky here." He'd revealed two Polaroid pictures. Dub leaned over and twisted his head to get a good look: Menzies, his back against blue curtains. A strand of his gray hair stuck up awkwardly. In the second photo his head was turned sideways and what Dub had taken for a shadow in the first picture was revealed in all its florid purple glory as a bruise. They were like police mug shots, except that the headline of the *Times-Picayune* was stretched across the bottom instead of a booking number.

"Oh, my God!" shouted Alma Louise, snatching up one of the photos. "It's Raleigh Lee!"

"Put that down!" said Campbell, jerking the Polaroid away from her. "That might have fingerprints."

"They beat him!"

"He's got a bruise! Just a bruise! He might have fallen. Will you please get out of here and let us do our work!?"

"What does the letter say?"

"Will you take this woman in there and get her something to calm herself down?" he barked at Dub.

"No," said Alma Louise petulantly. "I'm not taking anything. I need all my concentration. I have to remember what I'm doing. I have to be right to help Raleigh Lee. He *needs* me!" She said the last part as if it amazed her, as if it hadn't been true for a long time.

"Maybe just a steadying belt," said Dub. "You're not ready to—"

"No! Can't you hear me? No! He needs me."

Campbell closed his eyes and expelled a long breath. "Then please sit down and be quiet. Please!"

"Very Beirut that," said Horn-Rims. He was trying very hard to pretend he hadn't been a fool diving from the "bomb."

"The headline?"

"Um-hmm. That's this morning's."

"What time does it come out?"

"We'll find out."

"It means he's alive," said Alma Louise.

"It means he was alive until they got the paper," said Horn-Rims dryly.

"Okay, the letter," said Campbell. He summarized as he read. "A million bucks. Bills no larger than one hundreds. Old money, no sequences. Don't try to mark. No tricks with dyes. Put in a black briefcase exactly like the one Raleigh Lee Menzies always carries." Campbell paused. "Could be a switch," he said meaningfully. "They say they have electronic expertise and warn against transmitters. Don't follow, no helicopter surveillance, and so forth."

"Why would you follow when they sent a map?"

"They might intercept en route," said Horn-Rims.

Campbell tugged at Horn-Rims's arm. "Listen. They've seen all the movies. 'We'll be watching! The road! The skies! The water!' The water, yet. And further directions coming tomorrow, by noon, when the money should be ready. If we've got the message, we're supposed to call 'the bar' immediately and ask for Jack Hoff. What bar?"

"The same one?" asked Dub.

"There's no number."

"How would they know we knew about Les Amis?" asked Horn-Rims. "It's early. Is that place open? Maybe they've made a big mistake. Dumber things have happened."

"No. These are clever boys." Campbell seemed to get some satisfaction that he was up against "master criminals." He was already considering his memoirs, Dub decided.

"Who's Jack Hoff?" asked Horn-Rims.

"It ain't me." Dub smirked.

Campbell thought for a moment.

"Jack Hoff," said Dub, raising his eyebrows.

"Right," said Campbell. "Real funny, these guys." He spun on Horn-Rims. "How quick can we get some people to that bar?"

"We've got Gonzalez keeping an eye on it."

"I'll bet he loves hanging out on that corner," said Campbell sarcastically.

"We'll make sure he's in there at the bar and try to get some backup. We'll make the call in thirty minutes."

"You're toying with my husband's life," said Alma Louise. "Make the call! Now!"

Campbell seemed irritated, but he glanced at the cellular phone. "Signal Gonzalez and do it," he said.

"We have some options here," said Horn-Rims.

"Make the call. The circle around the quarantine station covers a lot of area. Nothing tells us exactly where in this circle they expect to make the pickup. The specifics will come tomorrow when they call, is my guess."

Horn-Rims covered the mouthpiece of his phone. "Gonzalez is going in. He says he'll get a date for you."

Campbell sneered nastily. "We'll need a boat in case they plan to take the ransom out on the river. And we'll stake some 'homeless' nearby, in the general area north of Socrates and east of Richland."

"Bar's ringing," said Horn-Rims. As expected, "Jack Hoff" did not come to the phone and the bartender insulted Horn-Rims. Gonzalez called in to say he had just got there when the bartender had answered. The bartender had hung up and blamed it on homophobes. There were only a couple of early-morning cruisers in a booth. No one had left abruptly or seemed interested in the call.

"Get Gonzalez to kick that bartender's alternative-life-style nuts. He must know something," said Campbell.

One of the agents from the living room touched Dub's shoulder to get into the room. "Kid knows nothing," he said. "I'll go down to his service and talk to his boss."

"Good."

"I'll help," said Dub. "I'll go scope out the wharfs."

"Forget it," said Campbell. "You're going nowhere. We don't know you're not in on it."

"Me?! Hey, sit on it, Jack Hoff!" said Dub.

"Get this asshole out of my presence," Campbell said to Horn-Rims. "We'll get this over to the lab—"

"Hey, fuck you! Who're you calling—?"

Horn-Rims had both palms on his chest, pushing him back into the kitchen.

"Get off!" said Dub. "Get the fuck off!" He spun, and pushed the man away. Dub's hip bumped against the cooking island. He flashed on having to fight for his life in such a kitchen once. It stunned his anger like an icy shower.

He took a deep breath. "Okay," he muttered, "okay." Mrs. O'Dell gave him a dismayed look and left the room. He shouldn't have lost his temper. All this waiting, waiting. "I'm okay," he said to Horn-Rims. "I'm okay. Sorry." Horn-Rims started to leave. "Just tell me one thing," he said. "How long you jerks been watching Menzies?"

"What?" said Horn-Rims.

"How long have you been watching this house?"

"I don't know what you're talking about, mister."

"And why'd you let him get snatched?"

"Yeah, right," said Horn-Rims. "It must be pecan season. They're all falling off the trees."

Dub struck the cooking island with the heel of his fist. Horn-Rims walked away. Loose ends like a goddamned fur ball. He had to do something, anything. What kind of detective was he, baby-sitting a drunk while all hell was running loose? He could have fried an egg on his forehead, he was so pissed.

THIRTEEN

Vonna pushed aside the battered metal door and peered into the dark hole called Chick's. An emaciated old man with wattles like a turkey's was frozen in the street light as if snapped by a press camera, his drink halfway between the cracked and stained Formica countertop and his greedy lips. "Close duh friggin' door!" said a phlegmy voice. The effort of shouting brought on a coughing fit. Stepping from the bright street into Chick's would be like diving into a pot of motor oil. It wasn't just the blackness that closed in, but the cloying smell and the feeling that the ancient piss, puke, blood, and spilled beer now memorialized for eternity in the floorboards was being stirred up as she walked and was soaking into her hair and skin. "Door!" said someone else. It thudded shut behind her.

She squinted into the darkness, slid her hand down the strap of her bag until she felt her Mace bulging against the flap. She oriented herself by a flickering Dixie beer neon and eventually bumped into the metal of a bar stool. No one seemed to be behind the bar. The pallor of the old man and his silvery week-old beard almost phosphoresced in the green light. He shuddered as his whiskey spread through his arms to his fingertips, then he stared at Vonna, blinking.

"Whore!" he said.

She looked behind her. There was no one else. "You mean me?" she said.

"Ahhhhh!" he said, waving his hand awkwardly across

the front of him. He made a fist on the bar and settled his chin on it, closing his eyes.

She heard the phlegmy coughing again, and she was able to make out a pool table and another man in a booth in the back corner. He smiled and raised his mug of beer to her. She had a sudden desire for a cigarette to wrap herself in a cloud with, to fumigate the air and create a ball of space that was her own. She ignored the man in the corner and rapped on the bar. The old man jerked his head, then settled back on his chin. He did not move when she rapped again.

"Anybody home? Yo!"

Nothing.

"How's a girl get a drink in here?"

"Help yourself," yelled the man in the corner. "Pal'll be back."

She waited. The trail led here and only here. And it had taken since yesterday. If it didn't pan out, she'd tell Devraix about it and let him tell Dub. She'd felt a little sorry for him when he looked so lousy at Menzies's house, like a bloodied, wet tomcat. But she'd been through enough to know you don't beg a man. It's better to let him go. If you beg, the problem either gets worse or the prick leaves anyway. What the hell was she doing living with some cracker anyhow?

She heard the creaking of the floor. "Yeah?" The speaker was a jowly man, the kind of fat man whose breath whistles when he begins to move and who sweats from the extra effort in breathing. He had squeezed in sideways through a narrow door beyond a rack of glasses.

"A draft," she said.

"Ain't hooked up."

"A Jax, then."

He fumbled in a cooler. The bottle hissed open. He waddled toward her, stopping in front of the old man still resting on his chin. He leaned over. The man sputtered, and the bartender twitched to avoid his breath. He shook his head and waddled on. The beer would be warm by the time he got here, thought Vonna.

He settled onto an invisible stool directly in front of her.

He set down glass and bottle without pouring. She could hear his breathing.

"Thanks."

He watched her pour. "I know you?"

"I don't know. Do you?"

"You one of Élan's girls?"

"Don't know any Alan." The foam slid over the glass rim.

"Élan. Ay-lan."

"Funny name for a pimp." The fat man grinned. He was missing a tooth. "Yeah. Listen, honey, freebirds get hurt in this neighborhood. They're Élan's or they're ugly. Élan makes them ugly."

"I getcha." She could hear his breathing. She sipped the beer.

"Nothing personal," he said. "I like your type."

"All blacks are cats in the dark," she said.

"Huh?"

"Nothing."

He leaned forward. "Maybe we work out a little something for the road, huh? I'll put in a word with Élan for you. Give him a personal recommendation."

This thing's got sex organs, she thought. I ought to call Jacques Cousteau and report it. She didn't want to imagine how he went about it or whatever he did. She let the nasty shiver that passed through her look like it came from the coldness of the beer. Let the bait float down the stream a bit, she thought. "Actually, I bet you could help me out. You know Gio Pantucho?"

"He don't run girls." The fat man winked.

"I know that, but I need to see him."

"About what?"

"Old friends."

"Maybe if I was in a good mood I'd remember something, you know?" He leered. His nose was whistling.

"I like to get paid up front."

"Smart girl. Gio's kind of lying low, though. He's retired."

"Ain't what I hear."

He leaned closer again. "Listen, friendly advice, honey. You don't want to get into that dude. There's some Chinks more in your league. They'll give you a better deal. The Chinaman kind of moved in when Gio got squeezed by the feds. You hear of the Chinaman? Scary hombre, I'm telling you. Gio's got to be careful he don't end up in somebody's moo goo gai pan."

"I got to see Gio. One of his skippers wants to settle up. Gio'd appreciate it."

"A skipper of Gio's who's alive? Ain't no such animal."

"Well," she said, shrugging. She turned slightly and watched the old man dozing on the bar. The bait was still drifting on the stream. Go for it, fat man, she thought. Go for it.

He wetly cleared his throat. "I don't know where Gio is, understand, but his brother Theo and I are thick."

"You let him use your upstairs room."

"How you know 'bout that?"

"I keep my mouth shut. Don't worry."

"It's the only honest game in town. Come back Friday two weeks, and I'll introduce."

"Naw," said Vonna, "might as well forget it. The money's too hot to wait." She made a movement like she was going to leave.

He put his wet paw on her forearm. "Okay. You never heard it from me, but I sort of found out that Theo's got a married chick. Name of Blevins. Apartment in a courtyard off Esplanade. That's all I'm saying."

"Well, ain't you a sweet thang!" said Vonna. "I'd best get going."

"Goin'? What about—?"

"Now, you don't want me till I'm washed up." She dropped a five-dollar bill on the bar and headed for the door.

The fat man raised himself to his feet. "You're a liar!" he said. "I knew it! You can't fool me."

She opened the door. The light blinded her eyes, and she looked back. The bartender had sagged to his stool, and with his head lowered said, "All you cunts are liars. All of 'em."

As the door closed behind her, the old man raised his head. "Whore!" he said, then settled down on his arms.

* * *

[121]

She was closing in, she could smell it. The Blevins apartment had been easy to find with a few phone calls. Two more calls got her the full names of the occupant and his occupation. No one answered in the apartment. One more call told her that wine importer Levi Blevins was on a buying trip to Argentina and Chile, probably for a couple of truckloads of *vino roja*. Good, she thought. Let's hope he hasn't been away for a while, that the appetite's strong. She checked out the building. It had been an expensive remodeling job to judge from what had been done in the courtyard, but if Theo Pantucho was meeting Katherine, the wife of wine importer Levi Blevins, here, then he wasn't coming in by the front. It would be too easy for the neighbors in the two adjoining apartments to see him.

Maybe a headknocker like Theo wouldn't care, or maybe Levi Blevins was too afraid of Theo to do anything about it, or maybe even Levi liked to hear all about it when he got back from wherever—it takes all kinds. But, judging from what she'd seen of adultery, odds were Theo would be going in the back door, especially if the man everyone called the China-man was after him.

She circled the block but couldn't find a back, just more fronts, but people rich enough to afford a place here would want somewhere to put their Jags and they wouldn't walk to them. On the second pass she spotted a narrow alley with an iron gate. A small security camera was mounted in a steel box high on the wall about twenty feet into the alley, and there was some kind of electronic lock on the gate itself. She saw a parking space open up on the street ahead, just big enough for her Chevette, so she took it.

She walked to the restaurant on the corner for a couple of burritos to go. She didn't eat, though it was getting close to six, and settled in for a long evening, positioning her rearview mirror for a clear view of the gate. He'd probably wait until dark, then might not come out again until morning. A group of Hispanics walked by. They seemed to be talking, but their boombox was so loud, Vonna didn't see how they could hear each other. She thumped the dashboard when she remembered she had forgotten to get batteries for her Walkman. It was going to be a long night. Dozens of cars cruised by, probably just looking for parking places. It hadn't been half an hour when she heard a dull ringing, as if someone had stuffed Kleenex in an alarm. The iron gate was opening out over the sidewalk. Somebody going out for the evening, she thought, but when the nose of the car edged out to the curb, she bolted upright. It was Theo's black Mercury. He was taking his tootsie out.

When the car passed her, however, he was driving alone. Maybe Mrs. Blevins had ducked down on the seat. Rich bitches were sometimes stimulated by that kind of thing: the heiress-and-the-gangster scenario. Vonna remembered a woman who'd admitted in Devraix's office that she had lost physical interest in the man Dub and Vonna had photographed her with, months ago, but she'd continued to go out with him because sneaking around was so much like a spy movie. "Takes all kinds," Vonna said to herself. Theo was now at the end of the block. Vonna started her car, but did not flick on the lights until Theo had turned. She had to be careful. If he decided to run, her sputterbug couldn't keep up with his Merc. The motor in his automatic windows probably had more power than all four of her oil-hungry cylinders.

Traffic was heavy. It meant she might have trouble at lights, but it also meant he wouldn't be able to get away too fast. Even if he saw her, he might not notice her, she thought. He'll be looking for the Oriental thugs that were trying to put Gio out of business. She hung about four cars behind him as he moved farther away from downtown. He made three turns, but always kept heading back to north, so she took a chance in one block and assumed he was turning east only to turn back north. She drove parallel, then turned east a block later. The light stopped her, but the Merc crossed the intersection in front of her. She was half a block behind him, stopped at another light, when he slid into the right lane and seemed to be getting ready to go up the ramp to Interstate 10. "Come on, light; come on, light," she muttered quickly, but he drove under the bridge instead. She visualized the map in her head, but couldn't see any particular reason for his going in this direction. Maybe Gio was hiding in the suburbs. Who could know?

After another ten minutes, he changed his general direction and began moving east. Later, when traffic started getting thin enough to make her nervous, he changed again and headed south. After he passed under Interstate 10 again, he slowed down a bit. He took turns less quickly but didn't dawdle at intersections so that he could be the last car through on yellow. He was relaxing, she thought. "Go straight to brother Gio," she said with satisfaction. "Fly away home, baby."

He was moving into an area slated for some kind of development. Many of the buildings were gutted and empty lots were piled with heaps of blackened joists and wallboard. A good area for a hideout. Too deserted for even a crack house. The only thing to worry about were the rats and maybe some homeless looking for shelter. But it was also too deserted not to notice a car behind you. She gave him a long lead. Finally, a block and a half ahead of her, he pulled over next to a row of boarded-up storefronts. She parked and fumbled her binoculars out of the glove compartment. This was a pretty lousy hideout, she thought, and felt a little peculiar about Theo's parking on the street in the open. But who would see his car in these ruins?

If Gio was out there, he wouldn't be alone. He'd have enough muscle to make certain the Chinaman couldn't get him. She understood, though, that Gio had always holed up in the middle of crowded areas, and the thought made her nervous. Even homicidal scuzbuckets like the Chinaman's gang wouldn't go after somebody where they'd risk killing tourists. Nothing could protect you, not all the graft in Louisiana, if you whacked a few tourists. But Gio had been in business a long time, and he hadn't stayed alive by doing the expected.

Vonna had just heard the crunch of gravel when Theo's pistol smashed the passenger window. Diamonds of glass scattered over the seat, and Vonna automatically covered her eyes.

"You get out over there," said Theo. "You get out real slow and real careful. This cannon's got a light trigger."

Vonna slowly lowered her hands from her eyes. Theo was

right. It was definitely a cannon. The kind of cannon where you wouldn't need two bullets to splatter an entire brain against a wall.

Keeping her right hand high, she lowered her left and gently opened the car door. He kept the pistol aimed at her until she was fully standing several feet from the Chevette. He circled the hood at a distance and checked the surroundings.

"Who are you?" he barked.

"I need to talk to Gio."

He chuckled. "Sure. You got money for him. Nobody's talking to Gio."

"I—" She swallowed. "I got nothing to do with the Chinaman. He's shit as far as I'm concerned."

He squinted. Theo was not a happy man. "Who are you?"

"My name is Vonna Saucier. I'm a private investigator."

"A private eye?"

"I work for Honoré Devraix."

"I heard of him."

"I think Gio knows him."

"He might. I don't like being followed, bitch. You think I'm a moron? I've been leading you around for twenty minutes. I'd just as soon blow your fuckin' head off. Tailin' me!"

She knew he meant it. Her lips went numb, like she'd gulped a quart of vodka in one swallow.

"So? What is it? You hauling subpoenas or what? That's how the Chinaman got Elvin MacDougal. Tailed him from the courthouse."

Vonna vaguely remembered a picture of MacDougal at the bottom of a staircase, swimming in a long, dark smear of blood.

"Fuckin' feds go after a guy like Gio and end up putting a gonzo creep like the Chinaman in charge. Maybe they make a deal with him. It's like welfare for the slants."

"I got no papers," said Vonna. "Search me. Search the car. I just want to talk to Gio."

He held the pistol at arm's length in front of him and shuffled closer. "You got a gun?"

"No."

It had become too dark to see. He opened her car door and glanced at the seat. "Keep your hands high," he said. "Turn around." He patted her back and under her arms. She jerked when he slid his hand over her rear and down the inside of her leg, but she kept still. "Turn around. Now don't take this personal." He pressed one breast and then the other.

She locked both eyes on the hole in the end of the barrel. "You prick," she said.

He stepped back. "Those real? You don't see real ones that good anymore."

"You shit."

"Hey, it ain't personal. I knew a lady mechanic kept her tools in there."

"All right, I put up with your shit. I just want to talk to Gio."

"Well, Gio ain't talking to you, so forget it." He lifted the pistol as if he were aiming it right at her nose.

"Oh, Lord!" she whispered, and closed her eyes.

The pistol cracked once, twice, three times. She had swarmed her arms over her head, crouched, and lifted one leg as if trying to curl into a fetal position while standing. There was no pain, dying had no pain, only the ringing in your ears, and a hissing, a loud hissing. She opened her eyes. The radiator of her Chevette was bleeding to death. There were two bullet holes in the hood.

My car! she thought. My sputterbug!

"I believe you got a cracked block there. Or at least you're supposed to. You keep your ass away from me or it'll be your head." He lowered the gun and began backing away.

"Damn you!" she said.

"Watch your mouth," he said, smiling, still moving away.

"What were you doing on Thibodeaux Road?"

His step stuttered slightly. "Fuck off." He continued walking.

"Who are you watching on Thibodeaux Road? Raleigh Lee Menzies? What you got on Raleigh Lee Menzies? Has he got something to do with the Chinaman?"

"Who's the Chinaman?" Theo laughed.

"I saw you parked there, Theo! In the trees!"

"You didn't see nothing, lady, and you'd better not forget it!"

"*I did!*"

He hesitated as if he were going to come back and finish her off. Instead he laughed. "You need glasses, lady!" He turned his back and jogged to his car. He moved lightly for such a big man. The Merc started and drove away.

She looked at all the emptiness around her, exhaled a long whistle, and then placed both hands on the hood above the tire of the dead sputterbug. "Poor baby," she said. "Where'll I get another like you?" She whirled and faced a vacant building. "Men!" she said. "Damn their butts!"

FOURTEEN

"What am I going to do?" wailed Alma Louise. "What?" She flung herself on Clementine O'Dell yet again.

"You're going to pull yourself together!" she said, gripping Alma's upper arms. "We have done all we can. Concentrate! You're going to have to hope they call again."

Dub noticed that Campbell had turned away in disgust. He probably felt his promotion going hinky. They had managed to get Alma Louise asleep last night only by calling in Mrs. O'Dell's private physician. He'd tanked the woman up on something that must have been Stop-a-Charging-Rhino, turbo-brand liquid Valium, because she dropped like a bloop single. To everyone's relief. They were all trying to imagine the size of the giant insects, pink elephants, and other wonders of non-nature she'd be seeing if the sleek doctor hadn't been willing to make his house call. For a handsome fee, no doubt. Mrs. O'Dell would be broke soon if she kept providing free medical care.

She'd be broke even sooner if she caved in to Alma Louise's begging. They had spent the previous day trying to raise the million. They were on the phone most of the morning, then in the afternoon went downtown to the Menzieses' broker and banker. There wasn't much equity in the house, and Alma Louise kept saying there must be a mistake in the brokerage records. The silver-haired man kept trying to explain that Menzies's holdings had been double-whammied by the fall in oil prices and then the October 1987 crash. The discussion ended shortly afterward when she started accusing the man of churning the account. In the end, she got fifty thousand on the home equity, seventy-five thousand guaranteed by her heirloom jewelry stored in a safe-deposit box, a hundred and forty-three thousand from liquidating the brokerage account. She borrowed twenty thousand against her life-insurance policy, and Mrs. O'Dell, against the advice of her attorney, cosigned a loan of sixty-two thousand to bring the total to a quarter of what the kidnappers demanded.

Dub kept telling Alma Louise about the case in South America in which some rebels had taken an American and demanded some enormous wad of money that his family in Missouri couldn't possibly raise. They took what they could to the rebels and got the boy back. Campbell backed him up for a change, though Campbell also said he had a feeling he was going to recover every penny. Alma Louise nonetheless had kept begging to get Mrs. O'Dell to cover the additional three quarters of a million. Sometimes the woman's eyes tightened like she was going to do it, but then the steel came back into her spine. She would not take a chance with that much of her late husband's money. That would be irresponsible to his memory and his children, even if one of them didn't decide to question her competence. When Alma Louise started grabbing FBI men by the lapel and saying they could use all that drug money they seize, Mrs. O'Dell called the doctor. Dub over the years had sometimes wondered if he was a problem drinker, but he'd never gotten as erratic or as forgetful. He'd never seen anyone as lonely for a drink as Mrs. Menzies.

Dub had quietly gone to Raleigh Lee Menzies's room as soon as Mrs. O'Dell went home. He paused at the door as if he were again violating its sanctuary. He again had the feeling he was being watched by the great man's possessions. Maybe it was just the neatness of the room: the brush and comb lying in their tray, the morocco slippers carefully placed beside the brass valet. It was like a photograph of a display room or, more to the point, a room being preserved in an historical mansion. Dub shook off the feeling as best he could. Menzies was a man like other men. Maybe a better man, a larger man, a living legend, but not a dead legend. Not yet. He might be in bad shape, but he still burped and picked his nose and scratched like everybody else. Kidnappers would need him alive. Dub hoped so, anyway.

Dub washed his socks in the bathroom vanity and hung them on the shower rod. He brushed his teeth with his finger and felt slightly more human. Almost, anyway. These kidnappers had the patience of a cat. They strolled around you like they couldn't care less, like they weren't even hungry, but you knew that any second the attack would come. He'd asked Campbell if it was usual for kidnappers to allow so much time. Campbell had answered evasively, and Dub knew from it that Campbell had about as much experience with kidnapping as he did: none. Menzies had been snatched on a Tuesday afternoon. The call had come at midnight. The demands were delivered on Wednesday morning. The frantic money-raising expedition had taken all that day. They still hadn't recontacted them by ten A.M. Thursday. They might hire another messenger. They might call. They might dump Menzies in a swamp and forget about the money. Maybe Menzies had dropped dead on them. He was trying not to think about all the different possibilities in the case until something specific happened, but his mind kept simmering nonetheless.

Maybe it was spending the night in Menzies's room, nearly finishing *Go Down, Moses* in there, that gave the Dub the sense that Menzies was like an iceberg, most of him underwater and not even understood by the man himself. There was this public man, an altruistic man, a man who had given of himself. And brother, he had! If half of what he said in his book was true, he had put his butt on the line a dozen times. He had broken his hand and wrist on the helmet of a policeman who had been beating a twelve-year-old black boy and probably saved the kid's life. During a march he had walked up to an armed Klansman and calmly taken a rifle out of the man's hand as an electrified crowd looked on. "You don't want to be a murderer, son," he had said. The man had wept. Later, when rednecks in the governor's office had tried to get him disbarred on the trumped-up "associating with Communists" charge, he used no defense in his hearing. He simply waited until he was to make his closing statement and recited the Bill of Rights from memory, so movingly that the panel refused to disbar him.

But the book didn't have the tone of someone who was trying to glorify himself. How he could tell these things without seeming like a braggart was what was interesting. The point about the cop and the kid was the kid's bravery and the cop's desperate cruelty. The point about the Klansman and the disbarment panel was that deep inside, there was good in them. His actions did not seem, at least as he wrote it, to be as incredible to him as they were. The Red Knight seemed to be an innocent. Not a Christ figure at all. Christ knew what he was getting into. It was as if Raleigh Lee Menzies was perpetually amazed that people could be so nasty in the face of what was right. It wasn't their true natures. Even when assaulted with human stupidity and brutality, he seemed to fantasize an underlying goodness, a childishness that made people want someone to watch over them. He seemed to imagine that when he reached down to suffering blacks, they would take his hand and climb up, not be offended by the offer. He seemed to feel that if he touched hatred in the correct way, it would see itself, drop its dark robes and stand nakedly good, remorseful for what it had done.

The parts of the book that had been so controversial seemed to come from this innocence, also. If several famous black leaders had gotten potted on beer and gin when Lyndon Johnson's Civil Rights Bill cleared Congress, what was important about that? U. S. Grant had drunk gallons of whiskey in saving the United States. If one of them cussed like a sailor, so what? George Washington had flayed his men with a withering tongue. If a few of the civil rights leaders had succumbed to the blandishments of the young women who worshiped them, well, Lancelot du Lac had fallen for Guinevere and still was the noblest knight of the realm. Menzies was no chaste Parsifal, himself. He'd had his Jane Thuxpin— though that was never mentioned in the book, either to protect her or Alma Louise, or simply because it had begun later. Raleigh Lee Menzies was probably astonished that so many people had taken offense, that black leaders had denounced him from the pulpit for sullying the martyrs and the living.

Mrs. O'Dell had told Dub that Menzies had been accused of writing *Go Down, Moses* as a kind of revenge for being pushed to the periphery of the struggle. When the Black Power impulse had arisen, even Martin Luther King's leadership was threatened. How much more irrelevant must the white Menzies have seemed? Black people had to take charge of their own existence, not depend on scraps from whitey's table. But there wasn't much bitterness in the book that Dub could see. Nostalgia, yes. Those were the days, my friend! What was it like to have been riding destiny's wave, only to fall off? It must be better than never catching the wave at all, Dub concluded. Like me. Maybe you just couldn't get any sense of the hidden part of the public man's iceberg because you'd never been there. What was George Washington really like? Robert E. Lee? Dr. King?

While Campbell was taking a nap, Dub borrowed the cellular phone from Horn-Rims and called the office.

"Emma? Dub. Honoré in?"

"No, sir, Mr. Greenert. He left with Vonna about ten this morning."

He hesitated a second. "She been working yesterday?"

"No, and Mr. Devraix was wondering if you knew where she was. She called and left a message that she had to find somebody for the Menzies case. Then she's here this morning talking for a long time and then they leave."

"Great," he said. If he hadn't acted like an asshole, she'd have kept him on line. Maybe she was off breaking the case just to show him up. He deserved it.

"Say, what's going on? What's this Menzies case about?"

"Everything, Emma. It seems to be about everything, and it's driving me nuts."

There was a sharp rapping on the front door. It opened immediately. "Get Larry," said the FBI man. He was holding a package, similar to the first.

"Gotta run!" said Dub.

"Black girl from up the street," said the FBI man to Horn-

Rims. "Father's the judge. She said the messenger delivered it to them by mistake." He held it up.

"That was no mistake," said Horn-Rims. "It says 'Raleigh Lee Menzies,' but the address is the judge's."

"What if it's a bomb?" said the man holding it.

"Are we going to go through this again?" asked Dub. Campbell then came out. They filled him in and waved a small metal detector, like those used in airports, over the envelope.

"Ever hear of a bomb with no wires, no metal at all?" Campbell asked.

Horn-Rims was still thinking when Campbell began working open the flap with a pen.

Alma Louise broke away from Mrs. Johnson and clambered over Dub. "What is it? What is it?"

"There's another Polaroid of your husband and more computer paper," said Campbell. "Directions, by the look of it." He began reading. "'Wait for the call. Take the map. Follow precisely. We have spotters on the route. After the bridge go north—' They underlined north. 'Then Newton to Meyer to Merrill to the high school.' That's also underlined. 'Trade briefcases by Dumpster near cafeteria service doors. Envelope in your case will tell you where to get Mr. Menzies.'"

Even his enemies referred to him as "Mister," thought Dub.

"'If anything funny happens along the way, Mr. Raleigh Lee Menzies is history. We will know if there are tricks. Alma Louise should come alone. Don't try to follow. No electronic devices. We have expertise. No helicopters. No funny money: no dyes, markings, sequential numbers. Nothing, or Raleigh Lee Menzies is a dead nothing. Remember—'" Campbell squinted. "What is that?"

"*Uhuru*," said Horn-Rims.

"Who is that?"

"Maybe it's like one of those names," said Horn-Rims. "Like the Patty Hearst kidnappers. What was the leader's name? Cin-que or something?"

"*Uhuru* is Swahili for 'freedom,'" said Alma Louise impatiently.

[133]

"Then it probably *is* an alias," said Horn-Rims.

Willie/Rasheed/Uhuru, thought Dub, though using Swahili seems a bit sixties, like somebody imitating the Black Power thing.

"Okay," said Campbell, unfolding the map. "We got options. Here it is: O. P. Walker High School, just at the edge of their circle. We get more men over there. Do a drive by, see if we can get one in the school as a janitor. Got to be careful, though. We can't get civilian kids in a cross fire."

"Cross fire?" said Dub.

Campbell ignored him. "See if we can locate a camera somewhere, and we'll put a radio beeper on Mrs. Menzies's car."

"You can't!" said Alma Louise. "They have electronic expertise."

"They won't know. We just need to verify the pickup, Mrs. Menzies, or we might not have a case later. We're experts."

"You know where she's going," said Dub. "Why take the chance?"

"We could tail her instead."

"But why, Campbell? *You know where she's going.*"

"They could intercept her on the way."

"If they spot your tail, Menzies is dead. Isn't the important thing getting him back?"

"No!" said Alma Louise, forcing her way between them. "No radios and no following. Nothing. I've got to save Raleigh."

"We're experts at this," said Horn-Rims.

"You'd better be," said Dub.

"When are you amateurs going home?" sniped Campbell. "Now, Mrs. Menzies, please. Reconsider. We've got an invisible ink *no one* can detect. If I used that stamp on my nose—"

"No," she said, "they have expertise. They said so."

"We have expertise. We're the Bureau, Mrs. Menzies. And anyway, they said 'electronic expertise.' "

"No! No! No! No tricks!" She spun and went into the corridor. She pressed her head against the wall at the end and quivered as she wept.

"Greenert," whispered Campbell. "Talk to her. Don't let her tie our hands."

"What can I say to her? 'Take a chance with your husband's life'?"

"You know as well as I do he doesn't have much chance, period."

"Aw, don't say that."

"Especially," said Horn-Rims, shifting his head toward her, "if she's supposed to pick up the package."

"The man's just a 'package' to you?" said Dub. He moved toward her slowly and touched his hands to her shoulders. She twitched, then settled back against the wall.

"I've got to do this for Raleigh," she said.

He shushed her gently. "You're doing the best you can."

"I've always let him down. Always. Now I'm too old and too sick to do him any good."

"Now, now. Listen to me. Everybody's got weaknesses. The past don't matter right now. What matters is doing what we can to get Raleigh Lee out of this."

She looked at him, her bloodshot eyes like red puddles behind her smeared glasses. "I'm going to be strong. I've got to concentrate. I'm going to save him. Raleigh Lee needs me."

"Can you do this?"

"I have to."

"It ain't gonna be easy to explain why the money's short."

"I can do it. I must."

Campbell suddenly interrupted. "What about a driver, Mrs. Menzies? Let us have a man drive you."

"You stop interfering or I'll throw you out of my house."

"Sssh," soothed Dub.

"Do you really think you can drive in the state you're in?" he asked coldly, and spun on his heels. "What a zoo this is!"

She stared at the shaking in her hands as if they were unfamiliar objects. "He's right," she said. "My eyes get blurry. I get confused. Sometimes I lose the feeling in my hands." She lowered her head as if she were about to break down again.

"Whoa," he said. "Whoa. Let them put one of the agents in. When they call you, you can explain you couldn't drive.

Mr. Menzies would know about your—" he avoided her oystery eyes "—health."

"But it will mess things up. I *have* to drive."

"This is messy to begin with, Alma Louise. When those boys sniff their money, they're going to be willing to overlook a lot. Even another driver. I'll drive you." It had slipped out without his thinking about it. There was a sudden dryness in his throat and his empty stomach seemed to be climbing up his esophagus.

"No," she said after some thought.

He took a deep breath. Oh, hell. "I'm sick and tired of sitting around here. I'll do it."

She shook her head timidly.

"Aw, Alma Louise, listen to me. I *want* to do it." Or had his anxiousness gotten the best of him? Does lowering your cholesterol short out your brain?

"I'll go myself," said Campbell. "I'm a first-class marksman. I—"

"Marksman?" shouted Dub. "Who you gonna shoot?"

"No!" screamed Alma Louise. The shrillness of her voice rang off the corridor walls. "I can trust Mr. Greenert. He'll drive or I'll drive. That's it!"

If Campbell had been a shark, he would have snapped off Dub's head with one bite.

Dub wiped his face with his hand. He'd wake up any second now.

"It's a long way to the college," said Alma Louise, raising her chin.

"High school," said Dub. "O. P. Walker." His heart was playing Sandy Nelson's solo of "Wipe Out." He glanced at Mrs. Johnson, who lowered her head, and he touched the vial of nitro tablets in his pants pocket.

Mrs. O'Dell gently pushed aside Horn-Rims. "You don't have to. No one will fault you if you don't."

"Beats sitting around thinking about food," said Dub.

"You said he would help me protect Raleigh Lee, Clementine," wailed Alma Louise. "You said so!"

They all seemed to be staring at Dub. He felt like he had just broken wind in a crowded elevator. "Aw, Jesus H. Christ . . ." He sighed. "She can't do this by herself. We're just playing United Parcel. Let's get this over with so I can get the hell out of this burg."

As if it heard him, the phone rang. No one moved for a second. Everyone's eyes widened except Alma Louise's. When it finally registered that everyone was looking at her, she leapt at the receiver.

Everyone heard the voice on the tape recorder. "You got the money?"

"I got all I could get."

"What?"

"The call's coming from Westwego," whispered Horn-Rims.

"Two hundred and fifty thousand is all I could get. No one will help." She looked at Mrs. O'Dell, who covered her mouth with her hand. "Raleigh and I don't have any more. We're not rich. Hello? Speak to me. Pleeease!" Dub grabbed her shoulders for support.

"It will do," said the voice. "For an installment."

The voice, thought Dub, sounded white, maybe Cajun.

"You'll let Raleigh go?"

"We'll decide later."

"But Raleigh—"

"Quit stalling."

"It's a pay phone on Lapalco Boulevard," whispered Horn-Rims.

"That fits," said Campbell.

"Leave right away. Now, Mrs. Menzies, you got that? *Uhuru!* Do you understand? *Uhuru!*"

"I remember. Yes." She seemed calmer. "You won't get any trouble from us." He had hung up before she finished the sentence.

"Get a rundown on this Uhuru business from Washington," ordered Campbell. "It might be a black revolutionary cell or something they have in the files."

"He didn't sound black to me," said Horn-Rims.

"Bingo," said Dub.

"We've got to go," said Alma Louise. "*NOW!*" She had plucked up the briefcase and headed for the door. Dub glanced back at Mrs. O'Dell and gave a wan smile.

FIFTEEN

They moved into the stream of traffic, and Alma Louise craned her head back over the seat for the third time since they'd left the house. "Are they following us?"

"I didn't notice anything," said Dub. "They could, but I don't see why. They know where we're going."

"Can't you tell?"

"I don't often have to 'spot a tail,' as they say on TV, Alma Louise. I usually do the tailing." It sounded obscene. Dirty business, he thought. Got to get a real job. When was the last time he'd called his daughters?

"You're going to do as I tell you?"

He glanced at her and then slid into the second lane. "Well, sure. What do you mean, Alma Louise?"

She noisily opened the road map. "They gave only one direction: north. So we go south."

"Hey," said Dub, "what the hell—?"

"We go south."

"I don't understand." He was so distracted he almost drifted across the lane line.

"They told us to go north, so we go south! What's so difficult about that? When we cross the bridge, go south."

Oh no, thought Dub. The bitch was in on it. Naw. Nobody was that good an actress.

"Alma Louise," he said sternly, "you tell me what's going on here or I'm pulling over and getting out."

She pored over the map as if she were trying to make out the individual paper fibers.

"Alma Louise, yoo-hoo . . ."

"Will you shush! I thought I saw— There it is!"

"There what is?"

"The high school. Archbishop Blenk."

"We're supposed to go north to O. P. Walker High School."

Alma Louise awkwardly folded up the map so that only the Gretna area was visible. She smugly laid it in her lap and tossed back her head. "We're going to save Raleigh Lee."

He waited for an explanation. Fuckin' drunks, he thought. "It ain't too far to the bridge, Alma Louise," he said. "Well?"

"*Uhuru*," she said.

"Almaaa . . ."

"It's a code. Raleigh Lee used it in the civil rights years. It reverses things."

"I don't get it."

"You don't need to. He didn't want anybody to know. When there's a direction, you reverse it. All the street names and such are just to confuse things. He said go north to the high school, never mind its name. We go south to the high school. And south is Archbishop Blenk."

He tried to think. He was driving slowly enough that a few people blew their horns at him. Alma Louise was almost too calm, too happy. She'd finally cracked. That was one explanation. He peered into the rearview mirror and glanced along the skyline, hoping there was some sign that Campbell had ignored her and was following them in a car, with a helicopter, anything. On the other hand, the kidnappers had put a lot of emphasis on *uhuru* and he'd had the feeling she was holding on to something desperately, concealing it from everyone else. She was off to rescue her husband and she hadn't had so much fun, hadn't really been a part of his life for years. What she didn't understand was that she could be rushing off to be part of her husband's death.

"Alma Louise, we will be awfully exposed if the FBI doesn't know where we are. These guys could steal the money from us and dump us in the river."

"They just want the money."

"That's what I'm saying."

"Well, you have a gun, don't you?"

"Hell, no, Alma Louise! Why would I have a gun? Jesus!"

She tilted her head as if she wondered what kind of bozo private eye was driving her. "Well, it will be all right. Raleigh must have told them about *uhuru*. We used to joke around with it back then. I'd say, 'Raleigh Lee, I'm not in the mood tonight,' and then I'd leave him a card on his pillow that said *uhuru*."

"This is a helluva lot to find out now."

"It was a long time ago," she said pleasantly, "but it is very vivid in my mind."

The bridge to Gretna was coming up. "Suppose I won't go along with this? What made you think I'd—?"

"I had to have a driver. You were right, I had to. It's the only way to save him."

"Aw, Alma Louise . . ." With the heel of his hand, Dub struck the dashboard. The glove compartment popped open. Receipts, maps, and repair papers cascaded out. "Close that tight," he barked. "You gotta kind of jiggle the latch. And pick up my damned papers. Aw, never mind. Just shove them under the seat."

"That's why I had to have you along instead of an agent."

They were now above the river. He had to decide what to do. Who might have known about *uhuru*? And who could have known Mrs. Menzies would remember it after all the highballs she'd socked away? Somebody in their house. Mrs. Johnson, thought Dub. Maybe her son. He would have been around the house. Alma Louise might have told the story to anyone she felt comfortable with, though, and that might be quite a crowd when she was potted. Mrs. O'Dell. Stavros. And who might Menzies himself have told? Dub didn't remember any business with code words in *Go Down, Moses*, but Dub hadn't read the whole book. All of Menzies's old civil rights vets would have known it. No. It had to be someone who knew that it had a special meaning to Alma Louise.

Of course, it could be the hostage thing. A terrorized victim often helps his kidnappers when it sinks in that his life depends on the crooks getting away with it. It happened in hijackings. It was Patty Hearst's defense. Some victims even felt grief when their abductors were killed, they had grown so dependent on them. Dub felt an acid nausea as he imagined what it must be like for Menzies, beaten, tied in a closet, begging stone killers for permission to take a piss. It would be like Menzies's worst nightmare from nearly thirty years ago suddenly come true. Alma Louise was right: the only way to help Menzies would be to go along. They'd have to hope that the kidnappers were men of their word. It was a slim chance, but it might be the only mote of a chance. They were now coming down on the other side of the bridge. He saw a huge barge headed toward the Gulf. He wished he was on it.

"All right, Alma Louise. It's your ball game," he said. "Tell me where to turn."

When she gave him the directions, she seemed to have lost twenty years. If she was making a mistake, it was still going to be her finest moment in maybe her whole life. "Half a league, half a league, half a league onward/Into the valley of death rode the six hundred." You always think you've forgotten those poems they force you to read when you're in school, but then they go off like tiny little time pills as if to pretend they were practical all along. "Theirs was not to reason why. Theirs was but to do and—" Well, never mind that, Dub told himself. Let's just hope this Light Brigade has a beeper hidden on it, that Campbell ignored Alma Louise's directions.

There was a little shopping traffic near the Westside Mall, but they soon spotted Archbishop Blenk. Dub slowed to a stop, licked his lips, tasted salt, and saw nothing in particular. It was obvious that the school was closed for some reason. The kidnappers had been delicate enough about that.

"We're going to save him," she said to herself. "We're going to save him."

Dub wiped his moist face with his hand and said, "Okay, Alma Louise, let's find the Dumpster." He drifted slowly past the school crossing signs and turned into the parking lot to circle the building. "It ought to be near the kitchen, wouldn't you think?"

She did not answer. Her eyes were wide as headlights. He saw windows decorated with colored paper cutouts. There were the usual basketball hoops, and he noticed a small statue of the Virgin on the sill of what was probably an office. Help us, Lady, he thought. He was leaning forward to see around the corner they were about to turn, when he heard the scraping sound of a vehicle hitting a speed bump too hard. He looked back. A white van was closing on them fast, much too fast. He had a moment to think—God damn you, Campbell—when he saw a familiar face behind the wheel.

He squinted.

John Wayne.

"Holy shit!"

The brakes on the van slammed and it shrieked to a stop, sliding, the tires smoking. It came to rest only a few yards back, angled across the pavement. Dub turned to see his avenue of escape. He snapped the car into reverse and rammed the pedal to the floor. His tires peeled back and he smacked hard into the driver's front.

"What are you doing?" shouted Alma Louise. "Stop!" She started clutching at him. He grabbed for the shift, but her hands were in the way, tangling him.

"Get back!" he said. "Get back!" He somehow got his hand over her face and shoved her hard against the opposite door. He dropped the transmission into drive, but in the split second it clicked in, John Wayne stepped in front. His plaid shirt strained across his big belly revealed a yellowish Tee-shirt and a tiny slit of white skin near his navel. He nimbly shifted slightly from side to side, ready to jump if Dub should floor it. The huge army Colt was leveled with both thick hands straight at Dub's head.

"Stop!" said Alma Louise. "We have the money! We have the money!"

Dub was tempted, very tempted. He could drop down and floor it and— And? And the cannon this cracker held could blow the whole car into hell. Shit, he thought. He turned off his engine.

By now another man had moved up on Alma Louise's side. He was wearing the Stan Laurel mask. He jerked her door open and yanked her out onto the pavement. "Get out," said John Wayne. "GET OUT!"

Dub raised his hands and leaned them out of the car window. As the gunman approached, he closed his eyes and mumbled to himself, "Be calm. Be calm. Be calm." He listened to his heartbeat. It seemed loud, but okay. He felt a moment of panic as he thought he might have left his nitro tabs back at the house. He opened his eyes, and John Wayne was reaching for the door handle. Dub couldn't check his pocket.

"Get out!" said the man. "Who are you?"

"I'm just driving," said Dub meekly. "Alma Louise was liable to run off the road."

"Keep your eyes down!"

Dub glanced toward the other side of the car. Alma Louise was on her knees on the pavement. Stan Laurel's western revolver was leveled at her head. He shuffled sideways to the car and grabbed the briefcase. "Is this the money?"

"Where is Raleigh Lee?" begged Alma Louise. "He's okay, isn't he? That's all the money I could raise. Honest. We are totally broke now. Pleeease . . ."

"Shut up!"

John Wayne suddenly made a half-kick at Dub's shins. "You run into me!"

"I didn't know who you were. We were looking for a Dumpster. You got your money now. Let Mr. Menzies go. He ain't done nothing to you."

John Wayne looked toward Stan Laurel, waiting as if he expected him to say something. It was an odd moment, as if they were communicating with their eyes. Slowly they turned toward the kneeling Alma Louise.

"Hey, y'all have an accident?"

A small man with a pasty face and two days' growth of silvery whiskers had come from inside the high school carrying a spray bottle and a broom. He froze when he saw the strange rubber masks and the guns.

"Go back!" said Dub.

The man's mouth opened as the situation sunk in. The spray bottle rose slowly, as if he were going to defend himself with it.

"Get the fuck outta here!" shouted Laurel. He raised his revolver and fired it in the air. Dub winced and crouched.

"Jesus Mary!" said the old man, skittering away.

"We gotta go!" said John Wayne in a panic. He shoved Dub toward the back of the van.

"Where are we going?" Dub asked.

"Shut up!!"

They roughly shoved Dub and Alma Louise facedown on the rough plywood sheet covering the floor. It smelled like an old dog.

"You move, you're dead!" said Laurel.

Dub shifted his head slightly to look at Alma Louise just as the back door clubbed the bottom of his feet. He bent his legs and the door thudded them into darkness. His glimpse of her quivering lip, her closed eyes, shook him strangely, more than anything that had happened yet. The bad guys had panicked. There was no telling what might happen next. As his eyes adjusted to the light, the truck began to move. Laurel was sitting on a wire cage for a raccoon-sized dog. His boots were close enough to see the layers of his sole.

The motion of the van was nauseating. The plywood sheet slid an inch or two each time they changed direction. Eventually the vehicle speeded up and moved more steadily. They were on open highway. It was then that Dub thought he should have tried to keep track of the turns. Some detective, he thought. How do I get myself in these fixes? He rolled his eye up. Under the edge of the eyehole of Stan Laurel's mask, he thought he saw dark skin. Laurel looked down, however, and Dub lowered his gaze.

Well, well. It was an interracial kidnapping. Americans of different races working together to pull themselves up by the bootstraps. Simple equal-opportunity crime. Not white crackpots, not black militants, just heartwarming money-grubbers of the sort that made America great. It might kind of put a catch in his throat, if he didn't already have one.

Stan Laurel's boot seemed to get more agitated the longer they went. It began to pat as if keeping time with some double-time rag. Then it added a little side-to-side movement that nearly clipped Dub's nose. Alma Louise seemed to be talking to herself, or praying in her sleep. They hit a dip in the road and she turned her head away from Dub. He was close enough to see a mole normally hidden by the hair on top of her head.

They were on a tilt, probably an exit ramp, and slowing. John Wayne said something that Dub couldn't make out. Stan Laurel's foot stopped abruptly for several seconds, then continued its nervous dance.

The van settled into a slow, steady pace.

"This looks good," said John Wayne. "It's time."

"Is Raleigh here?" asked Alma Louise.

"Shut up!" said Laurel.

Dub didn't like the tone of his voice.

The van eased to a stop.

"Well?" said John Wayne.

"Ease off," said Stan Laurel. His foot stopped patting and he stepped between Dub and Alma, his boot snapping the plywood down against the metal. The back doors popped open and Dub was blinded by the light.

"Is Raleigh here?" said Alma Louise, raising her head.

Laurel moved back to his "seat." "Get up," he said. Impatiently, he tugged at Alma Louise's collar, tearing it slightly. "Hands on your head! Get on your knees! You, too!" He turned them to face the open rear doors. Alma Louise made a noise and grimaced as if the plywood hurt her knees.

For Dub it was all too clear what Laurel had in mind. He straightened up. He wasn't going to unravel in these last few moments. "Be a man," he told himself. It sounded so silly: the kind of thing his father had said to him when he'd scraped his knee. The kind of thing that had been said so often in so many circumstances that it shouldn't have much meaning. But there wasn't much else left. Maybe it was lucky to know when Death was pointing his thin finger at you. Taking it like a man was better than wasting away or having a ridiculous, surprised look on your face when the grill of an oil truck crushed your nose into your brain. It didn't make dying easier. Maybe it just made it more decent.

He had to slow his breathing down or he was going to hyperventilate. "There's a quarter million there. All cash. She wouldn't let them mark it or nothin'. Honest. It's all good."

"Where is Raleigh?" wailed Alma Louise. "We brought money."

"Shut up!" said the man.

Dub swallowed. He'd been on the verge of begging. He didn't want to beg. Would your pride mean anything if you could go on living? Maybe it grows back. Maybe pride's just ego with an attitude. It has nothing to do with what you've done. He remembered every time he'd been close enough to hear Death's breathing. There was the undertow tearing at him when he was sixteen, the hangar in Vietnam, and the crushing of his chest that the doctors couldn't say for sure was a heart attack. He felt pressure in his chest now. Maybe he'd die before the man could shoot him. Was that a better way to go? "Be a man," he repeated silently, his lips moving.

"Have I got to do everything?" asked John Wayne.

The heavy gun abruptly snapped forward into the back of Alma Louise's head. The deafening report pinged off the metal sides of the van, then faded into the scrubby vegetation. Dub, hands still over on his head, folded his elbows in close, covering his eyes. He heard a wet sound like an expulsion of air and a patter like a tentative rain. When he opened his eyes, Alma Louise's body had toppled to the cracked and uneven pavement. One of her legs still rested on the edge, her thick ankle shining from the tight support hose, the foot twitching from the vibrations of the motor.

She had fallen facedown, thank God. A gun like that wouldn't leave a face if the bullet exited through it. He was surprised by how little blood there was on her, though the open van doors had tiny droplets of blood spray. They were in an area of old factories, one of which had an "1898" in a semicircle near the roof. The smell of oil and stagnant water mingled with the exhaust from the van. Most of the street had not been redone since it was cobbled. Large spiky weeds had forced themselves up between the stones. They'd wanted to live, too. Even if they'd had to split rock. He looked hungrily at the scrubby vegetation. There should be magnificent trees, mountains, running water, and a crisp sky. But there wasn't. Things never worked out like they were supposed to.

It was hot. The air was so humid, he was having trouble

breathing. He should have called Carrie and Elizabeth. How would they find out their father was dead? Would Beth tell them? Their new daddy? Who would pay for the funeral? Vonna? Devraix? Mrs. O'Dell? She'd paid for the doctors to keep his heart ticking, now she'd probably pay for disposing of the worthless thing. Maybe the man would let him write a note to Vonna. He just wanted to say he was sorry. He wanted to tell everybody he was sorry, but especially her.

"Whut the hell's the matter with you?" said John Wayne. "Get on with it."

"Shut up," said Laurel.

"You're sick, ain'tcha? Goddamn pussy. Have I got to—?"

"Shut up!"

There was a grinding sound and a distant roar. At first he thought it was John Wayne revving the engine, but there was a movement in the distance. A semi was awkwardly swinging into the lane.

"Hurry up," said John Wayne. He let off the brake and the van began to roll forward. Dub wavered on his knees, nearly falling out.

Dub felt the barrel touch the back of his head. He closed his eyes. It would be quick. Too quick to feel pain. That gun wouldn't leave a scrap of brain in one piece. When they found him, he wouldn't have a face. But that was all right. He wouldn't know. He concentrated on sending Elizabeth and Carrie a message. Wherever they were, hundreds of miles away in Charleston, they would suddenly think of him, know he loved them, feel it. No! No! He imagined spinning to knock away the gun. He was James Bond. He was the Cisco Kid.

Then he felt his head explode in a flash of white light that faded, faded, and he reeled into the velvet dark like a twisting diver tumbling into warm water.

SIXTEEN

Devraix leaned his tiny body across the leather seat and touched Vonna's arm. His white gloves were soft as velvet. "Are you prepared?"

"Yes," she said grimly. "I said I'd be okay."

"Very good."

He tugged each glove on a little more tightly and rested them on his cane. What *was* that cologne of his? The sweet aroma filled the back seat of the car like heavy water, and it was penetrating her clothes, her hair—probably her eardrums would smell like it for weeks.

Devraix touched Spyder Williams's shoulder. "There it is."

"I got it." Spyder turned into the semicircular driveway and pulled up by the canopy. Two large heavies in black flanked the double doors. The one with a mustache leaned over and squinted through the glass. "How ya doin', man?" asked Spyder. Devraix gave him a glance of disapproval.

The big man opened the door. The other never took his eyes from the street. "I anticipate we shall be some time," said Devraix. "Feel free to get yourself some coffee."

"I'll wait," said Spyder.

Devraix escorted Vonna up the pavement. There was an engraved brass plaque on the right side of the door shining like a mirror. "Menendez Brothers Funeral Home."

"To the right," said the man by the door.

Devraix squeezed her arm. They entered a dim foyer. Red, blue, and yellow light slanted from stained glass on each side of the door and mingled on the white marble floor. In the large chapel ahead, two women were dusting the pews. At the far end, sprays of flowers were scattered on the podium as a pale man arranged them around the space in which the coffin would sit. A giant horseshoe of chrysanthemums and roses was draped with a purple banner that said, "Bye Bye," in gold sequins. "Bye Bye"? Vonna's lip quivered as she tried to keep from laughing. Laughing wouldn't do at a time like this, but she often wanted to when she was nervous. They started up the winding staircase to their right.

At the top was another set of double doors. Another heavy moved forward, and politely said, "Excuse me" in a voice as low as a rumble in the earth's core. He passed a hand-held metal detector over their bodies. It booped near Devraix's waist.

"My watch," said Devraix, lifting it out of his vest by its amethyst-encrusted fob.

"Thank you, sir," said the big man. He touched a button under his Louis Quatorze desk and the door clicked. "You may go in now."

Devraix nodded and strolled calmly through the heavy doors. The room beyond also appeared to be a foyer. There was a silver dish for business cards. Devraix paused to drop one in.

"Can we trust these people?" Vonna whispered.

Devraix twitched his pencil mustache with amusement. "If they have the slightest reason to deceive, of course not, my dear. That is their nature. But they may certainly be helpful."

At that moment, a door with faux granite panels opened to their left. A man came through. He had froglike eyes and a head that looked like it had been dropped on the floor when he was a baby. "Honoré! Delighted!" Devraix neatly snatched off his glove and shook his hand.

"This is my colleague, Vonna Saucier. She is indispensable to me. Vonna, this is Arthur Carver, the eminent attorney."

Eminent shyster, she thought.

"Pleasure," said Carver, taking her hand. "Would you be related to Albertine Saucier, by any chance?"

"Not so's I know," she said bluntly.

"Miss Saucier's family is from the northern area of the state."

Carver nodded. She had the impression she had dropped a few thousand notches in his estimation. That was fine—she didn't like his looks, either. He dropped her hand. She rubbed the oily moisture from it between her thumb and fingers.

"Come in," said Carver. "Mr. Menendez is anxious to see you."

They passed into a library that might have been used to begin *Masterpiece Theatre* each week, except that it was so dark. The many lights on the mullions between the bookcases and the pair above the fireplace mantel seemed to have been adapted from old gaslights, but the black walnut shelves and paneling, the leather chairs and sofa, and the dark green drapes absorbed all of the light. The man they had come to see rose from his club chair and stepped into the puddle of light beaming down from a recessed fixture above.

"Honoré!" he said. "Too long! Too long!" The man was bigger than Devraix, barrel-chested, but about Vonna's height. For all the wealth implied by the room, his toupee was one of the most obvious Vonna had ever seen. "I thought of you just the other day, my friend. I had a meal of incredible Brazilian sausages. Yes, sausages! Who would think? Magic! Sheer magic! And this is the lovely lady?"

Lovely lady my butt, thought Vonna.

"Vonna Saucier, Oswaldo Menendez," said Devraix.

"I know who he is," she said.

"I'm very flattered," said Menendez.

"Don't be," she said.

Devraix cocked an eyebrow, but Menendez perused her without expression like a Mississippi farmer evaluating a sow.

"Call me Oswaldo."

It was going to be a long afternoon. She managed to force a smile. "Yes. Oswaldo."

"Coffee?" asked Menendez, as if she had been as gracious as he. Oh, he had the manners all right, but he wasn't truly refined like Devraix, not like generations of inbred etiquette could refine you. Running a funeral home was a kind of cornering the market for Menendez. It cut down on the overhead when he eliminated someone. The rumor was always that Oscar Menendez, his brother, had gone up the crematory chimney at the rear of this place and had been trickling down over the East Coast for some time in the form of acid rain.

"Espresso?" asked Devraix.

"Of course," said Menendez, spreading his hands. "Please. Sit." He gestured at a circle of four club chairs. A low circular table was in the middle. He lifted a small bell off the table and rang it. A thin woman entered and sat down a tray with four espressos and a selection of petit fours. Menendez's hand hovered over the tray and then pointed to one decorated with a miniature rose. "That one," he said. The woman picked it up and ate it. Menendez watched her in silence for a very long minute, then imperially dismissed her with a flick of the hand. If there was any poison, it wasn't the quick kind. Vonna's appetite dropped through the floor.

Devraix, however, immediately plucked up a chocolate cube decorated with a white dolphin and bit into it. He savored it. "Superb, Oswaldo. The touch of Seville orange makes it."

"Oh?" said Menendez. "I haven't tried those. A fish on chocolate seems a bit too adventurous to me."

"You gentlemen have such subtle palates," said Carver, smiling as if he'd plucked a fly out of the air with his tongue.

Menendez seemed to enjoy being called a gentleman, but he leaned forward. "I hate to rush your visit, Honoré. However, I have an appointment this afternoon. . . ."

Devraix hastily wiped his delicate finger. "Certainly, certainly. We are having a certain problem with Gio Pantucho."

"And Theo," said Vonna.

"A problem? Are you here to ask me a favor, Honoré? After all these years?"

"Oh, no," Devraix smiled, "the expense of a favor from Oswaldo Menendez is a bit larger than I would wish to pay."

The frog-eyed Carver sniffed like he was offended, but Menendez chuckled. "A favor from me is worth any price. It begins a relationship that goes on forever. Like a marriage. Isn't that right, Arthur?"

"Like a very special marriage."

"By the way, Honoré, how is your wife?"

"That has been over for some years now."

"For some years? Has it been that long?" Menendez clucked.

"I'm afraid so."

"Time flies," said Menendez.

Vonna caught herself staring at Devraix. She had never understood what sort of woman would date him—she knew he had a parade of fashion-model types all towering over him at the opera and so forth—but so do gay couturiers. That he had been married was harder to believe than Oswaldo Menendez as the secret potentate of New Orleans.

"Our situation is this, however. We wish to speak to Gio Pantucho on a matter of mutual interest."

"The Menzies kidnapping."

"Yes," said Devraix.

"How do you know about that?" asked Vonna. "It hasn't been in the press."

"I have many friends," said Menendez quietly.

Of course he did, thought Vonna. His enemies were all dead.

"Gio is evidently quite afraid of the Chinaman and assumes that we may make him vulnerable to him in some way."

"The Chinaman's an ambitious dude," said Vonna. "Word on the street is he's got notions about going into the funeral business."

Menendez's eyes narrowed. "It has been a profitable one for me, but the market is quite saturated."

"The point is," said Devraix, "that we have no relationship with the Chinaman. We are merely interested in certain business transactions of which Gio may have knowledge."

"I understand," said Menendez, "and I believe I may have heard some wild rumors that might be helpful to you. Gio will not see you, however. Under any circumstances. I fear he is not even willing to meet with me face-to-face, though we have chatted on the telephone."

"Where has trust gone?" said Devraix. Vonna concentrated on keeping a straight face. Only someone as odd as Devraix could get away with such an ironic remark and have others suspect he might be serious.

"I assure you Gio is quite unhappy that Theo overreacted to Miss Saucier's following him," said Menendez. "Theo is a bit paranoid, especially with all the pressures upon the brothers. If you can find him and his society wife, I certainly suspect the Chinaman could. It is very difficult to understand what rules the Chinaman plays by."

"You have no difficulty with him," said Devraix.

"I do not know the man. Why should I have difficulty?"

"Theo killed my sputterbug," Vonna insisted.

"Yes, Honoré explained on the phone that you were quite upset. You have an emotional attachment to the vehicle, such as it is. I understand. It is quite natural."

She had bought the car with her mustering out pay when she had left the Army. It might have had most of its original parts replaced, but it was still her sputterbug. All she said was, "It's the only new car I ever owned. The man got carried away."

"Perhaps," said Menendez.

"He has asked me, however, to offer you a settlement," said Carver. "If there is a police report, you'll withdraw it, won't you?"

"There isn't," she said. "This was more personal."

Carver extended a card. "Have the vehicle towed to this garage and it will be completely restored within three weeks. Or, if you prefer, perhaps a new car?"

"All I want is to be even. They don't make them like my sputterbug."

"They certainly don't," said Menendez dryly. Carver bowed his head to one side as if ready to shed crocodile tears.

Devraix interrupted. "I am personally very grateful at your treatment of my associate."

"This is entirely Theo Pantucho's doing," said Menendez. "You owe me nothing."

Nothing except the nuclear-tipped hint that shifted Theo's big butt, thought Vonna.

"Gio has also asked me that I convey to you his distress at your trying to locate him and his hope that he may continue his private life unmolested."

"Might we then," said Devraix, "satisfy our need to know certain facts?"

Menendez studied the crown molding over the doorway. "In this case, I may have heard certain things in passing, so to speak."

"Why was Theo watching the house of Raleigh Lee Menzies?"

"I would not know anything for certain," said Menendez. "Perhaps he was protecting certain business investments in the neighborhood."

"Someone in the neighborhood had borrowed money from Gio?"

"I do not know the nature of Mr. Pantucho's business."

"Yeah, right," muttered Vonna.

"Excuse me?" said Menendez.

"I didn't think you would," she added.

Menendez's eyes flashed. "I am only the director of a funeral home. I only care for my own business."

"Of course," said Devraix. "Of course. But these investments of Mr. Pantucho's, they involved Raleigh Lee Menzies?"

"I would imagine they were in that neighborhood."

"I find it difficult to accept that Mr. Menzies would have borrowed from Gio, Oswaldo. Perhaps your speculations are in error."

"That is up to you to decide." Oswaldo thought for a second. "Earlier today we spoke of marriage. It is unfortunate that yours came to an end—she was a lovely woman. Mine has lasted for over twenty-seven years, can you believe it?"

What choice would she have, thought Vonna.

"And do you know why a marriage lasts, Honoré? It can fail for a hundred thousand reasons, but it can only succeed because one partner is willing to assume a burden that the other has incurred."

Devraix was silent for several seconds. His eyes then locked with Menendez's.

"Let me be a little clearer. Suppose there is a wife who is a spendthrift. This is a common thing, is it not?"

Devraix nodded.

"Who knows why people are so careless with their money. Perhaps they feel neglected and buy lots of useless things. Perhaps they imagine they are going to make a fortune in the stock market. Perhaps they gamble. Perhaps they are subject to extortion. Perhaps their judgment is impaired. There are far too many people who ruin their minds with drugs. Or alcohol." He said the last word carefully.

Many of them thanks to you, thought Vonna.

"If you have taken the oath of marriage," said Menendez, "you have made a contract, and as part of the 'better or worse' part of that contract you ought perhaps to make arrangements to take care of your spouse's loans."

"Mrs. Menzies was into Gio?" asked Vonna.

"Who? I know nothing of Mr. Pantucho's business. I was speaking only hypothetically," said Menendez.

"Well, speaking only hypothetically, Oswaldo," Devraix carefully said, "how much might a wife require to satiate her profligacy?"

"It varies," said Menendez. His tone of voice was clear. The interview was over.

"Oh, gosh," said Carver, cued by Menendez's glance, "your next appointment, Oswaldo!"

"Forgive us," said Devraix. "We do not mean to importune your valuable time."

"Any time you need a favor," said Menendez. "Call again. I will send you a packet of the Brazilian sausages. I know you will appreciate them."

"Thank you *very* much!" said Devraix.

They climbed quickly down the curved stair and out through the door. "We better talk to Alma Louise, don't you think?" said Vonna. "She's got more tucked into that pickled brain of hers than she lets on."

Spyder was waiting across the street. He jumped out of the car. "Yo, boss," he said, "I tried to get in, but they wouldn't let me. I heard it on the news and then I called Emma. You'd best sit down for this one! Both of you! Dub went with Mrs. Menzies to pay the ransom."

SEVENTEEN

Devraix's single order "Drive!" was Spyder's cue to jump lights, cut corners, speed, and use every trick he'd learned in his juvenile days as top driver for a gang in Mobile. Swaying against the door, Vonna stretched out over the front seat rest and began working the radio dial.

"Ain't there an all-news station? Where the hell is it?" she said.

"I'll get it, momma," said Spyder.

She stared out the front window as he somehow turned the long car into an alley not wide enough to open the doors. "You keep your hands on the wheel, homeboy, and don't call me 'momma'!" Top 40, rap, top 40, rap, voices. She paused. A gravelly voice was insulting the Supreme Court. She moved the dial again. The car bounced as it dropped out of the alley and opened up on a street. Spyder did his mock Stepin Fetchit laugh, *"Heh-heh-heh!,"* teeth flashing in the sun. Putting down the pedal: he lived for this, but Vonna kept her eyes glued on the radio.

"It is not clear at this point," the voice said, "what action Governor Roemer will take on the bill. On the local scene, the body of Alma Louise Menzies, wife of civil rights activist Raleigh Lee Menzies, was discovered shot in the head about an hour ago in the River Road and Harvey Canal area. There are currently unconfirmed reports that Mrs. Menzies may have been the victim of a kidnapping; however, both local police and the FBI refuse to say at this hour. Mr. Menzies is also unavailable for comment. It is not clear yet whether the death of Mrs. Menzies is related to the recent explosion at the Menzies home. We will report further information as it is available. In other crime news—"

"My God!" whispered Devraix.

"Where's Dub?" said Vonna. "Did they kill Dub? Aw, tell us!" The memory of the victim of a mob assassination she had once seen in a morgue surged up like vomit. "And Emma didn't know?"

"Naw," said Spyder. "The client bought it, but nobody'd give Emma no details."

"Dub'd wouldn't've left her," she said.

"Never assume. Keep faith. He could still be alive. We shall soon know," said Devraix. Spyder whipped the car onto Interstate 10 with one casual rotation of his wrist. Vonna's rear bumped against Devraix's shoulder and she fell back onto the seat when Spyder accelerated. Devraix was resting his hands on his cane, looking out the window as if he were dawdling through the Garden District.

She had to find out, but she didn't want to know. It was her fault. She'd fucked things up again. She was the one who'd promise to diet with him. She was the one who'd invited him to move in and then she didn't take care of him. Her first husband had demanded and demanded and she had gotten hard. Dub had never asked that much, but she had kept that shell on her anyway. Sure, he'd acted like a prick, but he'd looked so pathetic at the Menzies house. If she'd just been able to cozy up to him when he started about the food, if she'd just not been so tired she . . .

Devraix's soft glove touched her arm. "If he had been found, I believe they would have said so. He may not have been with her at the time she was killed." Then, as if reading her mind, he added, "It is not your fault, my dear. In no way did your falling-out lead to this."

She nodded, but she knew she hadn't told Dub about spotting Theo Pantucho. You can't work with somebody and not communicate something like that. There was a knot in her throat, but she was afraid to cry. Crying would be giving in, admitting he had been hurt. She clenched her hands and thought of her mother praying, but she couldn't. The bad times at the orphanage with the reverend had destroyed whatever religion she had once had in her. Dub had to be all right. She wouldn't ask him to stay, she wouldn't ask anything for herself, ever, as long as he was okay.

Spyder was already charging up Thibodeaux. Television vans were parked in the road. "The vultures," murmured Devraix. The cream-colored Lincoln drew them like roadkill and they fluttered in. Vonna nearly knocked a woman down with her door.

"Who are you?" said a woman. "Who are you?"

"Get outta my face!" She went past the police line so quickly that the uniform made a funny shift trying to decide whether to go after her or hold his post against the press.

"Hey!" he said. "Hey! Halt!"

She glanced back, but kept moving. Devraix was getting out as if he could not be affected. "Excuse me. Excuse me."

The badgers of the press were undaunted. "Are you a friend of the family's? Are you with the NAACP? How is Mr. Menzies taking it? Was Mr. Menzies the target of the bomb?"

"Excuse me," he said with an elegant flick of his cane, nearly clipping the front of a camera lens, but dividing them like Moses parted the Red Sea.

Vonna crossed the flagstone patio and opened the front door. Campbell was on his cellular phone, pacing. Horn-Rims was huddled over the coffee table with two other agents.

"Just a minute," said Horn-Rims. Vonna ignored him and headed into the den. In the winged chair, Mrs. O'Dell held a handkerchief to her nose, weeping in the restrained manner of the rich. On the settee, Ben Hawkins, the New Orleans cop, was comforting Mrs. Johnson. Hawkins looked up. Vonna rushed to the kitchen. It was empty. Her head sagged. Mrs. O'Dell and Horn-Rims were behind her.

"Dub went with her? Is he dead?" Her eyes were wide, frozen.

"He's disappeared," said Mrs. O'Dell.

"Disappeared?"

"And the money with him," said Horn-Rims.

Her face asked the question. Mrs. O'Dell answered.

"He drove her to the rendezvous. They suddenly changed direction and the FBI lost the signal."

"Signal?"

"We put a beeper in his wheelwell."

"And you lost the signal? What kind of junk do you use? I never lost anybody's signal!"

"I'm sure," said Horn-Rims dryly.

"He ran on us," said Campbell. "Then ditched the car at a parochial school. He's got a good head start on us now, but we'll get him."

"Look, shitferbrains, Dub Greenert ain't—"

Campbell raised his voice to silence her. "He saw his chance and he scooted. He knew the bomb was in there."

"I refuse to believe that," said Mrs. O'Dell.

"He's going to have a good time with your money before we get him, lady. It won't be a long good time—"

"If you ever speak to me in that tone of voice again, Mr. Campbell, you shall discover exactly what a good time your job can be."

"I'm sorry, Mrs. O'Dell," said Campbell sternly. "But everything points to it. Somebody was on the inside, or they wouldn't have known Mrs. Johnson's private number."

"Anyone could get that number!" she said, quivering with anger.

"It's unlisted."

"Anyone!"

"Greenert was in there, called out, and they called back. On the morning Mr. Menzies was abducted, no one could find Greenert for several hours. He insisted he drive. As soon as they crossed the bridge he took over, drove south, and killed the woman. If he wasn't in on it, why didn't he follow the directions?"

"Maybe," said Horn-Rims, "he simply snatched the ransom. Either way, he's a killer and a fugitive."

Vonna was suddenly shaken from her reverie. She had stood there, stunned, allowing Mrs. O'Dell to do all the defending. She hadn't exactly been accepting their fantasy, but she had been hurt badly by men before. Love can do that, she thought, make you always expect the absolute worst ending. But, no, as hard as he was to read sometime, when he woke up sweating over some nightmare or sat staring at a blank wall for hours, Dub Greenert didn't have a mean bone in him. "You white-ass turkeys have BBs for brains! He's in danger, and you ain't doing anything about it!"

"You'd better calm down, Miss Saucier, or we're likely to find a charge that fits you. If Greenert were clean, he'd be as dead as Mrs. Menzies."

"Nonsense!" said Devraix. "This is more preposterous than the solution in some awful dime novel."

"We'll see," said Horn-Rims. "We told Mrs. Menzies not to keep him here."

"You lousy dumbass motherfuckers!" Vonna screamed. "You don't know that man. I know that man!" She raised both fists in the air, blinded with tears. She struck the kitchen wall instead of Horn-Rims's face. The clock crashed to the floor. "You dumbass—"

Devraix placed his hand upon her shoulder. "I refuse to believe it. Perhaps the kidnappers conveyed instructions to him. She was to divert your attention while Dub delivered the ransom." Horn-Rims and Campbell looked at each other. They hadn't thought of that. They shook their heads. No way.

"So where is he?" said Campbell.

"They killed him," said Hawkins stonily. A city cop was too used to the possibility for it to have any emotional impact. "He ain't crooked. Course, what do I know?"

"Where is Menzies?" asked Horn-Rims.

"They killed him, too, after they got the money."

"No, they killed Menzies after Greenert headed south," said Horn-Rims.

"And what, then, was the necessity of killing Mrs. Menzies?" asked Devraix.

"You ghouls!" shouted Mrs. O'Dell. "You hideous ghouls!" She slammed the bathroom door.

"So she couldn't finger Greenert. A quarter of a million is a lot of money," said Campbell. "If you two—" he cocked his chin toward Devraix and Vonna "—have any idea where your bird might have skipped to, you'd better speak up now."

"Accessory will go down hard on this," said Horn-Rims.

Vonna sneered at them, but when she looked at Hawkins, she knew he was willing to accept the theory, despite his earlier defense of Dub. Devraix's eyelids were half closed, his face as expressionless as a bronze Buddha's. She spun and charged out the sliding door to the swimming pool. She marched out to the far end, paced three steps each direction, then sat hard on the landscape timbers surrounding the roses. She choked up and silently wept.

Not again, she thought. Not again. A man couldn't betray her again. She was just cunt to them. Every time she'd loved somebody, she'd just been cunt to him. No, it was her fault. Him and his stupid diet. If she had calmed him down that night, he wouldn't have had a reason to run. She remembered the old trace dictum: if a man runs away, he runs to somebody. It may be another woman, his mother, a boyfriend, or the Foreign Legion, but he never just leaves. A woman, on the other hand, is more likely just to throw her life away and run. Where would Dub run to? She could trace him. No, she wouldn't do that. His daughters: that's where he'd run to. One afternoon Elizabeth and Carrie would disappear on their way to school. He'd never cut his tie to them. She thought about telling Campbell about the girls. Fuck him. If Agent Fat Boy was any good, he and his college-educated bloodhounds would find out about them. She choked up again. Oh, God! She was hoping the kidnappers had killed him, hoping he was dead. What kind of woman was she?

Devraix had come up on her without noticing. He whipped out a broad silk handkerchief from the inside of his vest and handed it to her.

"I'll just mess it up," she said, sniffing.

"That is the intention," he said. He patted her on the shoulder again and almost sat upon the timbers beside her. He thought better of it and quickly snatched up an aluminum chair near the diving board.

"There was a caretaker at the high school who saw the same kinds of masks that the kidnappers wore. He did say that Dub was removed at gunpoint with Mrs. Menzies. Or at least appeared to be being removed. The agents have also discovered white paint on Dub's car that may have come from a vehicle similar to the false Federal Express van that abducted Mr. Menzies."

"Oh God, Honoré, did you see Hawkins's face? He believes Dub did it."

"A policeman sees too much hypocrisy not to suspect everybody. If he does not, it will break his heart."

"Could Dub have done it?"

Devraix lightly touched her knee. "My dear," he said, "you are obviously and quite sloppily in love. Otherwise you would not even consider the question. Your judgment is impaired by the winged god, as my uncle used to say. I, on the other hand, am relatively uninvolved and furthermore an astute judge of character. Dub Greenert is incapable of treachery."

She buried her face in his densely cologned handkerchief and sobbed for several minutes. When the agony began to subside, she wiped her eyes, and saw that Devraix was sitting up stiffly in the chair, hands on the cane, his chin high and slightly turned away. He might have been one of his wealthy antebellum Creole ancestors holding a lengthy pose for a daguerreotype. One eye moved slightly toward her.

"Better? Well, I am considering whether it might be worthwhile to have a chat with Mr. Gio Pantucho."

"For what?"

"The nature of Mrs. Menzies's debt."

"The Pantuchos—" she wiped her eyes again "—are rough, but they don't just blow people's heads off. Not innocent people like Mrs. Menzies." She flashed on looking down the barrel of Theo's gun. "If they intend to make an example of somebody who's missing payments, they'd want the word out. They might cut her throat and dump her over Andrew Jackson's saddle in front of the St. Louis Cathedral but not just dump her by the road."

"Absolutely. However, consider the prominence of the man and consider the relative shabbiness of this dwelling."

"It don't look too shabby to me."

"Please," said Devraix with distaste. "Wall-to-wall carpeting! Corningware! Why did she find it necessary to go to a loan shark? Why? It is the sole inspiration I have at the moment." He raised a clutched hand. "Our only straw."

"Those dudes don't want to talk to us," said Vonna. "Remember my sputterbug? And Menendez won't see us again."

"True. Spyder has some interesting purviews, however. I believe he might—"

Hawkins interrupted them. "Honoré, Campbell wants to secure the house."

"We are being thrown out?"

"Everyone. Me. Mrs. O'Dell, even Mrs. Johnson. He says he should have done it days ago."

"Mrs. Johnson lives here!" said Vonna.

"Crime scene, Campbell says. She's going to O'Dell's. They want to play fed-ball now that the TV's out front."

"Well, let's boogie, then," said Vonna.

They had just gotten into the living room when Campbell blocked their way to the door. "This is a search warrant, Miss Saucier, to your apartment."

"You jive-ass . . ."

"Agent Monahan is going to escort you back to your apartment."

"You jive-ass motherfucker!"

"Now, listen, you—"

"This is totally absurd," said Devraix. "You shall hear from my attorneys!"

"You, little man, will stay out of my way or you'll need attorneys."

"We have cooperated on all levels," protested Devraix, "but your arrogance . . ." He quivered, unable to speak.

The front door slammed open. "Larry!" said an FBI man.

There was a yellow cab parked in the middle of the reporters. A squatty Greek-looking man peered in the door. "You mebbe know dis guy?" he asked, sticking out his hand. "Thirty-two fifty."

Raleigh Lee Menzies moved silently into the open doorway. There was a multicolored bruise on his left cheek. His windbreaker was dirty. He hadn't shaved for several days, and his silvery hair was ruffled. His hunched-over posture and subdued expression made him seem shrunken, almost wizened.

Vonna rushed past him. "Dub?"

There were many people looking back at her: reporters, the policemen, the curious neighbors. But there was no Dub, so the street seemed totally empty.

EIGHTEEN

Vonna parked Spyder's car in the quiet neighborhood and listened to a dog barking two houses down. It was nearly midnight, and the pavement, shiny from a brief earlier drizzle, reflected the red light blinking atop a radio tower at least a mile away. She got out of the car and closed the door gingerly. The faint battleship-gray light on the drapes told her that someone was still awake. She pushed the doorbell, and the light over the door came on. The curtain opened only a crack and then the door. Hawkins's eyes flicked from side to side behind the screen door, checking the street behind her. To be a cop was to live in permanent paranoia, she thought.

"What do you want?"

"To talk."

"You got something to tell me?"

She didn't understand him at first. When she did, it angered her, but she was too tired to argue. "Did it ever occur to you I might know some things you high-and-mighty police don't?"

"Is this on the record or off?"

"You don't get it, do you, Hawkins? I'm not here to confess. I'm not here to give you Dub, either."

"Then we got nothin' to say." He didn't close the door.

"Let me in."

"My wife's asleep. I just took my gun off. You know how tired I get of wearing that gun? That lump in the small of my back. When it comes off, I'm naked. I ain't a cop no more. I'm just another brother watching Arsenio Hall suck up to these 'stars' I never heard of."

"Tell me what Menzies said."

He laughed warily. "That'll be the day: I tell you, you tell your boyfriend. That'll be the day, girl."

She didn't like the way he'd sneered out "boyfriend." "He ain't my— We had a fight. He left."

"When?"

"The day before Menzies was kidnapped." She heard herself and knew what it sounded like. "He wasn't involved. We got to find him somehow. You're wasting your time trying to pin this on him."

"I don't even know *you* aren't in it. That's why Campbell sent you home, girl. It wouldn't be the first time a sister's been fooled by some white man."

"He didn't fool me. He's out there dead somewhere, and you want to close your file!"

"Girl, it's late. Anyway, I ain't privy. Feds don't share much with us. If I talk to you, Campbell will be putting me on his suspect list, and I got to get up at—"

A light came on. Vonna saw a pair of fuzzy pink slippers on the stairs. "Ben? Who're you talking to, Ben?"

"Police business, babe. Go back to sleep."

"Are they paying you overtime? They best be paying you overtime." The fuzzy slippers turned and disappeared up the stairs.

Hawkins opened the door wider and sagged in resignation. "Well, now we'll have something to talk about when I go to bed. Overtime! What is this 'overtime' stuff?"

"Ben, you're a cop a long time now, right? You got that look, like you seen enough, don't need to see no more. But that means you know when a man's crossed over. You know Dub ain't no kidnapper."

He snapped the latch on the screen door. "Don't know nothin' of the sort, girl, and even if I did I wouldn't trust it. Been fooled too many times. Come on in. We'll go out to the kitchen. You want a Coke?"

She started to say "Diet," but the thought gave her a

twinge. Before sitting, she had to take a plastic Robin Hood and a Happy Meal box off the seat.

"I tell Joanelle," he said, "not to buy the kids those things. The little toys are all made in China. Those old bastards shoot people." He popped open the bottles and straddled the chair opposite her.

"Cops sometimes shoot people."

"Only by accident." Hawkins winked. "When we're firing at two-legged cock-a-roaches." He rested his chin on the back of the chair and yawned. "So what do you know Campbell don't know?"

"The Pantuchos."

"Gio and his little brother Theo?"

"They're in this somehow."

"They never kidnapped nobody that I know of."

"Mrs. Menzies owed them money."

"Naw."

"We know it. We heard it from the Big Man himself."

"The Big Man? Naw, Oswaldo wouldn't tell nobody about 'investment opportunities' in his town."

"Devraix and him have some kind of old tie."

Hawkins was thinking. "You ain't been fiddling with Oswaldo Menendez? That's a real Tar Baby. Jesus, Devraix's not—"

"No. He's an unusual man—unusual ain't the half of it—and having a tie to Menendez without being tied to Menendez is pretty strange. But that's the whole of it."

"So Mrs. Menzies owed money. For what? Gio don't bank no five-hundred-dollar accounts. Not since drugs got big."

"We don't know. He's underground."

"He may be under the ground if the Chinaman has his way! We've been waiting for the war to start any minute." He sipped his soda. "Mr. Menzies never mentioned anything to me." He seemed hurt that the man hadn't. "How much was Gio into her for?"

"Don't know."

"How big could her bar bill be? Drugs? Naw. She was a gone babe, but it was the gourmet Thunderbird that done that. She shopped a lot, but not that much. Stocks and shit?"

"Honoré and I've been over this a dozen times, Ben. From what we can tell, she was real confused about raising the ransom, so she didn't seem like she knew anything about handling money."

"That don't mean she didn't screw up *trying* to get rich. I don't know anything about gambling and her. That's how Gio gets into a lot of high-priced spread. Even got some cops that way."

"Not a sign of it. We were thinking real hard about blackmail. Maybe somebody had something on her. She's supposed to've had some boyfriends."

"You got to have something to lose to be blackmailed. Mr. Menzies's a blue blood. He and she had separate bedrooms. You probably know he had a squeeze of his own until she died: a nice woman, a real good match. He was real messed up when she died. How much would he care if his old lady's riding the pole now and again? And then, you pay Mr. Blackmailer with this big wad of money that you borrow from Gio at nine million percent a week? Naw. How would Raleigh not know she was paying out like that? And then she'd have to explain and then the whole point of paying would be—you get the drift."

"Maybe you can find out what Mr. Menzies knows."

"Shee-yit, girl! Over something some wise guy told you just to jerk you around? Misinformation, girl. If the government will use it, the Nostra boys will use it. They practically *are* the government."

"But why would they lie to us? You've got to face the man with it and see what he says."

"I ain't gonna do that. His wife's dead. If it's bullshit, it'll just hurt him. I won't hurt the man. He's been hurt enough. He ain't the same man he used to be."

"What do you mean?"

"I mean he kind of lived for the struggle, you know. Then the struggle left him behind. He never got into the Vietnam protest too much because he didn't like the hippie/yippie assholes. And they didn't like him. What nobody really understands about the Red Knight is that under it all he's a kind of conservative. He believes in the old stuff: everybody's equal and such. He believed in law and order long after nobody else did, so they dumped him. So he defended a lot of two-legged cock-a-roaches in the criminal courts and fell hard for Miss Jane. Then there was the cancer. Since she died, he just seems to get smaller and older. I used to think he'd snap out of it, you know. But he's like an old silver quarter you find in your change, a real one. You say, 'Looky there, how'd that get there?' It's just hung around too long."

Vonna watched Hawkins's expression. It was like he was watching a film projected on the white cabinets.

"Now that Alma Louise is dead, he's really going to be a shadow. I used to tell him he ought to get back into it, you know. Uncle Ronnie and Kindly George and their Supreme Court gang are trying to take away everything we won. It's the Reconstruction all over again: the Republicans are tossing us away again like so much garbage. I'd tell him that and he'd agree, you know, but Raleigh Lee Menzies is a proud man. They didn't really want him anymore, so he took his ball and went home."

Hawkins was silent, watching the credits and final fade-out of his imaginary film: Raleigh Lee Menzies riding off into the sunset. He lowered his head and looked under his strong eyebrows at Vonna. "Okay," he said, "a lot of it will be on the news in the morning, anyway. And there ain't much of it's good for Greenert, I'll tell you right now. But maybe you got a right to know." He left the dinette and pulled a brown envelope from the suit jacket he had thrown on the sofa. He flopped it on the table in front of her. "The Chief's supposed to get this in the morning." He pulled out Raleigh Lee Menzies's preliminary statement.

ON THE AFTERNOON OF TUESDAY, NOVEMBER 6, 1990, I, RALEIGH LEE MENZIES AND MY WIFE, THE LATE ALMA LOUISE MENZIES (NÉE BERESFORD) WERE HAVING LUNCH ON THE PATIO IN FRONT OF MY HOUSE AT 16 THIBODEAUX ROAD. I WAS READING THE *TIMES-PICAYUNE* AND DID NOT NOTICE THE APPROACH OF A WHITE FEDERAL EXPRESS VAN. A MAN LEAPED OUT WEARING A RUBBER MASK IN THE LIKENESS OF STAN LAUREL, THE COMEDIAN, AND

POINTED A CHROME AND BLACK PISTOL AT MY WIFE AND
ME. HE ORDERED ME INTO THE BACK OF THE VAN, SHOVED
ME HARD, AND I STRUCK MY FACE AGAINST THE FLOOR. HE
GAGGED AND HOODED ME ALMOST INSTANTLY AND THE
VAN PULLED AWAY. THE MEN DID NOT TALK TO EACH
OTHER MUCH. THE ONE IN THE BACK SAT ON A MILK
CRATE AND KEPT THE GUN ON ME. I HEARD ORDINARY
TRAFFIC NOISES, AND THEN THE ROAR OF AN AUTOMATIC
CAR WASH. WE THEN DROVE FOR WHAT SEEMED CLOSE TO
AN HOUR, THOUGH I CANNOT BE SURE. EVENTUALLY WE
WERE BOUNCING SLOWLY OVER A DIRT ROAD AND I
SMELLED SWAMP WATER. I THOUGHT THEY WERE GOING
TO KILL ME, BUT THEY DRAGGED ME BY EACH ARM TO
A BUILDING WITH A WOODEN PORCH AND TIED ME IN A
CLOSET.

I WAS NOT ABUSED OTHERWISE. I WAS BROUGHT FOOD
TWICE A DAY. THEY GAVE ME A BUCKET TO USE AS A SLOP
JAR AND TOOK PICTURES OF ME WITH A POLAROID SX-70
TWICE. THERE WAS A BATTERY TELEVISION THEY LET ME
WATCH, AND THEY EVEN LET ME OUT ON THE PORCH
TO STRETCH SOMETIMES. I HAD THOUGHT THIS WAS A
TERRORIST OR A POLITICAL KIDNAPPING, BUT EARLY IN
THE SECOND DAY, I OVERHEARD THE TWO MEN TALKING
AND I RECOGNIZED THE VOICE OF RASHEED M'FULU, WHO
WAS BORN WILLIAM JOHNSON, JR., THE SON OF MY HOUSE-
KEEPER, MRS. MARTHA JOHNSON, AND JOHN JOHNSON,
LONG MISSING. I HAD ONCE DEFENDED RASHEED AGAINST
POSSESSION OF WEAPONS CHARGES AS A FAVOR TO HIS
MOTHER, BUT SHORTLY AFTER, HE FIRED ME IN ORDER TO
DEFEND HIMSELF. JUDGE MANNING HAD INSISTED (A
LEGALLY DUBIOUS ORDER, EVEN FOR JUDGE MANNING)
THAT I GIVE HIM LEGAL COUNSEL, BUT THIS HAD MADE
HIM ANGRY THAT I DID NOT REFUSE, AND HE MADE AT
LEAST TWO THREATENING TELEPHONE CALLS FROM JAIL.
LATER, RASHEED ESCAPED FROM A HOLDING CELL IN THE
COURTHOUSE AND I HAD NOT SEEN HIM SINCE. HE WAS
REPUTED TO BE A BLACK LIBERATION TERRORIST, AND I
UNDERSTOOD HIM TO BE IN WEST AFRICA.

I DID NOT LET ON THAT I RECOGNIZED RASHEED,

HOWEVER, FOR FEAR OF MY LIFE. I DID NOT THINK THAT HE WOULD KILL ME, BUT I WAS AFRAID HIS PARTNER OR PARTNERS WOULD. I DECIDED THAT IF RASHEED WERE INVOLVED, THE ABDUCTION WAS MOTIVATED PURELY BY MONEY, AS I DID NOT BELIEVE HE HAD ANY SERIOUS ILL WILL TOWARD ME. HOWEVER, FROM THE TONE OF THE CONVERSATIONS AND FROM THE WAY THE WHITE MAN ORDERED RASHEED AROUND, I NOW THINK IT POSSIBLE THAT RASHEED WAS MERELY A HIRED HAND IN SOMEONE ELSE'S PLOT. THE WHITE MAN TREATED RASHEED WITH LITTLE RESPECT AND SOMETIMES CALLED ME A TRAITOR OF MY RACE. MOST OF THE TIME THE WHITE MAN WOULD LEAVE RASHEED AND ME ALONE IN THE CABIN.

FINALLY, ON WHAT I BELIEVE WAS THE THIRD DAY, TODAY, RASHEED AND THE MAN SAID THEY BOTH WERE GOING TO PICK UP THE RANSOM. RASHEED TIED AND GAGGED ME. HE LAY ME ON MY BACK IN THE CLOSET AND SUSPENDED MY LEGS ABOUT EIGHTEEN INCHES OFF THE FLOOR WITH A CHAIN HE LOOPED OVER THE CLOTHES BAR. HE KNEW WHAT HE WAS DOING. KNOWING THAT I WAS ALONE, I STRUGGLED FOR SOME TIME BUT COULD NOT GET LOOSE. I RELAXED, ASSUMING THEY HAD ABANDONED ME AND WOULD TELL SOMEONE WHERE I WAS AFTER THE MONEY WAS RETRIEVED.

LATER, BOTH OF THEM CAME BACK. THEY WERE ARGUING OVER WHETHER TO LET ME GO BECAUSE THE RANSOM WAS NOT WHAT IT WAS SUPPOSED TO BE, AND THEY KNEW I WAS WORTH MORE THAN THAT. MY LEGS WERE NUMB, SO THEY BROUGHT ME OUT ON THE PORCH. I COULDN'T SEE TOO WELL FROM BEING BLINDFOLDED SO MUCH. THE WHITE MAN GOT BEHIND RASHEED AND SNATCHED OFF HIS MASK AND SAID, "NOW, YOU GOT TO KILL HIM, BOY. YOU GOT TO TAKE UP WHERE THAT AL-BERTS KID LEFT OFF." THAT WAS THE GIST OF HIS WORDS. THEN HE ADDED, "RASHEED'S GONNA SEND YOU TO YOUR WIFE."

I DIDN'T UNDERSTAND.

"YOUR WIFE'S DEAD," RASHEED SAID. "WE OFFED

HER." I DON'T REMEMBER IF I SAID ANYTHING OR NOT. I WAS STUNNED, I SUPPOSE.

AND THEN I'M NOT SURE WHAT HAPPENED. THEY ARGUED ABOUT HOW RASHEED ALWAYS DID THE DIRTY WORK AND OUGHT TO GET A BIGGER PERCENTAGE OF THE RANSOM. THE WHITE MAN SEEMED UPSET THAT RASHEED WOULD DEFY HIM BY ASKING FOR MORE. ALL OF A SUDDEN THEY WERE PHYSICALLY FIGHTING. RASHEED KNOCKED THE MAN DOWN THE STAIRS, AND THE WHITE MAN RAN TO HIS VAN. HE SOMEHOW GOT A GUN AND SHOT RASHEED.

HE THEN LOOKED UP AT ME, AND I COULD SEE THAT I WAS NEXT. I WAS DEAD, I THOUGHT, BUT I DIDN'T MUCH CARE SINCE THEY HAD KILLED MY WIFE.

THEN, I DON'T KNOW WHO DREW HIS ATTENTION AWAY. AT FIRST I THOUGHT THE POLICE HAD MANAGED TO FOLLOW THE VAN INTO THE SWAMP. NOW I BELIEVE IT WAS AN INNOCENT HUNTER OR FISHERMAN, POSSIBLY EVEN A LARGE DOG. WHEN THE MAN TURNED AND WENT AFTER HIM, I DECIDED TO TAKE MY CHANCES IN THE SWAMP. I HEARD THE WHITE MAN SHOUT, THEN I HEARD SHOTS AND I THOUGHT HE WAS CHASING ME. ABOUT TWO HOURS LATER, I CAME OUT ON A TWO-LANE ROAD SOMEWHERE IN ST. TAMMANY PARISH. I FOLLOWED IT TO A BAIT SHOP, WHERE I USED MY CALLING CARD TO GET A CAB. THEN I CAME HOME.

Vonna went back to the beginning and flipped the pages quickly.

"That answer your question?" said Hawkins, taking the papers. "Campbell's going to get more detail after the man gets some rest. Maybe even go the hypnosis route. I shouldn't've shown this to you. Your boyfriend looks like the link here."

"Well, he isn't," said Vonna grimly. "He didn't know this Rasheed Whatsizname."

"How do you know that?"

"You find the cabin?"

Hawkins nodded. "The white dude saved us the cost of one trial, anyway, and your boyfriend saved us the cost of another. Nobody noticed the white man off in the grass for a while." He slid a photograph from the envelope in front of her. "Rasheed and this one are getting their asses worked over by the god Mumbo Jumbo now." A headless torso was half sunk in the muddy earth.

Vonna grimaced.

"At first they thought this was your boyfriend. He's too big, though. They'll get him ID'ed eventually. But that means there were three of them. See, there was somebody who killed this guy."

"Menzies said it was a hunter."

"Well, he didn't see him. Why would a hunter do this? How would a hunter know to take the money? There's not a cent out there."

"He could have found it."

Vonna took another look at the photo of the corpse and turned it over. It might have been Dub. Whoever killed this man could have done the same thing to Dub. "Wait! Fingerprints?"

"In the cabin? Rasheed's. Menzies's. A bunch of unidentified. But it was a rental fishing cabin. There's a load of prints."

"But you were looking for Dub's. If any of those was a match, it would have been easy."

"Maybe. These things take time, sometimes days, weeks. The gun was there. Rasheed was there. A coupla pork-and-beans cans and lots of catfish bones. Television. A coupla bamboo fishing poles. Blue curtains like the Polaroid. *And* a dynamite box. No money, though. We found out Rasheed rented the cabin a week ago, the day after the bomb tore up the three punks."

"Why, just tell me why, they'd try to blow him up first, then kidnap him?"

"They wanted the man dead all along, but they got this idea to milk him."

She shook her head. "This whole theory is crap. Don't you think it's funny that Alma Louise didn't go straight to Gio Pantucho to raise the ransom?"

"Shit, girl, she probably knew Gio wasn't coughing up no more."

"Well, suppose she thought Gio had snatched him to get the loan paid. She thought everything was her fault. That's why she acted like she did."

"The woman acts funny all the time. It's the booze. Don't try to tell me it's the Pantuchos. The feds'll find your boyfriend and then you'll see." He stood up. "Now please get outta here and let me get some zees."

She sat there trying to make sense of it. The easiest way to sort it out was to think Dub had jumped with the cash. But that couldn't be. "He's dead," she said numbly. "You're going to find Dub dead and then you're going to have shit. The bad guy will be long gone because you're looking for Dub."

"If he's in the river, it would take a few days for him to float." Hawkins blinked. "I didn't mean to say that," he explained. "I'm beat."

She nodded.

"Go home, girl," he said. "At least Mr. Menzies got out alive."

She rose from the chair. The kitchen clock shaped like a cat said one-thirty. It didn't matter. She wouldn't sleep until they found Dub, and if he was in the river, he might be carried by the current halfway to Mexico. If they found his body out there, they'd probably try to say he was swimming to South America to escape.

"Tell me, Hawkins," she said at the door. "What is it with you and Menzies?"

"Old times," said Hawkins.

"Meaning?"

Hawkins quickly stepped to his bookshelf and pulled down a copy of *Go Down, Moses*. He turned to the photo section. He pointed to the boy being beaten mercilessly by a cop, the cop who had later beaten Raleigh Lee when he threw himself against him to save the boy. "That's me," said Hawkins. "I was only twelve, and full of piss. I'd seen my daddy eat so much shit. So much. I near got killed. Might've been. I got enough pins in my arms to set off a metal detector." He shook his head. "Now go home, will you, please? Go on."

NINETEEN

Bobby Alberts rubbed his eyes and tried to figure out whether the gritty feeling in them came from spending two nights in the car or from the chemicals Menzies had sprayed in his face. His butt was damp from the log he was sitting on, and his arms and neck were peppered with mosquito bites that grew itchier as he sweated. It had taken a long time to relocate the van after he had lost it, but now he knew exactly where Raleigh Lee Menzies had been taken. If he could only figure out how to deal with whoever was inside, he might get his shot at Menzies and finish Billy's payback. He just needed to make a plan.

It hadn't been easy getting here. Bobby remembered Billy's advice about how to deal with the police and had played meek throughout his brief hospital stay. A day and a half later, when the boy had finally come up before a judge for formal charging, Perlie had gotten him a free lawyer who had just passed the bar. The lawyer had argued so excitedly that the woman judge had been amused. Eventually, however, she said she would grant Bobby bail until his trial in order to give him a chance to keep away from the type of people he might meet in prison, providing he would solemnly swear to stay a long way from Raleigh Lee Menzies. She was willing to accept that what had happened was a youthful indiscretion, particularly since the state had chosen to charge him with assault rather than attempted murder. The prosecutor fumbled with his papers, saying he wasn't sure why that was, but that the state opposed bail. He wanted a brief postponement to call his office, but the judge was short with him. Bobby had surprised himself by how sincere he had sounded when he had sworn to leave Menzies alone. Maybe there in the courtroom with the impression of the handcuffs still on his wrist, the memory of the Lysol smell of the holding cell still fresh in his mind, he had even meant it. Billy had always bragged that the jails weren't as tough as they liked to make out, but from what Bobby'd briefly seen of them, he hadn't wanted to see more.

But when Perlie dropped him off at home, his father was asleep on the sofa snoring loudly. A puddle of drool had formed on the armrest. Mrs. Jones was conked out on the floor, as if she had numbly rolled off Bobby's father. Her dress was hiked up and her underwear was torn. Bobby went to the kitchen and stood against the sink. There was a ring of orange grease near the top edge and over the drain a cracked plate covered with chicken bones and beans. Bobby snapped. He grabbed an RC Cola can off the counter and flung it against the opposite wall. It flattened with a *thup*, gushing droplets of liquid dark as blood. When it caromed to the linoleum, several startled roaches fled under the stove.

Bobby went straight to his father's room and searched his closet for the old shotgun. It was dusty, but the shells were right next to it. He paused to look in Billy's room, but still couldn't find any of Billy's other weapons. He stopped in the kitchen to pick up a carving knife. As he was about to leave, his father snorted like a hippopotamus clearing his nostrils. Bobby looked down at Mrs. Jones, her pubic hair speckled with gray and her thighs etched with broken veins. He almost reached down to lower her dress, but couldn't bring himself to touch her. He angrily kicked the sole of her foot. The woman rose, squinted through the mucus in her eyes, smiled, and dropped back to the floor, just as exposed as before. Bobby took his father's car. He was going to be more careful this time. He would stalk Menzies until he had a good opportunity, then blam, both barrels in the face.

He remembered the car parked in the woods near the edge of Menzies's property, so he came into the woods from the other end, easing his way in the general direction of Menzies's house. When he spotted the fence surrounding Menzies's pool, he followed it, creeping to a spot of tangled brush. He crawled under it, the shotgun slung over his arm, snagging his shirt every few feet. When he parted the veil of honeysuckle at the edge, bingo! It was Christmas. Menzies was on the front veranda having breakfast with his wife. The driveway was empty. He lifted himself onto his knees to charge straight across at them, but lowered himself when he thought that's how he'd goofed it up the time before. This was hunting. He remembered his grandpa's teaching, "Impatience makes a mighty po' hunter." He had to think of a way in which to cross the seventy-five or eighty yards before Menzies had a chance to see him and get inside. He'd watch and—

Menzies's housekeeper brought out a tray. Menzies sipped at his coffee, then reached behind his seat. He took out a newspaper. He unfolded it in front of him. Mrs. Menzies had her back to Bobby. Menzies lowered the paper to turn the page, then raised it again.

Bobby lifted himself, crouched to spring. The next time the paper went up, he would charge. The paper went up, he started forward, but before he had gotten clear of the brush, there was a roar to his left. A white van was climbing the driveway. He skidded to a stop, falling hard on his rear, and scrambled back into the brush. His face clawed by the branches, he twisted around and heard shouting. They had seen him! Heart pounding, he looked through the leaves.

What he saw made no sense at all. The rear of the van was open. A man with a weird face was yanking Menzies by the arm while waving a pistol at Mrs. Menzies. He pushed Menzies to the rear doors and climbed into the van together. Something was shouted to the driver, then Menzies and the gunman each pulled a door closed. The van ground its gears and plummeted down the driveway. It took him a second to know what had happened, and even then he wasn't sure. Nor was he sure what to do. The police would be there any minute. Instinctively, he got up and plunged back through the woods. Whoever they were, they had stolen his sitting duck. It wasn't fair! He jumped into his father's car, carelessly tossing the shotgun to the passenger side. The van exited Thibodeaux

Road just ahead and roared past him. Bobby made a screeching U-turn, clunking loudly over the opposite curb.

He had hardly known what he was doing or why, so he made it up as he went along. He had seen enough cop shows to know he ought to hang back to avoid being seen. He had little trouble keeping the lumbering van in view, even when it was ahead. He rushed through a couple of yellow lights, and almost got up on the van's bumper when it turned to get onto the interstate. The chase became the goal in itself. When they stopped, would he try to join these kidnappers? Would he take a chunk of ransom for himself? Maybe he would rescue Menzies, make the bastard really feel safe, then "Hasta la vista, baby!" Bobby Alberts, Terminator. Dirty Bobby: "Make my day!" Yes. They couldn't steal his pigeon. He'd earned it. Who did they think they were?

Just when he began to believe that tailing someone was a lot easier than the cop shows made out, he lost them. They had left I-10 and gotten onto I-59, but just before they would have entered Mississippi, they abruptly cut across from the left lane. Horns blew, tires squealed, but they managed to exit. They had been as obvious as an overturned tanker truck, but when they got out on the winding two-lane country roads Bobby was afraid he'd stick out. He let the gap widen, and they disappeared. He rounded one bend, then another, and the paved road narrowed to a single-lane dirt road disappearing into a forest of southern pines. Bobby pulled over and leaned out the window. He thought he saw road dust still hanging in the air. There was a swampy smell, and he thought maybe the road wandered into some bayou. He'd heard you didn't want to mess with the swamp Cajuns: some of them didn't speak English and fed the gators with anybody who messed with them. That's what he'd heard, anyway.

He was pacing beside the car trying to decide what to do when he heard the grinding of tires on the dirt road. They were coming back out! There wasn't time to get away. He fumbled for the door handle and dived for the shotgun. Shells rolled under the dash, but he managed to get two in the chamber. A dusty, but fairly new, Lincoln rumbled out of the trees. An old man was driving. He was wearing a fishing hat and his head was tilted back as if trying to see through the bottom of his glasses. He glanced at Bobby and drove on.

Bobby decided to walk in. It had seemed easy enough, but when he got into the woods it had gotten even more complicated. The dirt road split into other roads, which split into lanes wandering among crude hunting and fishing cabins and lots with camping trailers and bloodhound runs and picnic shelters. The whole area was a warren of getaway lots. He tried getting a sense of the layout of the area by walking along the main road, but there seemed to be no particular scheme to it. Not many people seemed to be there, but he smelled barbecue, which made his stomach growl. After a couple of hours of walking around, his feet hurt, he hadn't spotted the van, and a woman hanging clothes behind her rusty trailer had cautiously nodded to him. He thought how obvious he was, walking around with the shotgun in the crook of his arm, and returned to his car. By the time he left to find a Mc-Donald's, it was already dark. He knew they were in there somewhere, but where?

He scoured a road map and figured out these camps were somewhere among the branches of the Pearl River. The reason the camp roads weren't on the maps was probably flooding. He tried to think like the kidnappers. He'd seen a number of roads with chains or steel cable across them. Some had warnings about dogs. Menzies was probably behind one of those. After eating he felt a little less frustrated. He listened to the radio, but they said nothing about Menzies's being kidnapped. He thought about going home for the night, but wasn't sure about finding his way back. A police car passed him on the highway, and he suddenly thought maybe his daddy would report the car stolen. He called home, got no answer, then called Perlie to tell her. He told her he needed to get away to think things out, so he'd gone hunting.

The next day was a disaster. After sleeping in the car in a truck stop on I-59, he'd even lost track of which exit led to the camp area. It seemed like he was going to drive over half the pavement in Louisiana when he realized he had somehow crossed over into Mississippi. It was late Wednesday afternoon, and he was exhausted. He was cussing himself for being stupid, banging the steering wheel in anger, and even saying he ought to use the shotgun to kill himself. By the time he recognized a white house he had passed in following the van, he had decided to give up. And then, there it was: the dirt road. Like an omen. He decided to make a little map of the camp area as he searched it. He walked the lanes until dark and then sneaked up a few of the blocked roads. Sometimes there was a barking dog, sometimes the silver light of a TV on the cabin shades. But no van. No Menzies.

He had started again Thursday morning, this time daring to drive about half a mile into the woods to search the far end. The junctions were more spread out down there. The ground was marshier and many of the trees had been killed by high water. The humidity was junglelike, and the Spanish moss was swarmed by insects. A bearded man with elaborately tattooed arms was cleaning his Harley and eyed him suspiciously.

"Hey, buddy," he said. "You need something?"

Bobby wasn't sure what he meant. Drugs? "I think I took the wrong path," he said.

"Oh," said the man. "That way's out."

"Say," said Bobby suddenly, "I heard there's a guy back here with a white van for sale. You know where that is?"

The biker glanced at Bobby's shotgun. He had to see it was nearly an antique. Only a kid trying to pop squirrels would have a weapon like that. Bobby blushed.

"I don't know the dude," said the biker. "But you go back to the fork and wind to the left and there's a wire gate. I seen a white van going in there. I think it's an old Fed Ex van."

Bobby's eyes widened. It couldn't be that easy. He didn't want to show how much it meant. "Thanks," he choked out. He backed several steps, then tried to walk away slowly. He could only endure it for a few yards, then he began to run. It was farther than he thought, and he was soaked with sweat when the gate came into view. As he approached he peered both directions, then peered into the undergrowth. A small animal rustled the leaves and startled him. Near the road was fairly dry, but it seemed to get wetter farther in. There might be water moccasins, maybe even gators. If he walked straight down their access road, he'd be a sitting duck. He went around the gatepost and skirted the edge of the road in order to be able to slip into the brush if he heard anything. He moved along this way, tormented by gnats for a long time. Eventually the sky opened up. The woods had turned into a wide clearing of high swamp grasses divided by the raised road. At the end was a ramshackle cottage with a rusty tin roof, and beyond that the open water of the river. The cottage was lifted several feet off the ground by a forest of green-stained telephone poles. There was no sign of the van unless it was directly in front. He bent and could not see it through the poles.

He heard a television and the creaking of someone pacing the thin floor. He could take a chance on going straight in, hoping that whoever was inside didn't look out the window. Not again: impatience makes a po' hunter. He moved into the grasses, the greasy, stinking mud sucking at his feet. He took each step as if he were surrounded by water snakes. The sun was low when he reached the huge fallen log, but he was close enough to hear the television. It was the local news. Something about Menzies. Maybe they had already killed him and dumped him. Who was inside the cottage? Maybe he, or she, or they, would come out—it had to be hot as hell inside—and he could surprise them. Maybe he'd have to break in on them after dark. He settled down to wait it out.

The grinding of the van on the road startled him, and he dropped flat on the mud. Shit! he muttered to himself. Suppose the driver could see over the grass. He heard it shut off and the doors close. A man was whooping. "Get me my money and get me a beer!"

"Sssh!" said the second voice. "We don't want to rub it in the man's face."

"Yeah, yeah," the first said tiredly.

"Come on out," said the second.

"Is it—" This was a third voice. "I heard on the news . . ."

"It's over," said the second.

"My God . . ."

"They sent some FBI agent to drive Alma Louise," said the first man. "Well, don't look at me like that. We done what we needed."

"We didn't kill him!" said the second voice quickly. "We just give him a tap on the head. He'll be all right. Everything went fine."

"I didn't think she could drive herself," said the third voice sadly.

"Menzies!" Bobby said to himself. He tried to raise himself on his hands to peek.

"Well, let's go inside and get the payoff settled and then we can get this old boy home," said the first.

They were climbing the stairs that led to the front porch of the cottage. Menzies, his head low, was climbing slowly in front. A thin black man carrying a briefcase followed him and was trailed by a big-bellied white with a wispy red beard.

So they *were* kidnappers. Bobby's first thought was that he should call the police. He blinked. That was a strange thought. He had come here to kill Raleigh Lee Menzies, and now he was envisioning himself trapping his enemies. He didn't know what was happening to him. The anger was gone. Instead there was an emptiness. He was just tired, he told himself. He had to go through with this. He owed it to Billy. Daddy had failed Billy, everybody else had failed Billy. Menzies had blown Billy up, he insisted to himself. It wasn't the time to get buck fever, it was time to kill. What was making him hesitate? Hands shaking, he loaded the shotgun in both barrels. He couldn't shoot all three of them if he had to, but maybe he could hold off the kidnappers or get one of their guns.

He was startled by the crashing of a screen door. The fat man stumbled backward across the porch, caught his heel, and rolled down the stairs. The black man charged out as the fat man scrambled for his van. Just as he opened his door, the black leveled his pistol and shouted, "Don't make me do it, motherfucker! I'll blow you to pieces!"

"Come on, Rasheed," said the white man. "He ain't no fucking good to us. How many goddamned witnesses you want to leave?"

"We didn't need to kill no FBI man, and we don't need to kill Menzies. He can't finger us!"

[182]

"Get serious, Rasheed! We earned the money. Let's off the dude and go party."

"You ain't doing it. Nohow. No way."

The fat man lowered his head. "All right. Shit. Have it your way. You'll be sorry, I'm telling you."

Between the grass blades, Bobby could see that Menzies had walked out onto the porch. He looked down at Rasheed, who began lowering his pistol. Bobby rose from his hunched-over position to see if he could get a clear shot at Menzies. He could now see that the fat man's hand was easing its way under the dash. He saw the flick of an elastic snap.

"Look out!" shouted Bobby.

Rasheed looked toward Bobby, and the fat man fired. Rasheed spun back against the stairs and the fat man turned on Bobby, who dived into the mud. The grass around him whizzed as the man's pistol cracked three times.

"Come on out of there," said the fat man. His breath whistled. "I got a load of money. I'll give you plenty to keep your mouth shut. How 'bout it, buddy? A thousand? Two thousand? All right. Drive a hard bargain. Three thousand. Three thousand U.S. dollahs! Whuddya say?" Bobby could hear the man wading into the grass. Each step made a squishing, sucking noise. "Who are you?" said the fat man. "Have I got to come get you?"

There was a clattering noise and the sound of someone running through the swamp grass.

"Hey!" yelled the fat man. He fired in the opposite direction. "God damn you!"

Bobby clutched his old shotgun and saw water trickle from the barrel. If there was mud in it, it could blow up. If the water had penetrated, the shells might misfire. He wanted to give up. He wanted it over. But the man was coming to kill him, and he was shaking, afraid to move, perhaps unable to move.

He heard a laugh. "Well, looky there!" Wood shattered on the log next to Bobby. He screamed, and spun up to a sitting position. Before he could raise the shotgun, both barrels discharged. Instantly he was blinded by pain as something that felt like a cannonball thudded into his crotch. The man had shot him in the gut. He dropped the shotgun. He was going to die. When his eyes eventually cleared, the man had disappeared. Through his nauseating pain he tried to see his own wound. There was none. The pain had come from the stock kicking back into his groin.

He tried to stand, but couldn't. His legs were like fishing worms, writhing on the end of a hook. He climbed up on the log and heard Menzies still crashing through the brush. He breathed deep and tried to control his feelings. He could not. He sobbed like a baby. He should have died here. He'd failed to get Menzies. He'd been scared like Billy had never been. He'd let his brother down. When the throbbing in his testicles finally subsided, he managed to stand.

What he saw made him sag back to the log. Less than five feet away lay the fat man. He was on his back, his legs and arms spread as if he were skydiving backward. His head, however, was gone.

TWENTY

The smell was first: a stale, rancid, acid stench that seemed to burn his skin.

It turned to violet perfume thick and sweet as maple syrup, then faded.

Immediately then there was a confusion of voices. Jostling. The scurrying of quick hands into his pockets. He stirred, waving his arm to fight them off. He tried to speak, but his mouth was filled with oatmeal and all the words blended. "Geawwwwwr! Whaaaadder!"

Laughing, echoing like the deterioration of a bell clap. A sharp plink as a can struck the heaving pavement. Then something on his face. A rat! No, his hand. His own hand. Wet with vinegary slime from the brick pavement. He raised his head. The asphalt pitched as it crested a wave, then, struck broadside, whirled. He lowered his head and felt the hard edge of the curb behind him. A shift and he was resting on it, using it as a pillow. Back to sleep, he thought. Back to sleep. He twisted his hip, and his hand touched the sheets. The woman next to him touched his hand and rustled as her hip collapsed under his touch. He went up on one elbow, then lurched onto his full arm. The sheets were plastic bags. The woman under them was a mound of potato peels, napkins, half-gallon cans. An inch-long cockroach sat on the back of his hand waving its antennae.

"Aack!" He flicked his hand, striking more garbage, and tried to stand, his one foot slipping from under him. He was moving forward on the foul pavement. He heard unearthly music as if through a long tunnel and slowly, slowly, rose, his arms spread to catch himself if he fell. The slanted pavement was rocking like a detached roof in a Mississippi flood, and he was riding it like a surfer. *Endless Summer.* The Banzai Pipeline. He looked back to the garbage bags and heard someone say "Wish they all could be California girrrls!" But he had lost his concentration, and the wave changed and tossed him. He staggered into the brick wall and clung to it, resting his cheek against it. He moved along, clinging to it to stay up, and reached an old iron pole, thick with years of black paint. The unearthly music came from beyond.

The gate wasn't pearly at all, and where was Saint Peter? He squinted back down the alley as if he expected to see his life back there. A dog barked. The echo made him dizzy. Cerberus. The gates of Hell. He looked up to see the warning over the top, but there was only some scrollwork, some intertwined initials that were unintelligible. He rested his back on the wall as it accelerated, spinning like the blades of a ceiling fan. Like the blades of a Huey. *Thup* it went round. *Thup. Thup.* Faster with each rotation. *Thup. Thup. Thup.* Stop, he begged. Please stop. *Thup. Thup.*

It was his heart. It was beating once with every spin. He couldn't breathe. Oh God, he was dying! The pavement pitched. He heard "Wipe Out" again. His heart was playing it, and each touch of the drumstick upon the drum was a heartbeat, a stabbing, painful heartbeat. Through blurred eyes he saw people dancing, swirling, laughing on the other side of the gates of Hell. I don't want to die, he thought. I don't want to die.

He fumbled in his jacket pocket and came out with the bottle of nitro pills. Spreading his legs to hold himself against the wall, he opened the lid. The circle of the bottle lip doubled, spread like two interlinked rings, then came back to one again. He tried to shake one of the tiny pills out, but the bottle vanished. He collapsed to his knees to find it. The little white pills were scattered. He desperately picked one out of a crack in a brick and slipped it under his tongue.

"Wipe Out" ended. He was in an alley. As he raised himself to his feet again, the little pill became a hot coal burning. The warmth spread into his face and head. The people in the street were swirling, shaking. Fat women in cutoffs careened like ten-year-olds. Gray-haired men dropped to the sidewalk and leaped back up again. "Feet don't fail me now!" clapped the crowd. "Feet don't fail me now!" A rail of a black man was wearing a cowboy hat, knee-high boots, and a sequined shirt. Where was his big revolver? The blatting of a trumpet started the procession moving again, and the thumping of a drum seemed to vibrate even the brick wall behind him.

The headache came on like a rising note of music, starting beyond the audible range of hearing and then becoming higher and louder until he could hear nothing else. It filled his head from the very center, growing larger until it pressed against the bony walls and he squeezed his temples with both hands because he thought he heard cracking as they gave way.

He was in the street, staggering, spinning. "Feet don't fail me now! Feet don't fail me now!"

A woman stopped in front of him, shook her hips, and cackled. "Dance it, baby! Dance!"

He lurched on, holding his head. The crowd stopped, and he bumbled into the back of a small light-skinned woman. "Hey! Watch it. Goddamned drunk!"

"Feet don't fail me now!" people chanted. "Feet don't fail me now!"

He could see the sunlight blazing off the brass instruments ahead and thought it was the light glaring off windshields. Saigon drivers plunging ahead. Look out! He tumbled to one side. The air was jungle thick and the Vietnamese were closing in around him and any one of them could be carrying a knife, a satchel bomb. He panicked and crashed against a man selling jewelry on a card table. Cheap watches and chains slid to the ground. Something hit him in the back. Where were the rickshas? He moved faster, but the ground seemed more uneven and he fell against a tourist with a video camera. Someone cursed and shoved him and he was in another street, clinging to a cast-iron fence.

"Oh, mister," said a voice, "you are hurt, are you not?" The voice was clipped and quick. He rotated his head slowly and saw a brown man with black hair and spectacles. Behind him was a woman in a sari. She had a red dot on her forehead and was carrying a girl with a single braid at the back of her head. The woman said something. "No, look, he is bleeding. Very much."

He craned his head forward, cautiously. "You are very much hurt, mister?"

"My head," he forced out. He wanted to vomit. His shirt and jacket were stained with slime. He had wet himself. He swallowed hard. The man went to the crowded street and said, "Please. Please. There is a man hurt. Very much hurt."

He clung to the iron fence. He didn't want to let go or he might fall. The woman, no more than five feet tall, watched him suspiciously. The child had lovely dark eyes. The man was back. He had his hands spread. The woman yammered in a high-pitched voice. The man moved close and shifted his head from side to side, assessing the damage. "Aaah!" he said. "This is very nasty! Very nasty!" He talked to the woman again. She seemed angry, but he raised his voice and came back. "You will wait here. Do not try to walk. I will bring car, eh? You wait."

It seemed like days passed, but the woman stood ten feet away, watching the crowd gradually thin out as the band moved farther along. The little girl rested on her mother's hip, her doelike eyes riveted to the strange, fetid man desperately clinging to the iron fence. He tried to remember where he was and why. This wasn't Saigon. It must be Charleston. The iron fence was like . . .

"Please to lean on me. Here, there."

He fell onto the clean back seat of a silver car. The upholstery smelled new. The door closed up against his feet and he felt the cool, clean air-conditioning rolling back from the dash. The horn beeped. They moved. The horn beeped again. He heard the man talking to someone else and looked up at the child peering at him over the seat. The car swung from side to side, surfing the fluid pavement for some time. He was nauseated, but he swallowed hard and didn't throw up. His face pressed against the back of the front seat and then the door popped open. He was leaning on the man again, staggering through automatic glass doors. The man lowered him onto a plastic seat and rushed forward to the counter.

There was some problem. The man was gesticulating and speaking even more rapidly.

"This is a private hospital!" barked the nurse.

"But you have doctors, do you not? This man is very, very hurt! His head bleeds profusely! You are telling me to take him away? This is an outrage, a veritable outrage! It would never happen in Montreal. Never!"

"Then take him to Montreal, buddy. He's just one of the homeless. They have places to go. There are no charity cases here. You pay or you go. So go!"

"I want to see your supervisor immediately! Immediately! You will not trifle with me!"

A man in a white coat appeared. "What is this disturbance? Shall I get security?"

"Ah, thank God! We are here visiting your city and we encounter this man. He has a nasty, nasty wound on his head. He is needing a doctor immediately."

"He is an indigent, doctor," said the nurse.

"I understand your concern," said the doctor, "but you should have taken him to the city hospital. We only accept patients with insurance, we cannot afford—"

"Please," the Indian pulled his arm, "his head is very nasty."

"We can call an ambulance for him to take him to the Emergency Room, but—"

"This is an outrage!" said the man, still tugging. "An outrage. You will be looking immediately or I will hold you responsible. In Canada you would be arrested for such behavior. Arrested!"

The doctor seemed confused. "You're Canadian? I thought they were mostly Cajuns. Lovely country, Canada. So clean. Vacationed at the lodge at—what was it?—Lake something or other."

"If he is dying, I will be making certain you are well known in the press. Yes, indeed! In American papers as well as Montreal papers! Yes, indeed."

"No need to get excited," said the doctor, "Mr.—?"

"Savanandra."

"Yes, well . . ."

The doctor leaned over and gingerly looked, his nostrils flaring at the smell. He touched him as if he were afraid of catching something. "Umm, it has clotted. He will keep. Happens all the time. Probably cracked his head falling in the gutter. Have a good time last night, did you?"

He shook his head.

"Well, we'll telephone for the ambulance."

"But what of internal injuries?" said the Indian.

Where was he? He touched the crusted blood. His head still hurt, but the roaring pain had subsided to a dull thud. The floor seemed less fluid. "Call," he said. "Call Honoré Devraix." He raised his arm and gestured toward the pay phone. He carefully articulated the number.

The doctor looked at the nurse and shrugged.

"Yes," said the Indian. He examined his change and asked the doctor for a quarter.

The doctor sighed and fished it out of his coat. "He's probably delirious."

"Perhaps it is his family," said the Indian, still angry. He leaned over and asked quietly, "And who is it I am to say is injured?"

He looked up and blinked. Who was he?

"What is your name, Gomer?" said the doctor condescendingly.

"Dub," he said. "Dub Greenert, you fucking leech!"

Then, quite noisily, he vomited on the floor while the doctor tiptoed wildly backward like one of the parade dancers.

TWENTY-ONE

Vonna rushed toward the doors so quickly she nearly collided with the glass before they glided open. The waiting room was not very crowded because of the time of day. Children were running between the connected plastic seats. A black man with a woolly beard was talking to himself. A skinny white girl was crying as her mother rocked her against her bosom, and a pregnant woman leaned back, stroking her enormous belly with all ten fingertips. The nurse at the Emergency Room desk barely raised her eyebrow as Vonna moved straight past her, around a gurney carrying an old woman, and into the treatment area. She reached up to pull aside the curtain around the closest bed when she heard Dub's voice.

"—I don't need to be admitted, I'm fine, and I just want to get out of here."

"Mr. Greenert, in head injuries—"

"Just what part of the word 'no' do I need to explain, doctor?"

"Hey!" said a security guard to Vonna, but she was already halfway to Dub, then sweeping aside the curtain, then frozen looking at him, his hands stretched out in front of him toward the young Hispanic doctor. Dub was red-faced, his eyes bulging with anger, but he was alive. She hadn't thought it possible, but there he was, gaping at her as if he could not believe she existed either. She quivered, afraid to touch him, afraid he would dissolve into the light of her awakening like an aspirin in water.

"Lady!" said the security guard, touching her shoulder

and breaking the spell. She plunged against Dub, moving the examining table with the force of her body, clinging to his neck, squeezing his shoulders.

"That's no lady," said Dub. "She works with me."

The tears gushed out of her. "You're alive! You're alive! Oh, baby, you're alive!" She held him back to look at him through her blurry eyes. He was sheepish, like a little boy caught peeking in a window. "Are you all right?"

"I reckon," he said. His eyes met hers. "Better now. A lot better."

She gently touched one finger to the adhesive patch on the side of his head. "Does it hurt?"

"It's all right," he said. "They X-rayed my head. Guess what? They didn't find a thing." He forced a weak laugh.

She threw herself against him again and buried her face in his shoulder. She rubbed her forehead against him. "I'm not surprised. You're such a bonehead. How could they hurt you?"

The security guard touched her shoulder again. "I'm sorry, there's no visiting in this area."

"That's all right," said Dub. "We're going."

"Please," said the doctor. "I won't be responsible. You've taken a serious blow to the head. You were unconscious for many hours. There might be brain swelling—"

"It might just be gas," said Dub.

"Are you disoriented, Mr. Greenert?" He plucked a penlight out of his scrubs to shine in his eyes again.

"I'm all right," said Dub. "I'm not paying for a room just to be observed for twenty-four hours."

"If you cannot afford to pay, you need only fill out—"

"No!" said Dub.

"Maybe you ought to listen to the man," said Vonna. "I thought I'd lost you, and then here you are." She hugged his ribs. "I don't want to lose you again."

He stared into her eyes and she thought he was going to lose his temper, but with a quick movement he took her head in his hands and pulled her mouth against his. When she opened her eyes, he pecked her on the forehead. The security guard had averted his eyes to the fluorescent fixtures above him. His thumbs were stuck in his belt and he impatiently drummed his fingers. "Okay," he said as the kiss lingered. "That's enough. You can't—"

Dub rolled his eyes toward the security man as if to say, "So kissing's not legal in here, either?" The guard suddenly turned, however. A man had stuck his head between the curtains behind them. Bald on top with neat silver hair around his ears, he had bright pale-blue eyes that studied Dub as if he were a doctor, but he never moved closer. His stare quickly became eerie as each moment passed and he did not speak.

"Can I help you?" asked the guard.

"Nurse!" said the doctor.

The man kept staring at Dub. "Help me," he said in a voice as expressionless as the tinny thank-you from a bank card machine. "There are mice in the refrigerator." Something about the man reminded Vonna of Raleigh Lee Menzies: the patrician chin? the close trimming of what was left of his hair? The stare was chilling, as if the man were the ghost of Menzies, and she felt a quiver pass through Dub.

A short nurse yanked the curtain wide. "There you are, Mr. Lamb. Let's go back to your chair." She took his arm and tried to turn him.

"Help me," he repeated.

The nurse glanced at the doctor. "He wanders off," she explained. "His family tries to keep him at home, but somehow he gets out. Alzheimer's. This is the second time somebody's found him wandering and brought him here." She turned him with both hands and he shuffled off.

"He's lucky somebody brought him here," said Vonna.

"Like me," said Dub.

"I thought he was a nutter," said the guard.

"Me, too," said the doctor. "Too clean for a wino," said the doctor.

Dub gave him a nasty stare. The guard smiled. They were all trying to shake off the eeriness of the old man's interruption. Dub kissed Vonna on the forehead, his lips sliding on her skin as he tasted her. "I'll come home if it's all right," whispered Dub. "*You* can observe me. If it's all right."

She pressed her face against him again and sniffled.

"Then you sign here," said the doctor, holding up a clipboard. "We don't have time for this. If you drop dead it isn't our fault, that's what it says. Don't be alone. Don't go to sleep before ten tonight. You get yourself to a doctor if your vision blurs or you feel dizzy. Tingling in your fingers. Anything weird could be neurological."

Dub scratched out his signature. "No alcohol," the doctor added, "and I mean beer, too. No drugs. If you need something, take aspirin, Ibuprofen, Tylenol, something like that—and don't go over the dosage. *Comprende?*"

Dub nodded. The doctor walked away yawning. The security guard said something about a wheelchair and ambled away.

"Let's get out of here," said Dub. "I just want to go home and take a bath. I smell like puke and garbage. They dumped me in a fucking alley."

"You smell like roses to me, baby."

"Now don't get corny on me."

She laughed. Of course it was corny. She felt corny.

He lowered his head sheepishly. "Listen, I was way out of line. The other night, I mean. I was, I don't know, just stupid. I don't know what got into me. Maybe the killer knocked some sense into me, but . . ."

He reminded her of a guilty puppy. She swallowed hard. "That's ancient history. You were tired. You were hungry. This diet's been hard on you."

"Don't make up excuses for me. I acted like a prick. I just—I've tried to figure it out. I just lost control. I don't know."

"I'm gonna take you home. I'm gonna give you a bath. Then I'm going to broil you some snapper and mix you up a nice salad. From now on, I'm gonna be more like a wife to you." She grinned. "I'll fetch your slippers and get you your pipe."

"Don't even mention tobacco."

"All right, then, slippers and the *Times-Picayune*."

"Aw, now," he said, "don't go sucking up to me. I don't deserve it. If I'd wanted Donna Reed, I wouldn't have let that other dingledick marry her. Nothing has to change with you.

Honest. You're perfect like you are. Don't go *Good House-keeping* on me. Just be your old mean self."

Her eyes brimmed with tears again. "Well, I'm gonna stay on that awful diet with you, like I promised. I'm gonna be lean and mean, baby."

"Fine," he said, "we'll both be in a rotten mood. We'll live to be eighty and fight like an Orange and Green Irish marriage."

She kissed him again. He slid to his feet, and she took him around the waist. "I was sure you were gone," she said numbly. "I was sure of it."

"We agree about something," he said. "Are we gonna make it, do you think?"

"Do you love me?" she asked. "I love you."

"Is love enough?" he mused. "When you're eighteen you're sure, but later you see how love gets run over by things. Like the way I act."

"Look," she said, "now is all what matters, baby. I ain't gonna think about no future I'm making up and I ain't gonna let you do that, either. You don't look like no Nostradamus to me, Delbert Greenert the fourth, so quit trying to get a warranty on your love life. Sears don't have them. This is the present, baby. Live in it."

He kissed her forehead again. She closed her eyes with the pleasure of it. "Okay," he said. His tone of voice told her he really wished it was possible to live only in the present, but that the wish was what mattered in his feelings, not what was possible. "Whaddaya say we take a vacation, drive over to Charleston? You never seen Charleston, right? Elizabeth and Carrie are always asking about you. I think they think it's 'radical' or whatever that their daddy's got a woman with such a deep tan."

"God's tan," she said. "The permanent kind. They're just curious whether I wash it off at night."

"Naw. They're my kids. They're the best. They got to like you."

"Let's go home," she said. "Honoré brought me."

"Aw, shit," said Dub.

When she looked into the waiting room, Campbell and

Horn-Rims were waiting. A third agent quickly slipped up and put his hand on Devraix's shoulder. There was a movement behind them, and Dub slowly twisted his head. Two other FBI men had cut them off.

Campbell coldly pushed Vonna aside and patted Dub down. "You have some questions to answer, Mr. Greenert," he said.

"You bastards," said Vonna. "He could've been killed!" Horn-Rims stepped between her and Campbell.

"Can't I at least get a bath?" barked Dub.

"They have all kinds of showers in the federal pens," said Campbell.

"He could've been killed!" shouted Vonna.

Campbell curled up his lip like a cheap Elvis imitator. "But he wasn't, was he?"

"No thanks to you," said Vonna. "No thanks to you!"

Campbell had started with questions, then played the "we already know, so why not clear up the details" bluff. He brought out photographs of the kidnappers' cabin, inside and out. The white van. Blood on the porch. A garbage bag that some animal had ripped open. Finally Campbell snapped down the photos of the dead Rasheed, blood oozing from his chest, and the headless fat man, his arms spread, the big, chrome pistol still clutched in his hand. Looking at the corpses didn't affect Dub, but the sight of the .357 raised the hair on his neck. Campbell hammered on. He was desperate, Dub thought. The kidnapping had turned messy, and his promotion was evaporating.

For the past hour, each question by Campbell was having the effect that the nitro tablet had had in the alley. It was as if it came into Dub's ears and then expanded, pressing against his skull from the inside until it was ready to burst.

"And this Canadian Indian," asked Campbell again, "what was his name?"

"Mohil or Moheel, something like that. The last name started with an S."

"And what was he? A Montreal Mohawk?"

"You know goddamned well he was an Indian, subcontinent of, or Pakistani, Hindu or Tamil or whatever. He was from Canada, he said, and he was a nice guy. You also, by now, have talked to that prick of a doctor at the private hospital who kicked me out and you know that the nice guy from Canada was a real guy, so stop trying to play Perry Mason with me. You *know* I came to in that alley."

"No, we know that Mr. S., supposedly of Montreal, brought you to the hospital. He could have been your accomplice. Probably he was just another duped tourist. For a quarter million I'd be willing to take a crack on the head. Honor among thieves. Great concept. Your fat friend kills Rasheed. You killed your fat friend. So where's the money?"

Dub sighed to slow the pounding in his head. "Campbell, when I first came in here, I looked at that wall there and I said to myself, that color—I mean where do governments buy paint like that?—it's the visual equivalent of the way I smell. But you know what? It's actually the visual equivalent of your fucking logic, which stinks ten times worse than I do!"

"Was that a simile or a metaphor?" said Campbell.

"It's a 'talk to my lawyer,' asshole. You're sitting here trying to make me your pigeon. I agreed to cooperate. I told you every goddamned thing that happened to me. Now I've said enough. Arrest me, or send me home. Either way, I got nothing to say."

"I don't know," said Campbell. "This could make you look guilty. In fact, you already look guilty. You're driving Mrs. Menzies. You suddenly go off the route. You meet your buddies. You execute her and they give you a love tap on the head just for show."

Dub shook his head and laughed. It hurt to do it. "Will you listen to yourself? First you got me faking a crack on the head. Next you got them cheating me. Now, sometime after I've been dumped in the alley, you've got me killing the fat guy. You're all over the place, Campbell. None of it makes no sense. Who was this fat guy, anyway?"

"You tell us. He was your pal. You blew his head off with a shotgun. One of our magnets will fish it out of the Pearl, don't you worry." Dub just stared. "Hey, maybe they decided that since they didn't get the full million, they'd just dump you. Maybe they killed each other. If that's the case, why don't you come clean?"

It was the old "a guilty guy will clutch at straws, so offer him one" routine. "Are you on some kind of hallucinogen, Campbell?"

"And where's Bobby Alberts? It looks like he jumped bail."

"Bobby Alberts? What's Bobby Alberts got to do with it?"

"You tell me. You talked to him in the hospital, didn't you? He disappears about the time the kidnapping goes down. He's one of your partners, isn't he?"

"God almighty! Two kidnappers have now turned into four. Look, here I am. I'm no lawyer. But you are. All the Fat Boys are. I know that if I shut up that has no effect whatsoever in evidence. I know that since I've asked for my lawyer, you've got to get him here. How come I know this and you don't?"

Campbell looked like he was going to call Dub's bluff and say, "Okay, who's your lawyer?" and Dub tried to think of who he could get. "We're not talking evidence," said Campbell. "We're talking truth."

"And then there's my bump on the head. Duress. Poor me! Badgered and harassed while I'm in pain. Why, shit, I might say anything. I might call you the peabrain you are. I might confess. A court would sure believe the first one, but they'd never believe the last. Can I go home now?"

Campbell's lips curled in amusement. The cat and the canary. He believed he'd gotten his man. He was seeing "promotion" scribbled on Dub's forehead. Horn-Rims, on the other hand, would have been great at poker. "We'll get you," said Campbell. "Your alibi for the time of the kidnapping is weak. No one knows you were in that motel room, even if you paid for it. Why did *you* insist on driving?"

"Can I go now?"

"Why aren't you dead? There was no reason to kill Mrs. Menzies, unless she saw more than she was supposed to. Like you palling up with Rasheed."

"So arrest me."

"You disappear. The money disappears. Why would they

sap you and then dump you in town? Why not leave you where you fell? That's to give you an alibi."

"Maybe I'm asking wrong: *may* I go now?"

"If Rasheed and his supposed pal were going to dispose of Menzies, why wouldn't they do the same to you? They had already wasted Mrs. Menzies. You three were a cozy little trio, that's why, and now you're the only Musketeer left."

"Where would I know Rasheed?"

"Mrs. Johnson can fill us in on that once she knows the trouble she's in."

"Aw, Campbell, this ain't the Lincoln assassination. Your conspiracy theory gets bigger every five minutes. Leave that woman alone, fer Christ's sake. Her boy's dead and you want to say she's part of it."

"You have any other reason they wouldn't put you out of business, gumshoe?"

"They didn't. Is that too simple for you? I got no idea what these people's motives were. I'm not sorry they didn't blow my brains out, but I got no idea why not. But since you understand it all so well, you don't need me, do you?" He unsteadily rose from his chair. "Good day."

Campbell kicked the chair. It clanked into the corner.

"Oooooh!" said Dub. "Bad cop!" He leaned toward Horn-Rims. "That means it's your turn to play good cop."

"Get him out of here!" barked Campbell.

Horn-Rims led Dub to the elevator. When the door closed, he asked, "You don't really believe I did this, do you?"

"I follow the clues where they lead," he said.

"You think I could send a woman face first into a cannon?"

"I just act on the evidence."

"Well, you're wrong, you prick."

Horn-Rims did not react. He was doing his Jack Webb to the max. "Maybe you did her a favor, but the law doesn't see it that way." The elevator door opened.

"What do you mean, 'favor'? People get off the sauce all the time, don't they?"

Horn-Rims blinked. He was new at this and he'd been so intent upon being a tough guy, he'd let something slip. Maybe it was the thing that made them so hot to break Dub. Something that pointed to Dub. "What do you mean?" he repeated.

"Nothing." The grim set of Horn-Rims's jaw told Dub that whatever it was, he wasn't going to find it out tonight.

Vonna was waiting in front of the building. "About time," she said.

"It's part of the cure," he said. "They kept me awake past ten."

"Honoré said to call his lawyer. Or Welch Everman."

"Never mind this thing. All that matters is me and you. I been stupid enough for one year—maybe for the next five," he said, taking her shoulder. "Take me home, woman, and give me a bath!"

Despite his head, he felt a warm tingle in his belly, the kind of feeling you'd get if you came home from school and smelled the new Christmas tree in the parlor.

TWENTY-TWO

He had forgotten how sweet it was to be bathed. He couldn't remember when it had happened last. He couldn't even remember when he had last taken a bath instead of a shower. Usually he came home eyes throbbing, rear aching from a long wait in a car, his skin greasy from the humidity, and all he wanted to do was to wash the crud off and sleep. The only pleasure was in getting it over so that he could be clean again. His first wife Beth and he had made love in the shower, but they had been too full of hormones then to appreciate much more than soapy skin on soapy skin. And then, that wasn't bathing. Bathing was full immersion. Like the southern preachers said, you can't get to heaven without full immersion.

And this was good enough to be heaven. Warm water lapped up the slope of his chest between the bulge of his loose pectorals, flowing back down when he shifted, straightening the hairs on his chest and thighs like an invisible comb. He had lifted his pruney feet out of the water and propped them on the tiles next to the spigot. When he gently pressed against the wall the water rushed through his pubic hair like a tide through the great Sargasso and his penis bobbed like some weird invertebrate attached to the ocean floor. The steam grayed everything, coated everything, filled the air like music. It smelled of the old after-shave that had been collecting dust in the medicine cabinet. Vonna had sprinkled it in the water, and the scent was everywhere. Sandalwood? All was pleasant.

All was soft. Even the cool curve of porcelain supporting his neck.

Vonna soaped him with her hands, leaving the washrag hanging on the shower pull at the front of the spigot. "I can do that," he murmured halfheartedly, his eyes closed.

She stopped sliding her hand along his thigh and clawed him gently with her fingernails. "I want to," she said, pouting.

"Mmmmmm," he said. God, he thought, he was the one who'd acted like a son of a bitch and she was the one making it up to him. "I love you, woman," he said without opening his eyes.

She kissed him on the soapy forehead. "You better, you old bastard." He lifted his head slightly to catch her lips with his own, but she had pulled away and was squirting shampoo into her hand. With one hand gently cupping the adhesive bandage over his stitches, the strong fingers of her other hand massaged his scalp.

God, maybe he hadn't been bathed like this since the first grade, when Opal, their black housekeeper, would have done it. He tried to remember it. He'd had a gray battleship. The cannon on its foredeck was bent and would not straighten. He'd had a Wild Bill Hickok he had gotten from a cereal box— Sugar Pops, he thought. Didn't Sugar Pops sponsor Wild Bill Hickok? He would put him straddling the cannon turret as he attacked the giant atomic rubber alligator, guns blazing. The bullets always bounced off, and Wild Bill would wrestle the creature to the bottom of the sea with screams and splashing. And was it afterward, while toweling him, that Opal had intoned, "Blessed are the peacemakers" and told him about Jesus going down to the sea and calling the fishermen to follow him? He could hear her saying it, but the picture wasn't clear.

Was the memory of that why this was so good? Back to Opal taking care of his cuts and examining his bruises. Back to the servant who had been more mother than his blood mother. Back to the womb. He could picture some psychologist—the kind who knows it all and is damned certain to explain it all to you—outlining every event in Dub's life as if it dated back to Opal bathing him. The imaginary psychologist squinted over his spectacles and said in his German accent, "You are in luff vit a black voman because you are searching for your mommy." He laughed.

"What?" asked Vonna.

"Nothing," he said. Yesterday, tomorrow: neither mattered. Everything was in the present. All he cared about was loving her. It was what living was for. Alma Louise, Rasheed, Bantam Billy Alberts: they couldn't love anymore. That was the worst part of dying, even if they couldn't know it.

He woke the next morning on his back, totally naked, his legs splayed out like a frog's on a dissecting table. Martin Luther King was looking at him from his portrait on velvet on the opposite wall. Dub pulled the sheet over his midsection in embarrassment. "Sorry," he said to the icon. He tried to sit up, but all his muscles shrieked. "Oooh!" He exhaled a long stream of air. He had stiffened up like he'd gone ten rounds with Muhammad Ali the day before. Even his toes hurt.

Vonna appeared in the doorway, arms crossed. "Sleepyhead's awake."

"Wish I was dead. It can't hurt as much as this." The joke didn't seem so funny.

"You got a couple bad bruises on your shoulder and butt."

"They probably weren't too careful when they dumped me in the alley."

"How's your head?"

"Throbs, but only around the cut." He squinted. "We didn't—?"

She grinned. "No, baby. You took the aspirin and went out like that." She clicked her fingers.

"I'd remember it if we did."

"Damn straight you would." She said sternly. "I'll make you breakfast."

He struggled into his boxer shorts, but gave up on any other clothing for the time being. He looked at himself in the mirror. He was a mess, but the paunch was now down to a pot. He was a skinnier beat-up guy, anyhow. He remembered regaining consciousness in the alley and thinking his dizziness was a heart attack. He hadn't thought of his nitro tablets since Campbell had interrogated him. Where were they? He suddenly didn't care. Maybe he ought to try to get the money together for the angiogram the doctors had wanted. Aw, what for? he thought. They had said that if he'd had a real heart attack, the enzymes in his blood should have shown it. They didn't. Nothing else showed it. You've been thinking about death too much, and it's screwed up your thinking. Middle-aged crazy. You should be old enough to know how to live.

He creaked into the dinette and saw a big plate with an omelet, two link sausages, and toast. He glanced up at Vonna. She smiled.

"Now don't get yourself in an uproar, Delbert. Those are those Egg Beater things and no-meat sausage. That's wheat bread, tub margarine, and the coffee's black. If there's choles-terol in this room, it's in your mind. So sit down and eat."

He had tried to stay away from most of the substitute foods because he figured it would only build up the craving for the regular foods. But, man, did it look good! "What about you?" he said.

"I been up for a while. Bran flakes, skim milk. Three hundred calories."

"I shouldn't't've been such a prick."

"Sit down," she said.

The omelet was like any omelet. She had cut some green onion into it and green pepper. "Good!" he said with a full mouth.

"How's the sausage?"

He felt guilty eating in front of her. She was probably famished.

"To tell the truth, it's gross. It looks right, but it's like cardboard. Oh, it ain't your cooking. It's just . . ."

"Gross," she said. "I did try one. Fifty calories."

He laughed, but it hurt. He slowly chewed each mouthful and savored it. "I think its good for the environment, though. Recycled cereal boxes, I'd guess." Soon they were sitting silently, looking into each other's eyes as if they were kids on a date. She gently stroked his forearm with her hand.

"You're okay," she said, choking up. "You're okay."

"I'm just an old bull elephant," he said, "full of scars, but

[204]

not fit to eat and too ugly to kill." He touched her cheek. "Maybe we could slip back into the bedroom and—"

Someone rapped on the door. He wiped his face with his hand. "What's the matter with my luck lately?"

Devraix stood in the corridor in a white suit with a red bow tie. He held out Vonna's newspaper as if it were infested with chiggers. "You have heard the news?"

"No," she said.

"Gio Pantucho has been found, missing most of his blood. The Chinaman has disappeared. There is a great deal of speculation that gang warfare is about to erupt." He rushed in past her. He quickly sat opposite Dub, who felt naked when Devraix noticed his bare chest. "Bodies are falling like Amazonian trees. Mrs. O'Dell has retained Everman's firm to represent you when Campbell charges you."

"When?" said Dub.

"I am led to believe it is inevitable, and since they believe they have their man, I doubt whether they are making a conscientious effort to discover the truth."

"You can't be serious!" said Vonna.

"They're blowing gas. If they thought they had a case, they would've held me."

Devraix made a helpless gesture and plucked what was left of a sausage link off Dub's plate. He made a face when he tasted it. "What in the name of Lucifer is this?"

"Well, they won't find *my* fingerprints in the cabin."

"Mr. Greenert," said Devraix, "you are hardly so naive as to imagine that Mr. Campbell would not be perfectly content to close his file by charging an innocent man."

Dub started to say he didn't think Campbell was totally an asshole, but then he remembered that Campbell had once insulted Devraix in a way he'd taken as racial. There was no point in defending the FBI man, especially when Devraix was in such high dander.

"We must reseize the initiative," said Devraix, "and locate the other culprit ourselves. Someone killed the fat man. Perhaps the hunter Menzies mentioned. I've got Spyder looking for him."

"Oh, sure," said Dub. "You don't think I've tried every

angle I can think of? There are so many people and things in this that I can't simplify it. There's something else we haven't thought of."

"What of young Bobby Alberts? Could he be involved? He absconded on the day of the kidnapping."

"Honoré, I can't buy that. Maybe he just run off. The kid's mixed up. But he's no killer. Maybe he'd like to be, but everybody likes to fantasize that when they're seventeen. He's a hothead, maybe. There was no sign of him when the kidnappers grabbed me and Alma Louise."

"Kids get carried away by their feelings. They do stupid things," said Vonna.

"Just like adults," said Dub. "But, naw, he ain't the criminal type. Well, that's what I think, anyhow."

Devraix considered it for a while. "There are some things that Vonna and I know which perhaps you do not know. Perhaps there are things you can tell us. This is no time for a lover's spat to interfere with direct communication."

"It won't anymore," said Vonna.

"Paper," said Devraix. "We shall brainstorm." Other than a tiny spiral notebook, all Vonna could come up with were some brown paper bags on which Devraix began jotting his notes. They told Dub about their visit to Oswaldo Menendez. They batted around possible reasons why Alma Louise must have borrowed the money. Devraix listed them, but got nowhere. He listed those who might have known why: Alma Louise and Gio Pantucho. And those who still might know: Theo, Menzies himself, and Martha Johnson. It wasn't a good time to talk to any of them, so Devraix suggested they try a different angle.

Vonna brought up Rasheed. Why would he put his mother in that spot? He had grown up as a part of the Menzies household and then suddenly he turned on it. "The man was a paranoid revolutionary," said Devraix. "Perhaps he saw in Menzies just another patrician paleface." Dub suggested maybe he was heavy into drugs. The white man had ordered him around, according to Menzies's affidavit. That wasn't the Rasheed who had run away to Africa. They thought about a possible drug connection to the Pantuchos, and Vonna thought maybe the fat man's killer could have been Theo. They got excited about this idea for a while, but couldn't connect the bomb in the mailbox. "Why would Theo watch the Menzies house, be seen near the Menzies house, if he set the bomb?" asked Dub.

"Maybe the Alberts ain't what they seem," said Vonna.

"Perhaps they have a relationship with the Pantuchos?" Devraix squinted.

"Who knows," said Dub. An hour had passed. Vonna made more coffee. Dub heard her stomach growl, but she didn't go after anything to eat. He didn't deserve her.

"Perhaps we are not ranging far enough afield. Let us consider the absurd."

"Stavros," said Dub. "Nobody's thought about him for a while."

"Who?"

Dub explained. "He boffed Alma Louise at least once. Maybe she borrowed the money so he could open a restaurant."

"Has he?" asked Vonna.

"Not that I know," said Dub. "But if he killed her maybe he figured he wouldn't have to pay the Pantuchos back."

"Do we know anything more about Stavros?" asked Devraix.

"Not much. He's staying in the servants' quarters at Mrs. O'Dell's."

"I can put Spyder on him if you believe anything might be discovered."

Dub thought for a moment. He shrugged. "Maybe I'd just like for the lounge lizard to be the bad guy. We got nothing else to link him in at all."

"Maybe the bomb was to clear his way to Alma Louise," Vonna said. "And the kidnapping was really just to kill her and pick up some more money on the side."

"She would have talked," said Dub.

"Not while Stavros had her man in that cabin."

"Excellent idea," said Devraix. "I shall unchain Spyder in that direction."

"It'd be a waste," said Dub.

[207]

"What about Mrs. O'Dell?" asked Vonna. "She's always around. Stavros is in her house. She knows things about Alma Louise. Maybe she's got something for Menzies."

"Get serious!" said Dub, but he started thinking. "No," he said. "I can't buy that. I don't want to believe that. We're just making up things."

"Maybe she knew what the loan was about," said Vonna.

"She says not," said Devraix. At their puzzled looks, he explained. "I asked her. If she knew, she isn't saying."

"No way," said Dub. "If you try to tar her with this, I'm out of it. If she did it, man, I don't know shit about human nature." He paused. "Which is entirely possible. But if you want to go after somebody, what about Ben Hawkins?"

Devraix's pen froze in midair.

"There is something tight between him and Menzies. Maybe he knows more than he's letting on."

Vonna silently went into the bedroom and came out with *Go Down, Moses*. She opened to the photo of Menzies rushing up to protect the fallen twelve-year-old Hawkins, and then flipped to the text. "You see what it says here. 'When I saw the deputy beating Ben, Jr., I suppose all the anger that had built up burst out of me, and I rushed to his aid.' Ben, Jr. is our cop."

"So maybe Ben whacked Alma Louise to protect Menzies from her cheating. Aw, hell," said Dub in exasperation, "what am I saying? You're right. Hawkins is a tough son of a bitch, but he's a cop son of a bitch."

"It would be just like a man to kill his wife for cheating when *he's* been at it for years," said Vonna.

"Yeah," said Dub, thinking of several divorce cases he had worked. "You think maybe Jane Thuxpin—what do we know about her?"

"She never married," said Devraix. "She was devoted to him. She had no brothers and sisters. She was a very talented photographer."

"And she's dead," said Vonna.

"Of an extremely hideous cancer," said Devraix. "I had her history excavated while Mr. Menzies was being held."

"Another dead end," said Dub. "My head hurts. Not to

mention the rest of me. Will you bring me a file on visiting day? I'm beginning to believe *I* did it. It's the best theory. The trouble is, everybody must know more than they're saying. Mrs. Johnson has to know more about her son than she's saying. Menzies had to know it was Rasheed from the moment the van pulled up."

"He hasn't seen him for years."

"Okay, I'll accept it for now, but don't you think maybe Mrs. O'Dell knows more than she's saying about Alma Louise's money problems?"

"So why'd she give her more money for the ransom?"

"Vonna," said Dub, "there's an answer for everything and no answer for anything."

They went on for another hour and a half. They continued circling over the same points, thought Dub, like weak-eyed buzzards who couldn't see whether the roadkill was dead. The image led him to think about Alma's Louise's getting him to drive. Her helping the kidnappers had helped them kill her. So why hadn't they killed Dub? Poor old drunk. Funny, come to think of it, he hadn't actually seen the woman put drink to mouth that often. She was clever at hiding her flasks, he supposed, like a lot of sneaky Petes, but she sure enough acted drunk enough.

Vonna interrupted his thoughts by standing up. "We don't know shit. I'm going to get the mail." She left the apartment.

"Vonna is on the money," said Devraix. "We do not know enough. We are going to have to look further if we are going to outthink Campbell and his men."

"Maybe the FBI did it," said Dub. "I would love to put it to Campbell." Horn-Rims had let something slip, he was sure of it. What was it? Alma Louise was lucky. What did it mean?

Vonna was back. "Nothing but shit," she said. "Car insurance, I already won a million—that'll do the insurance, and whoa, Jesus, the hospital bill's here already."

"Bill?" asked Dub.

"From the Emergency Room."

"I was only in there yesterday morning, fer Christ's sake."

"It looks like one of them computer things. As soon as they put it in upstairs, it's printed out in their mailroom."

"Fucking leeches," said Dub. He flicked the bill away from him. It spun and toppled to the carpet. Dub's eyes settled on the brown paper on which Devraix had been making his notes. He thought of the old man who had stuck his head through Dub's curtains.

"Well," said Devraix, "on that note of elegance I shall leave. Think about it tonight and we shall decide what avenue to pursue in the morning."

"If we could only have gotten to Gio," said Vonna.

"It might well have been another dead end," said Devraix. "Now he is playing bridge in hell with Crazy Joe Gallo, Al Capone, and Joe Columbo. Bridge, I am convinced, is the only game allowed in hell."

Joe Columbo, thought Dub. What was it about Joe Columbo?

"Maybe it's like the Orient Express," said Vonna. "*Everybody* done it."

Devraix was already halfway through the door when Dub raised his hand without taking his eyes from the paper. "Wait a minute," he said quietly. On the paper, Devraix had written the initials "RLM" for Menzies and drawn lines out to indicate connections. RLM to Alma Louise, then the line branched to Stavros and to Mrs. O'Dell. Another line branched off Alma Louise to the Pantuchos. A line ran from RLM to Mrs. Johnson and then to Rasheed. Hovering nearby was "Rasheed's father, John Johnson?" A line led from RLM to Jane Thuxpin, and another to the Alberts, Billy and Bobby. Yet other lines went toward "White group? KKK? AVCN?" and "Black terrorists? Muslims? Panthers?" His lines branched out from RLM like imaginary rays spreading out from a sun, but there were no connections between the various lines. Hovering outside the cluster of definite connections were a few others. "The so-called Chinaman," Devraix had scribbled. "Campbell," "Hawkins," "someone mentioned in book?," "an unknown?" Everyone's life was like this, an intricate network of relationships leading to other relationships, branching out like trees. A forest of them.

"Jesus!" moaned Dub with his hand on his head. "The forest and the trees. We haven't seen it because it's so obvious.

I can't prove it, but it's the only thing that makes sense. I don't like it. Damn, I don't like it. But it's it. Joe Columbo! The Emergency Room! It plays like a compact disk!"

Devraix and Vonna looked at each other. Dub could tell they were wondering about his knock on the head. He must have looked like a lunatic.

TWENTY-THREE

Devraix urged caution. "See if you can produce any more evidence. There is nothing that would hold in a court of law. You need more supporting evidence." He also urged Dub to stay home and keep his head out of harm's way for a few days. In the end, however, Devraix grew silent. He had accepted Dub's thinking. He said it sickened him, however, and he had Vonna and Dub drop him at a taxi in front of the Clarion Hotel. "I want a full report in the morning," he said. He stared blankly at the sidewalk. "Human nature," he mused, "is so endlessly generous, so infinitely disappointing."

It had just turned dark when they pulled up to the Menzies house. He turned off the engine and touched Vonna's thigh. "Are you sure you won't wait here?" She gave him a nasty look. "Ready?" She nodded, and touched his shoulder. At the door, they glanced at the black wreath and then each other. Dub took a deep breath and stretched his finger toward the bell. Before he touched it, however, the door snapped open: Ben Hawkins.

"What are you two doing here?"

"What about you?" asked Dub.

"You ever hear of condolences? You didn't answer my question."

"We want to talk to Mr. Menzies."

"Well, I doubt he wants to talk to you. I'd've thought you'd jumped the country by now. Come back to finish your job?"

"You know I didn't do it."

Hawkins's bulldog face tightened into horizontal lines. "I know nothing of the sort, rentacop." He glanced at Vonna. "You had me fooled good, girl."

They heard a voice behind Hawkins. "Who is it, Ben?"

"Nobody," sneered Hawkins. He pointed with his hand. "I was just leaving. I'll escort you to your car."

"We're staying," said Dub. "And maybe you'd better stay, too."

Menzies's silver hair materialized out of the shadows. "It's you," he said. "Haven't you done enough?"

Dub riveted his eyes to Hawkins's.

"We know who killed your wife," said Vonna.

"Come in, then," said Menzies.

"It ain't a good idea," said Hawkins.

"I'll hear them," said Menzies. "The sooner they've said their piece, the sooner they can leave."

"You got a gun?" Hawkins reached out to pat Dub down.

Dub shoved Hawkins out of the way. The fire in the policeman's eyes was so sharp, Vonna thought he would lash out, but he didn't. Menzies led them into the den. Vonna took a chair in the corner, Hawkins leaned on the writing desk, and Menzies sat behind it. Dub hesitated by the big winged chair in which he had seen Alma Louise in so much turmoil while she waited for news about her husband. He sat. After all, she was still his client as far as he was concerned, and he was speaking for her. He shifted, and bumped his elbow on the top of Mumbo Jumbo. "I see you got your protector fixed."

"You can still see the split," said Menzies. "Some things cannot be repaired. We all grow to learn that."

"Yes, we do. But we gotta try."

"Well?" said Menzies. He looked tired, very tired, and twenty years older than when Dub had first seen him out by the swimming pool. A man in mourning, Dub thought. A man lost in his troubles.

"Mr. Menzies—"

"Call me Raleigh Lee." It was a reflex with him.

"Naw," said Dub. "You're a great man. A great man ought to be a 'mister.' What you done has helped a lot of people. It was dangerous and it was gutsy—it was more than gutsy. I know what you were up against. Hey, I grew up in Charleston, and that ain't much different from Louisiana in a lot of ways. Yankees coming down to stir up the 'nigras,' as they used to call them—" he rolled an eye toward Hawkins, whose jaw muscles were flexing enough to crush a car "—that was bad, but being betrayed by a son of the Old South, a lawyer, a man whose family owned a plantation, well, that was worse. It wasn't just that friends you knew all your life stopped talking to you. Suddenly they wished you were dead. Some of them might've winked and encouraged a cracker or two to drag you out for a whipping. And you knew it. But you didn't stop. You're stubborn. You can't help helping people."

"You've got to leave the world a better place, is what my father used to say."

"Yes, sir. But you weren't recycling aluminum cans. It took a lot of charging right into the cannons: the Light Brigade, Pickett's Charge. It's all in a southerner's blood."

"I'd like to think I made some difference, but you never know. Maybe the problem's too deep. Look what happened in the governor's race. A Klansman was almost in the governor's mansion." Menzies was no longer looking at Dub; he was staring out the open French doors. A humid breeze stirred the trees, but brought in no coolness. The mixed weariness in his expression had been replaced by a total sadness.

"The why of all that interests me, you see. You were a man of privilege. You had River Bend. You could've been a judge like your daddy. In the legislature like your uncle and your granddaddy. Maybe governor, senator."

" 'What profiteth a man if he gain the whole world, but lose his own soul?' "

"Yes, indeed," said Dub. He thought of Opal, who had often quoted the line. "But, you know, I read your book, and something was kind of nagging at me. I mean, I don't like to be cynical, but it's kind of an occupational hazard when you're hired by greedy wives to follow lying husbands, and vice versa, when you spend six or seven hours staring out through a peephole to catch somebody pilfering VCRs off a loading dock."

"Your point?"

"Puleeze," said Hawkins through his teeth.

"Well, it's just that you're really wrapped up in being the lord of River Bend."

"Excuse me? I sold River Bend."

"What I mean is, you got this thing about taking care of your people. *Go Down, Moses*: you're Moses. You're going down to Egypt-land to save your people."

"I don't understand. We are put here on earth to help our brothers and sisters, aren't we?"

"Yes," said Dub, "we gotta try to fix things. But you see yourself as the older brother, the leader. You got this noble obligation to sacrifice yourself for the good of others, so that you can be the older brother."

"I have never sought political power. What are you speaking of?"

"Political power isn't the point. The first thing you say in your book is that your daddy said that you have a duty to take care of your people."

"Excuse me?"

He leaned forward. "*Your* people. They aren't *your* people. They're people."

"What difference does that make?" shouted Hawkins. "The man saved my life. He saved lots of lives from ignorance and poverty. Me included."

"And he gave them hope," said Dub. "So maybe his fantasy of being the savior of his people don't matter too much. He helped. The South changed, and is still changing. All of America is still changing. I hope."

"And this has something to do with the kidnapping?" said Hawkins.

"Let Dub speak," said Vonna.

"It has a lot to do with it," said Dub. "You expected gratitude, didn't you, Mr. Menzies?"

"Don't be absurd," he answered.

"I mean, it really hurt you when they left you at the station. You helped them get a taste of their freedom, and suddenly they were all head up with it and they didn't need you. When a man or a woman sees the Promised Land, they don't follow somebody to it. They run."

[215]

"There is a long way to go to equality in America."

"Don't tell me!" said Dub. "But what we're talking about is you. You, along with a lot of others, some before and some after, many more important than you, showed people how to play the game, and then you found them playing the game without you. They didn't need you. You were alone. Society moved on."

"The kidnapping, Dr. Sigmund Fraud," snapped Hawkins. "What do you know?"

"You'd paid a big price. Your law practice was shot in any big-paying sense. Oh, they probably offered you some think tank, pro bono jobs. Maybe a teaching job, but maintaining a place like River Bend was an expensive proposition. Just the taxes—"

"So I sold it," said Menzies indifferently. "Sugarcane is better grown elsewhere. Times change. I have no regrets."

"And you put your money in stocks. Oil looked great in those days."

"That was a mistake, true, but—"

"And then you got a nice, hefty advance on your book. That helped tide you over, but it didn't do well. Civil rights is out of style. I expect the publisher figured the controversy would help, but it didn't."

"I didn't say a word that wasn't true."

Dub leaned forward again. "No, but don't you think maybe people got a sense of what was really going on? Maybe they couldn't articulate it, but they could feel the self-serving taint to the thing: 'Look, I saved you people. Where's your gratitude?' Maybe there was a little taste of bitterness in there that put people off. There's a lot of truth people feel but don't see."

Hawkins almost exploded off the writing desk. "Where do you get off running down this man's motives? I got pins in my arm. I got a metal plate in my head from a redneck deputy. Maybe I'm bitter he don't get what he deserves either."

"Ben . . . ," said Menzies gently.

"But then there was Jane Thuxpin," continued Dub. "*She* saw the hero, didn't she?"

Menzies lowered his head.

"She was a good photographer. Nobody ever caught you better. You can see the love she had for you. You can see your pride in being loved. That book-jacket picture was you, the hero, the lord of River Bend. She fed you everything you needed."

Menzies pressed his hands over his face.

"For God's sake," said Hawkins.

"I known a lot of men who got themselves in a bad way by supporting mistresses. Well, you could afford that. She didn't ask for much. She loved you. The thing went on for a long time."

Menzies shook his head.

"But the cancer. How could she pay for that? Mistresses don't get medical insurance. How could you pay for that? Where'd you take her for treatments? Mrs. Johnson told me you took Miss Jane anywhere you thought there might be a chance. Mexico?"

Menzies lowered his hand. He was pale, weak. "And Switzerland," he sighed. "And Morocco. It was in her brain, then it was everywhere. They cut her breasts and they scraped her womb and they made her sick with vitamins and they burned her with radiation and they killed her beautiful hair with chemicals. And the cancer nibbled until there was nothing left. She didn't recognize me at all the last eight weeks. Some things can't be repaired, no matter what you spend."

He bit his lower lip, staring as if her ghost had appeared to him. "It's a shame. In a country rich as this."

"You know," said Dub, "I got whacked on the head a few days ago." He touched the bandage. "I don't think it knocked any sense into me, but I had a bitch of a time with the doctors. And if it wasn't for Mrs. O'Dell—I guess she likes taking care of her people, too—paying for all them worthless tests and things after my heart attack that wasn't a heart attack, I'd owe more than I'll ever make. Or maybe not. Nobody'd have done the tests if she hadn't been paying."

"Society has an obligation," said Menzies as if he'd said it a thousand times but was now hearing a hollow echo. "This is America."

"The oil crash. Then the stock crash. You tried to turn

your grief into a weapon. You tried to write a book on the medical crisis, both in memory of Jane and for the money. You didn't have any buyers."

Menzies stared at him.

"I saw the letters in your desk," said Dub. "I'm sorry. We thought you were in danger."

Hawkins sagged against the desk. The tough guy was melting.

"So you somehow turned up Gio Pantucho. You told him the money was for Alma Louise. That's why she didn't turn to that scumball when she was trying to raise the ransom. She never knew him."

"I told him it was for my wife. I thought Pantucho wouldn't dare hurt me if I couldn't pay on time. I expected the book to— I told him it was because of my wife."

"You meant Jane?"

"She was already . . . But I was nearly bankrupt. I thought I would be able to get back on balance with the book, but the offers—I had two—were nothing. They said the book needed a personal touch to sell. I couldn't use the memory of Jane for that."

Menzies had opened one vein, and Dub expected him to keep bleeding. Instead he stared, an ancient warrior who no longer knew if the suffering had been worth the victories.

"Gio was draining you. Theo started watching to make sure you didn't skip, but also to let you know the threat. You needed to support Mrs. Johnson. And Alma Louise." He paused. "What was it with Alma Louise? Another brain tumor?"

Menzies looked Dub directly in the eyes.

"She can't be hurt no more," said Dub. "And we'll get the medical records one way or another. I think the FBI already knows."

"It wasn't a brain tumor," said Menzies.

"Then what? Huntington's disease? Alzheimer's? She didn't have a serious alcohol problem, like everybody thought. She was sick."

Menzies began opening and closing his desk drawer, as if he were testing the silkiness of its slide.

"You were tired of giving. You'd stuck with Alma Louise because you felt the obligation. Most men wouldn't've."

"No, they would not."

"But now you were going to have to watch her die slow. Like Jane. You couldn't do that again. You couldn't afford it."

Menzies' eyes flashed anger like an arc welding torch.

"So you decided to kill her."

Hawkins jerked to his feet. "After all these years of sacrifice you think this man is an ordinary wife-killer? He killed her to pay off Gio?"

"Her insurance wouldn't have covered it," said Menzies. "For money? Ha!"

"All right, then. You knew about her adventures with other men."

"Do you think I could care about that? *She was suffering! And it wasn't going away!*"

"Okay, so which was it, then, money or mercy? And mercy for her or mercy for you? Whatever the reason, you done it. You got hold of Rasheed. You've probably been in contact with him for years. He made you the bomb and you put it in the mailbox. You were going to send Alma Louise to the box for you. Along comes Bantam Billy and the dumb fuck blows himself to hell. It never made no sense for the supposed kidnappers to try to blow you up and *then* kidnap you. You came up with the kidnap scheme afterward. You figured you were worth a million. You asked for a million-dollar ransom hoping some of your old friends might be able to raise the money. You imagined that invoking the name Raleigh Lee Menzies would bring money out of everywhere. You expected that gratitude. You deserved it. You'd get out of hock, and when she got bad put Alma Louise into a home where they could take care of her. But only Mrs. O'Dell helped with the money. And, by the way, I want hers back."

"You can't prove a thing in this fairy tale," said Hawkins. "Is this your defense? I ought to kick your butt."

"You watch it," said Vonna, raising her cylinder of Mace.

"It's all right," said Dub.

"Nothing is all right," said Menzies. "Everything's wrong.

Suppose I were to say Rasheed had another partner who sounded like you. Who would be believed?"

Dub cleared his throat. "Well, you might, but your story still don't wash. If the FBI'd found one fingerprint of mine, one hair of mine around that cabin, hell, I'd be in a cell right now. Come on. You fished, ate catfish. Relaxed. So who was the other, really? A friend of Rasheed's? He's messed up, I understand, but they'll identify him. Was there a third man, or did you kill them both yourself?"

"You lousy motherfucker!" barked Hawkins. "You know you were part of it."

"I kidnapped myself! What a fairy tale," said Menzies quietly. "You're just trying to smear me." He lowered his head and sighed. "I can live with that."

"Look out!" said Vonna, jumping to her feet.

Dub thought she meant Hawkins, but Menzies had plucked a gun from his desk drawer. He didn't point it at Dub, though. In the open French doors stood Bobby Alberts. His old shotgun was under his arm.

"You killed Billy," he said.

"Nonsense," said Menzies.

"It took me a while to know, but I ain't stupid. Nobody kidnapped you."

"You put him up to this," Menzies said to Dub.

"I don't know nothing," said Dub. "Bobby, don't fuck your life up. Put down that gun."

"I want to turn him in. I want him to tell the truth."

"What truth?"

"I saw the fishing place. I saw the fat man kill Rasheed."

"Just as I said," said Menzies. "They fought."

"Then I—" he choked up "—I killed him."

"The fat man?" asked Dub.

Bobby nodded.

"What does that prove?" said Hawkins. "Put down the hardware, son. Let's talk about this."

"No. You don't understand. He was in the cabin alone. He could have gotten away any time he wanted. He was watching TV. He was *alone*. It didn't register with me for a while. I was upset. But he was *alone*."

"I was imprisoned in the closet."

"Chained?" asked Dub. "I seen the pictures of the cabin. There was no chain in there."

"Ropes," said Menzies.

"There's no marks on your arms."

"It's been days."

"Shut up!" shouted Bobby. "I heard you walking around. I heard you!"

"You could not have heard that. I was locked in the closet."

Bobby looked like he was going to cry. His hand leveling the front of the shotgun nervously twisted around the barrel.

"Son," said Hawkins, "you got to put down that gun. I am with the police. Let's talk this out. Look, I'm going to reach for my wallet real slow."

"Tell him to put down his gun," said Bobby. "Are you going to arrest him?"

"Look," said Hawkins, "I'll just slide over in between you two. Then both of you will lower the weapons. Okay?"

Dub looked at Vonna. She was slowly raising her Mace. He shook his head. There was a sad calmness about Menzies. It didn't look like he'd start shooting. On the other hand, he hadn't ever looked like the kind of man to try to blow up his wife. What if Dub was wrong? Menzies wouldn't kill a woman with a bomb. Somebody else could have been hurt in the process. Broke and bitter, Menzies couldn't face another slow death. Could he kill, though? He was calm, very calm, as if he knew what to do. Bobby, on the other hand, was certainly no killer. He had put himself into a situation where he might kill by an inadvertent press on the trigger, but he was sweating and licking his lips as if both guns were pointed at his head.

"Okay, now," said Hawkins, "I'm just going to start sliding over. Okay?"

Bobby blinked. Hawkins stepped sideways around the end of the desk and shuffled one step, two steps, three between them.

"All right now, son, put the shotgun on the floor."

Bobby stared at him. The shotgun would blow Hawkins's guts through his own spine.

"There's been enough killing, son. Put it down."

Bobby screwed up his face and abruptly threw the shotgun into the French door. The bottom panes shattered and the shotgun thudded against the floor. "Jesus!" said Hawkins. "I said put it down. The damn thing could've gone off!"

Bobby's shoulders sagged. He looked up at Hawkins sheepishly. "It wasn't loaded," he said.

"What?"

"I ran out of shells."

Hawkins put his hands on his hips, looked toward the ceiling and expelled a long stream of air.

"What about you?" asked Dub. Menzies still held his gun aimed at Bobby through Hawkins, who now rotated his head to look back at him.

"I suppose it is pointless," Menzies said. He gently lowered the pistol into his lap.

"What about what the boy said?" Vonna asked.

"He was mistaken," said Menzies.

"I wasn't," said Bobby. Aroused by Menzies's words, he tried to move toward him. Hawkins blocked him with a wide hand.

"I was kidnapped," said Menzies flatly. He was quivering. He looked like he was about to collapse. "It is past my bedtime," he said. "I was forced to borrow money from a loan shark. That's true. Perhaps you'd like to try to pin Mr. Pantucho's murder on me, too. Good night. Good night, Ben."

"Wait a minute!" said Dub. Still keeping his hand on Bobby, Hawkins blocked him.

"You put this boy up to this," said Hawkins.

"Me?" shouted Dub.

"You've got to arrest him," said Bobby. "He killed Billy!"

"Time to go home," said Hawkins. "I ought to kick your butts. If anybody gets arrested, it might be you three."

"Have you totally lost it, Ben Hawkins!" shrieked Vonna.

Dub heard a door slam. Menzies had left the room. "Hey! Goddammit!"

"He's getting away!" said Bobby.

"The door's this way." Hawkins shoved Dub.

Vonna menaced him with her Mace. "You're in on it, too, ain'tcha?"

"Go!" growled Hawkins. "Before I forget myself. And you, Bobby Alberts—" he picked up the shotgun and checked the empty chambers "—you're coming with me. You got a statement to make about being at the cabin."

Vonna was grinding her teeth. She might give Hawkins a squirt of her Mace if Dub didn't get her out of there. He grabbed her by the upper arms and pushed her backward toward the front door. "We'll get him later, baby. Let's go home."

They were going down the sidewalk. When they reached Dub's car, Vonna exploded by kicking the front tire. She stood there, arms crossed, her breath puffing little clouds into the humid night air.

"Of all the stupid!" spat Dub. "What ever gave me the idea to accuse Mr. Menzies? When I got here I was sure. Now?" He shrugged. "He's no bomber."

"We fucked up," said Vonna.

"I was the one that fucked up."

"Don't argue with me. You convinced Honoré. You convinced me. We should have done like he said and got more evidence, that's all."

Dub wryly smiled. "Don't argue with me. We can't prove nothing. Maybe there's no evidence to get."

Vonna's expression softened. "Let's go home," she said.

A patrol car pulled up on the street. Its lights were blinking, but the siren was off. Transport for Bobby Alberts. "Maybe we ought to call and see if Everman will help Bobby," said Dub.

"Whatever," said Vonna.

"The FBI's gonna arrest me, and I'll spend twenty thousand years in Sing-Sing."

"Over my dead, fat body," she said.

TWENTY-FOUR

They were curled up in the bed like two spoons in a drawer, his face pressing the soft brown skin between her shoulders, his belly curving into the small of her back. He partially awoke, breathed in her scent until the skin blocked his nostrils, and listened to the boom, boom, boom of his heart.

Vonna moved. Boom. Boom. Boom. Somebody was yelling. "The door," she said sleepily. He clung tighter to her when she reached for the clock. "Ten-thirty." As she turned, one of her breasts rubbed his elbow. "The door, baby. JUST A MINUTE!"

He winced, blinked, and unsteadily swung to his feet. She put a pillow on her head while he tried to lift his feet into his boxer shorts. Boom. Boom. Boom. "All right! Goddammit! All right!"

He bumbled down the hallway to the door. The peephole made Hawkins's face look like a varnished ebony mask. "Open up, Greenert, damn you!"

Dub popped the deadbolt and Hawkins pushed his way in. Dub saw that the neighbors had opened their doors at the racket and were peeking over their door chains, then Hawkins slammed the door behind him.

"Jesus," said Hawkins, "you still sacked out? Get your clothes on."

"What for?"

"I said get your clothes on. We're taking a ride."

Dub blinked. Hawkins obviously wasn't arresting him. "What's the hurry?"

Hawkins paced, his forehead shiny with sweat. "I'm not in the mood to shoot the shit. You get your clothes on or I'll drag your butt out of here like you are."

Vonna stood in the corner in her bathrobe. Dub shrugged as he passed her. "This is *my* house," she said. "You don't come busting in here like this."

His voice was not as forceful as he leaned on the dinette table. There was a tinge of pleading in it. "Go back to sleep."

"I'll go with you."

"No," said Hawkins. "Just me and Dub. He'll be back soon enough."

Dub had slipped on the clothes he had worn yesterday. He touched her shoulder. "It'll be fine, baby. Take a nap. We'll go to Skeeter's or somewhere for dinner. Right?" As he turned sideways in the hallway, she gave him a quick peck on the mouth. Hawkins seemed annoyed by it, but also distracted. His eyes were puffy. He turned his back and left the apartment.

"Are you sure this is okay?" she asked.

Dub patted her butt. "You make me indestructible."

Hawkins hadn't bothered to park his car. Dub had barely gotten halfway in when he was thrown back against the seat. He managed to get his door closed and caught his breath. He waited for some explanation. Hawkins merely drove. His bulldog jaw set as if he had a criminal by the throat.

Dub turned sideways and noticed Mumbo Jumbo lying face down on the back seat. Some broken things can't be fixed. "What's up?" said Dub.

Hawkins did not answer. He would speak when he was ready. Dub peered at the raised houses along the street. They looked as if they were built to imitate the old-fashioned New Orleans style rather than being original. The heat made him notice he should have taken a clean shirt. He and Vonna had made love half the night. The taste of her breasts and neck was still on his lips. People were such dopes, he thought. I'm a dope. You should be old enough to know how to live, Dub Greenert. You know one day your life's gonna evaporate on you.

"Tell me how you knew about Mr. Menzies," Hawkins said.

"Huh?"

"Tell me what got you to his house last night."

"I thought he had to've done it. It's the forest and the trees. All these people. All these possibilities. Only one thing connected them. Him. There he was in the center of it all. We didn't really look at him, didn't really think about him. He was a great man. Everybody sees what they want to see in a great man. That's what makes him great. But it's hard, maybe impossible, to see the man."

"Well, you don't see shit, white boy, if you think Raleigh Lee Menzies would kill his wife for money! Jesus H. Christ!"

"Okay, so I'm wrong. But then there was Joe Columbo," said Dub.

"Say what?"

"Joe Columbo. He faked his own kidnapping."

"Shit for brains," laughed Hawkins. "Absolute shit!"

"It seemed good at the time. I'm wrong, you're right. I don't really see Raleigh Lee Menzies blowing up Alma Louise. Not for money. Not to save her from a slow death."

A thick envelope plopped into Dub's lap.

"What is this?"

"Sixty-six thou," said Hawkins.

"Who I gotta kill?"

Hawkins twisted his face. "It ain't for you, cracker. It's Mrs. O'Dell's."

Dub lifted the flap. That much money didn't look real.

"You don't have to count it," said Hawkins nastily. "Just make sure she gets it all."

"You were in on it?" Dub asked in amazement. "You expect me to be quiet about Menzies because of this?"

"Praise the Lord, you are a dumbass!"

"I get caught with this stuff on me and Campbell will be tossing me in a cell with some slasher lonely for love."

"Don't flatter yourself, white boy. Just get the cash to Mrs. O'Dell. It's laundered. In six months or so, some of the ransom will start showing up in the Caymans or somewhere.

If she wants to talk about it, I can't stop her, but I think she won't."

"Why not?"

"To protect you, maybe. Maybe even to protect me. But mostly to protect—" He turned away and nearly rear-ended an old Pontiac.

"Raleigh Lee Menzies. What's going on, Ben? Last night you tell me I'm full of shit. This morning you're here telling me I was right. If I'm right, the man has done some heavy crimes, Ben. You can't ignore those. I don't think you would ignore them."

"You can't prosecute a dead man." There was a hitch in Hawkins's voice.

"Huh?"

"Menzies got himself shot last night."

"Got himself shot?"

"What part don't you understand?" said Hawkins sharply. "Mrs. Johnson busted in on him."

Dub wiped his face with his hand. "*She* was behind the kidnapping? I *was* wrong, then."

"No. He had asked her to shoot him. He left a note. She tried not to interfere, then couldn't help herself. When she tried to take the gun away . . . There was residue on her hands."

"Slow down, Ben. Am I still asleep?"

"Why're you such a dumbass, honky? She said he came to her room. He said he couldn't go on living. She was supposed to hold the gun for him against his heart while he pulled the trigger. That's what she says."

"Like the noble Roman getting his best friend to hold his sword." Dub watched some children jumping rope under a tree. "Were they lovers? How do we know she didn't just kill him?"

"Naw. You know better than that. One detective wants to make it out that way. But they know he was despondent. Alma Louise had been killed, his ticker wasn't too good, he was broke . . . I don't know if the full truth will have to come out, or whether it matters. His name may be tainted enough."

"So what is the whole truth? What is this money?"

Hawkins silently reached in his pocket and handed Dub a cassette tape. He pointed to the glove compartment, where there was a small player. Menzies's voice came out clear and precise, as if he were arguing again before an appeals court.

I'M SORRY, BEN. I GUESS MAYBE THE OLD SONG IS TRUE. YOU ALWAYS HURT THE ONES YOU LOVE. JANE, TOO. I COULDN'T HELP HER, SO I HURT HER, TOO. BUT I KNOW WHAT TO DO ABOUT IT NOW. I LET TOO MANY THINGS SPIN OUT OF CONTROL. ALMA LOUISE WAS HAVING SOME FUNNY THINGS HAPPEN TO HER, SO CLEMENTINE O'DELL TOOK HER TO SEE A NEUROLOGIST. HE WAS VERY CERTAIN, HE SAID, OF THE PATTERN OF THE DISEASE. I ALMOST HAD A BREAKDOWN. I COULDN'T HELP HER. THERE WAS NO MONEY. I STILL OWED FROM THE . . . THE SITUATION WITH JANE. AND THEN MY ANGIOPLASTY. ALMA LOUISE WANTED TO BORROW FROM CLEMENTINE O'DELL, BUT I SAID, NO, I'D TAKE CARE OF HER. THERE WAS NO QUES-TION BUT THAT SHE WAS GETTING WORSE SOME DAYS, AND I KNEW IT COULD GO ON FOR YEARS. SOMETIMES THEY'RE BETTER, SOMETIMES WORSE, BUT THE END IS INEVITABLE.

Menzies choked up. He seemed to be weeping.

ONE DAY I COULD TAKE NO MORE. I TOLD MARTHA I WANTED TO HELP ALMA LOUISE PASS ON BEFORE SHE LOST ANY MORE OF HER DIGNITY. I ASKED HER TO PUT A POISON IN SUPPER. SHE WOULDN'T DO THAT, BUT AFTER I BEGGED I GOT HER TO TELL ME HOW TO CONTACT RASHEED. HE HAS KILLED MORE THAN ONCE. HE BRAGGED ABOUT IT WHEN I WAS DEFENDING HIM. HE MET ME ONE AFTER-NOON IN JACKSON SQUARE AND TOLD ME I SHOULD SEND ALMA LOUISE OUT TO THE MAILBOX AT EXACTLY MID-NIGHT. I DIDN'T KNOW HOW TO PERSUADE HER OF THAT, BUT SHE ALWAYS WANTED TO PLEASE ME, PARTICULARLY SINCE JANE DIED, SO I KNEW SHE WOULD.

RASHEED PROMISED SHE'D NEVER FEEL A THING. I DIDN'T KNOW WHAT HE HAD IN MIND—I DIDN'T WANT TO

KNOW. I JUST TOLD HIM SHE WAS NOT TO FEEL ANY PAIN.
IT WAS TO BE INSTANTANEOUS. I THOUGHT HE INTENDED
TO SHOOT HER, OR ABDUCT HER AND USE A FATAL DRUG,
BUT WHATEVER IT WAS TO BE, HE PROMISED SHE WOULD
NEVER KNEW WHAT HIT HER. AFTER THAT I WAS SURPRISED
HOW UNMOVED I WAS BY THE ALBERTS BOY'S DEATH. I
GAVE RASHEED THE DICKENS FOR HIS STUPID BOMB, THEN
I GOT THE CRAZY KIDNAPPING IDEA. I MADE THEM PROM-
ISE NOT TO HURT ANYBODY, BUT RASHEED SEEMED TO
KNOW THAT I STILL WANTED TO HELP ALMA LOUISE. HE
THOUGHT OF SHOOTING HER WHEN HE KIDNAPPED ME,
BUT HE COULDN'T DO IT IN FRONT OF HIS MOTHER. I'M
GLAD I DIDN'T HAVE TO SEE IT. LATER, HE SUGGESTED HE
. . . WELL, YOU KNOW. IT WAS JUST TOO EASY TO SAY YES.

THIS IS ALL BUT ABOUT TWENTY-FIVE THOUSAND
DOLLARS. MRS. O'DELL'S IS THERE, PLUS INTEREST. THERE
IS A HUNDRED THOUSAND FOR THEO PANTUCHO. I KNOW
YOU'LL TELL HIM THAT HE HAS HAD ENOUGH AND YOU'LL
MAKE SURE HE LEAVES MARTHA JOHNSON ALONE. HE HAS
NO REASON TO TRY TO SUCK HER BLOOD. THE THIRD GOES
TO BOBBY ALBERTS. IT'S FOR HIS BROTHER. I DIDN'T
MEAN TO END ANYONE'S LIFE BUT ALMA LOUISE'S. IT WAS
AN ACCIDENT. FORGIVE ME, BEN. I DON'T KNOW IF GOD
CAN. I CAN'T. MAKE SURE NO ONE ELSE IS HURT. I, OF ALL
PEOPLE, AFTER WHAT I'D SEEN IN THE SIXTIES AND SEVEN-
TIES, OUGHT TO HAVE KNOWN THAT ONCE THINGS GET
STARTED, THEY CAN'T STOP. I SHOULD HAVE KNOWN
THERE WAS NO GOING BACK.

Menzies sobbed for several seconds, then his voice weakly
returned.

FORGIVE ME.

Dub listened to the hiss of blank tape. Being right wasn't
very satisfying.
"He wanted to do it himself, but couldn't," Dub stated.
"Not Alma Louise, not himself."
"So now he's dragged Martha Johnson in."

[229]

"If she keeps to her story, she'll just get aiding a suicide."

"The detective could say she murdered him, Ben."

"Just in case, I'll keep the tape safe. If something happens to me, you'll know about it."

"You ought to make a copy." Dub stuffed the big envelope into his inside jacket pocket. "What you wanta bet the ambulance bill gets to his house before he's buried?" Two kids were waiting for a bus and dancing to a boombox. "A lousy goddamned mercy killing. That's all. A lousy goddamned . . ." Dub struck the dash in frustration. "Damn!"

"He meant well," said Hawkins, then winced at the absurdity of the remark. "He lost it. Maybe he was sick, too."

Hawkins pulled into a Jitney Jungle parking lot. He rested his elbow on the door and stared at the Fotomat. When he had composed himself, he said, "It's stupid, you know. They had to do an autopsy even though her head was blown up. The brain tissue confirmed the neurologist's earlier diagnosis."

Dub remembered the deafening flash of Rasheed's gun. Alma Louise tumbling. The stifling day became chilly. "It must have seemed to Menzies that God, his ally, had betrayed him. The disease was eating his wife's brain and she would slowly fade. Perhaps it would have been worse than Jane's cancer, perhaps easier, but he couldn't do anything about it but end her suffering. It was the only way left for him to take care of her. Then the scheme to get enough money to pay off Pantucho and protect his own old age. What must he have felt like as things spun out of control? How long had he been thinking about the hard barrel of a soothing bullet passing through his heart? The heart, appropriately, not the head. What would Dub do if he knew Vonna were going to die slowly, horribly? He closed his eyes and shook his head to erase the thought. Thinking about it might make it come to pass. No. *No!*

They were silent with their thoughts for a long time. Finally, Hawkins broke down and sobbed on the steering wheel. Dub watched the shoppers scurrying with their carts. Hawkins blew his nose. "He lost it. He just lost it. Shit!"

"You ain't gonna give that money to Pantucho, are you?"

"Fuck Pantucho," said Hawkins. "Mrs. Johnson needs it. He shows up and I'll send him to party with his brother."

"Sounds good to me."

Hawkins started the car. "Bobby Albert's supposed to be at Boss Mayhew's garage."

"What about the assault charges? And whacking the fat guy?"

"I'll get him off somehow." Hawkins didn't say he would do it even if he had to hurt Menzies's reputation, but Dub felt he was thinking it. Dub was sure when Hawkins added, "Like Mrs. Johnson."

"I'll talk to Bobby," said Dub.

Hawkins said nothing. His eyes were cold, too sad to cry.

You can't fix some things, Dub thought. What was Dub going to say to Bobby? The boy probably wouldn't take money if he knew it came from Menzies. Boys his age could get real proud, and poor people could be as arrogant as a Menzies. He would say an insurance company had gotten him to find him. He would say that Billy had a policy. It was so ridiculously absurd that Bobby might believe it. Whether he did or didn't, Dub wanted to tell him to get on with his life. To face up to his brother's flaws, not make him into anything perfect, but not hate him either. He wanted to try to explain to him that he shouldn't let his brother's death eat him up, like Jane's had eaten up Raleigh Lee Menzies. Bantam Billy had let his bum leg eat him alive. He'd always been out to prove something, and it was always the wrong thing he needed to prove. Dub wanted to convince Bobby it hadn't been Bobby's fault that Billy died, that he shouldn't let himself feel guilty that he didn't die with him. You've got life, live it, boy! Take something from it before it beats you down! Find somebody warm and hold on until your arms ache.

Fat chance. Dub knew he could never explain these things well enough. He was old, and Bobby was young. Words weren't enough. You couldn't grasp it until you had the scars. He would simply say that Billy had bought educational insurance for Bobby. When he finished high school, there was money waiting for Bobby's college or trade school. It wouldn't matter whether Bobby believed it. Bobby'd want to believe it.

[231]

The car pulled over. Boss Mayhew was sitting on a folding chair, greasy and sweating, sipping a Coke. He eyed Hawkins suspiciously. Bobby Alberts was at the side of the garage, his head stuck down in his brother's Mustang. An older man was helping. Well, maybe there was enough money immediately available to fix up the car. But no more.

Bobby Alberts looked up at the disheveled man moving toward him, this bull elephant with an adhesive patch on his head and a weary expression. "What do you want?" he said.

Boss Mayhew raised his newspaper. There was a Jane Thuxpin picture of Raleigh Lee Menzies at the bottom. He was smiling and holding up his fingers in a victory sign. The modest headline said:

RED KNIGHT DEAD